I0523409

KEEP YOUR GUARD UP

TARA MERILAID

Copyright © 2025 by Tara Merilaid

All rights reserved.

No parts of this publication may be reproduced, distributed, or transmitted in any form or by any means, including photocopying, recording, or other electronic or mechanical methods (including Generative AI), without the prior written permission of the author, Tara Merilaid at authortaramerilaid@gmail.com.

This story, all names, characters, and incidents portrayed in this production are fictional. No identification with actual persons (living or deceased), places, buildings, and products is intended or should be inferred.

Paperback ISBN 9780646725734

Ebook ISBN 9780646726274

Editing done by Anna Bishop @ Creating Ink.

Cover art by Kari March @ Kari March Designs

1st edition 2025

To the survivors past, present and future, I believe you.

1800 737 732

Author's Note:

'Keep Your Guard Up' contains potentially triggering content. Please read the following trigger warnings before continuing.

Domestic violence; emotional coercion/manipulation; physical abuse; kidnapping; physical violence; gun violence; death; mention of suicidal thoughts (spoken about in memory); descriptive sexual content.

Written in Australian English.

Glossary

Alco - Alcoholic

Ambo - Paramedic

Arvo - Afternoon

Avo - Avocado

Barbie - Barbecue

Biccies – Biscuits / cookies

Bird - A lady

Bloody - Another word for very

BO - Body odour

Bogan - Uncouth/uncultured person

Bottle-O - Bottle shop where alcohol is sold

Brand spanker - Something that is brand new

Brekky - Breakfast

Brickie - Bricklayer

Bubbler – Water fountain

Buckley's Chance - Little chance

Bugger - Something annoying

Buggered - Exhausted

Chippie - A carpenter

Chock-a-block - Really full/busy

Chook - Chicken

Chrissy - Christmas

Ciggy/dart/durry - Cigarette

Copper - Police officer

Cop shop - Police station

Crook - Sick/unwell

Cuppa - A cup of tea or coffee

Devo - Devastated

Dunny - Toilet

Eggs benny - Egg benedict

Fire engine - Raspberry lemonade, usually served at a pub in a schooner with sprite and raspberry syrup

Flanno - Flannel shirt

Footy - Football, typically AFL or Rugby

Garbo - Garbage truck driver

Goon - Cheap boxed wine

Green-eyed monster - Jealousy

Have a crack - Try and attempt something

Hit the bricks - Leave/go somewhere else

Kay - Kilometre

Mozzie - Mosquito

Occa - Heavy Australian-ness, usually referring to an accent

Pineapples - 50-dollar bills

Root - Sex

Rubbish bin - Trash can

Rubbish - Garbage/trash

Scull - To chug/drink quickly

Seccy / seccies - Security guard/s

Servo - Service station, where you go to get fuel for the car

Smoko - A morning or afternoon work break, usually to eat and/or have a cigarette

Sparkie - Electrician

Stubby - Can of beer

Thongs – Flip-flops (and underwear ;))

Togs - Swimwear

Tradie - A tradesperson

Ute - Pick-up truck/utility vehicle

Woop woop - Really far away

Vaso - Vasoline

CHAPTER 1

Mari

"We don't need another coach though, Nan," I whined. "We go through this every year, and we always end up getting rid of them anyways."

I set the cuppa in front of Nan and shook her sugar packet. I'd brought in her favourite mug from home the minute we moved in closer to the gym. She never took it back with her, only drank out of it here when she came to visit each morning.

"Thank you, dear," she said, stirring the sugar I'd poured. "Al wants to retire, Mari."

I fought the urge to scoff and roll my eyes, as it would definitely not impress present company.

"Al says that every year. And as soon as we get someone in, he's all, 'No one can do it right like me, *yada, yada, yada*'." My voice lowered a few octaves, and I poured some cold water into my black coffee before switching the kettle off at the wall. It was here when Al had arrived in Soggla, according to him, and liked to steam itself four to five times a day. But Al had an odd sentimental tie to it, so no one was allowed to get rid of it.

Even when it had rattled itself so hard it tipped over, spilling scalding hot water *everywhere*.

Nonetheless, Allen Burke was one of Australia's best mixed martial arts coaches. With a professional record completely clean of defeats, Al had brought MMA to Soggla. He's the sole reason why our tin-shed gym, in a small, *small* town, had a name for itself. There hadn't been, and still wasn't, much here in Soggla—just *The Allen Burke*.

He had been my father's first coach, mine, and *hundreds* of other successful fighters'. Al and my dad had opened Knock's Mixed Martial Arts five years after my mother passed, taking over the financially failing gym they had both been spending their days at. My dad, the famous Elijah Trevino, had been at the peak of his career, meaning I spent a lot of time with my grandmother. His reign as champion in the light heavyweight division of the Ultimate Fight League was second to none. Though there were rumours if he hadn't retired when he did, he would have soon been inducted into the UFL Hall of Fame.

Elijah Trevino, the champion fighter, lives on in this gym. Who my father was to the people watching the big screen; the kids with his poster in their room; the screaming fans in the stadium—his legacy remained in Knock's. But that was what lasted. Elijah Trevino the fighter, not Elijah Trevino the single father to a young girl.

"I know he does; he cares about this place too damn much to hand the ropes over to some stranger," Nan replied. "I told him if he wanted to retire, he had to find his own replacement."

This time I couldn't help but chuckle. "So, in other words, Al'll be here until the day he dies, and then some."

Nan pursed her lips and smirked as she lifted her mug to her red-stained lips.

"He's comin' in on Monday."

***

It took a solid five minutes for me to pick my jaw up off the floor. Al retiring was a conversation we'd had many times over the last few years, sure.

But now?

He had a replacement *already*?

"Who is it?" I asked, taking a long sip of my coffee.

Soggla was a small town, four hours inland from the Harbour and with a declining population of around four hundred people, so I didn't really need to question whether I knew the person or not.

"Some young fella JJ's mates with; both think he's real talented," she replied.

I narrowed my eyes; that was a tough combination. If it was someone my goofy, extroverted, shaved-bear-looking best friend suggested, it could literally be a circus monkey walking through the front door. But Al? If it was someone with his approval? They had to be good, *better* than good. Al didn't make mistakes like that, not when it came to Knock's.

"What do you think?" I asked warily. Nan was very intuitive. It was unusual for her not to throw her opinion—which usually turned out to be right—into the mix.

"Why, I haven't met the lad yet, have I?" She wiped the lipstick off of her empty mug. "He's very polite and professional on the phone though, and anyone who Al speaks highly of can't be all that bad."

I sighed. Getting Al's approval was never an easy feat. Lord knows my shockingly low number of boyfriends over the years had always tried ... and failed. "Why would someone young want to move out here?" I asked, taking our mugs to the sink for rinsing.

"JJ seems to think he wants to take a break from the fighting scene for a minute or two, regain his 'soul in the sport' or so he says," she replied, pushing her chair in and packing up the obnoxiously floral handbag JJ had bought her for Christmas last year. "You'll be able to ask him yourself next Monday."

I huffed and folded my arms across my chest as I leaned on the faded grey countertop.

Nan came over and pressed a red-lipstick-coated kiss to my cheek as she hugged me. "I know you and Al have a special bond, dear. I wish he could stay too. But the man has dedicated his whole life to this sport—it's time for him to start living again," she said, patting my cheek as if I was still just her little granddaughter.

***

"I hear you're hanging up the pads for good, Al?"

The old man sighed and turned to face me. His grey eyes bore into mine, and the drop in his expression revealed how incredibly unenthused he was to have this discussion. He tossed aside a set of hand pads he had been cleaning; his favourite pair. The exact pair that had been featured in all of the photos on the walls in the office.

"Sure am, darlin'." Gloom washed over his face as he flashed me a sad smile, scuffling his feet over the mats as he crossed the open space to where his shoes were waiting behind the timber edging.

For the first time, I looked at Al. I really looked at him. The wrinkles that I'd never really seen before. The droopiness in the skin around his jawline. For the first time ever, Al actually looked *old*.

At the age of sixty-nine, I was surprised he had made it this far. But I guess that was what happened when you loved something the way he did. He'd rebuilt this place with my dad, watched it grow and flourish. He'd seen it become some peoples' second home. Hell it had even been my first home. I've spent more time in this oversized shed than I had in any house, slept on the floor more times than I could count.

Kicking my thongs off at the edge of the mat, I quickly moved in to wrap my arms around him. The smell of cigars and meat pies filled my nose, the smell that was indisputably *Al*.

My eyes turned misty at the sight of my inked hand wrapped around him to his far shoulder. The same little diamonds, triangles and circles that were on his hand—the ones my father had tattooed onto him and JJ onto me. A symbol, a permanent representation of what we were a part of, of what we'd built together.

"I'll miss having you around here, Al," I croaked.

"I could never fully leave this place, Mari. I'll still be floating around here somewhere," he replied with a chuckle.

I pulled away and playfully punched his arm. "You know what I mean. I'll miss having you by my side to run this show."

He put his arm around me and pulled me into his side. "I been in this industry for sixty years, and never in my time have I ever come across someone quite like you," he stated. "You're ambitious, coura- geous, smart ... Everything that one needs to run a ship as big as this, you have. Part of the reason why I felt now was the right time to retire was because I knew you were ready to step up."

"You say all of these things, but I don't necessarily feel like I can agree with them," I countered.

"You don't need to when everyone around you already does. If you can't believe the words, let your community do the believin' for you."

CHAPTER 2

Mari

Nan had deemed tonight—'Al's last night before freedom'—a worthy celebration and promptly dumped me on pizza duty. I'd called Lozza's about an hour ago and been told it was *wicked busy* by the young guy with colour-varying dreads, affectionately nicknamed 'Noodles' after his lovely, knotted locks.

Only one of the locks on the doors of JJ's ute clicked, the dingy old thing. Reggie, the old tradie-typical ute JJ's dad had given him, was an extremely faded blue and cream white with over a dozen scratches and dents on it. I was responsible for probably about half of them—JJ the other half. Both of us had learned to drive in the ute, with JJ's dad as our teacher and the other lounging in the back seat as 'moral support'. Really, it had just been to jumpscare each other every now and then, causing the driver to stall.

I tucked my keys into my shorts, along with my phone and the cash Nan had given me. The smell of pizzas cooking wafted through the air, and I swallowed the saliva that immediately filled my mouth.

The neon green sign hung above the wavy metal roof, flickering and humming. The poles holding up the little amount of shelter outside of Lozza's were rusty, and little of the original white paint remained—the paint that did was faded and dirty. Several of the glass windows needed a clean, and the community board they'd stationed over one side still had advertisements from ten years ago pinned up. Two sets of cheap metal chair and table sets sat underneath the windows on either side of the bright red door. They were the kind of table and chair sets that screeched so loud when you moved them an inch, everyone within a block's radius knew someone was sitting down for a feed.

Despite the roughed-up conditions of this place, it was still a thriving part of the Soggla community. Unlike a lot of other restaurants, Lozza's was busy every night of the week.

Danny, Lozza's second husband and father to their affair-driven lovechild, was the full-time manager of the restaurant. One thing you could never fault him for was his work ethic. What Danny did wasn't 'full time', it was 'all of the time'. He felt a passion for Lozza's I don't think even Lozza felt.

I looked up to see the man himself fixing something for Noodles on the register. Not only was his button-up, grease-stained black shirt done up with the buttons in the wrong order, it was also getting uncomfortably tight around his beer-belly region. Neveah, his chubby, pink-cheeked daughter, reached down from his arms to touch something on the screen. Danny groaned and rolled his eyes before handing the little girl over to Noodles, though his lips tilted up into a soft smile for the briefest of moments. Her little orange ringlets bounced up and down as Noodles twirled her around, high and low, to keep her entertained.

"Your dreams of a career in childcare coming true?" I asked Noodles, leaning my elbows on the counter.

He wiggled his fingers on Nevaeh's pudgy belly, and she giggled before latching onto one of his newly lime-green dreadlocks.

"Best part of hanging out with other people's kids is getting to hand them back," he joked, seemingly not noticing that he had a small child gnawing on one of his prized dreadlocks.

"Y'know she's currently using your hair as a teething toy?" Danny grumbled, looking over his shoulder.

"She can chew on them as much as she likes. Bobby-Joe said the only way these bad-boys are coming out is with a pair of scissors." Noodles grinned. Bobby-Joe's barber shop had to be one of his favourite places on earth—he visited nearly every week.

"How much do I owe you, Danny?" I asked him, pulling out the small wad of coloured notes Nan had given me.

"On the house tonight," he grumbled in reply, his wispy beard the same colour as his daughter's hair fluttering about. "System's down."

"Pizza's in the oven, Mari!" one of the boys out back called.

I gave them an appreciative nod before turning back to Danny. "Where's Loz?" I asked, leaning in further to avoid all of Soggla listening in.

"Girls weekend in Darlington. One of her crazy-ass friend's hens weekend," he replied, rubbing a hand over his forehead.

"Need a hand with Nevaeh?" I pointed up at Noodles. "You know Nan's offer still stands. Think she gets a little lonely waiting for me to make her some great-grandchildren."

That got Danny to laugh.

"You're only twenty-four. There's still time."

"With the amount of shit I've gotta do around here? Not enough," I replied, shifting the subject off of me. "Invite always stands for you and little miss."

"Thanks, Mari, but I wouldn't wanna trouble youse. She's a bit of a handful at the moment," he replied, gesturing to the baby still chewing on Noodles' hair and gripping tightly on to two other locks.

"Don't say we didn't offer." With a joking smile, I held my hands up in acceptance.

"'preciate it." He nodded at me just as a ding sounded from the register. The cash drawer popped open and receipt paper spewed out from the machine.

"Order up!"

"You're up, Mari!" Noodles called, moving my order from the metal bay onto the counter.

"Fucking *hell*, how much did we order?" I gaped at the stack of pizzas and multiple garlic breads being piled on top. Noodles, still holding Nevaeh, opened the fridge door and pulled out three bottles of soft drink. My eyes narrowed.

"JJ called and said you'd forgotten a few things," he explained.

"*Of course* he did." I made a mental note to throw the bottle of Sunkist at JJ when I got home. "Righto then, Noodles. Load me up."

After careful stacking of our gigantic order, I turned to head towards the door, taking small and cautious steps and stiffening my muscles to keep from any wobbles. I was *not* a two-tripper. There was no way JJ's gigantic pizza order was going to beat me.

The door creaked loudly as it opened, and a series of jingles followed from the rusty bells hanging above. I assumed Noodles was lending me a hand, despite me refusing and telling him to help the crew out back instead. My shoe scuffed the floor and I staggered, sending one of the bottles rolling off my mountain of pizzas and said mountain into the poor victim walking through the door. Pizzas flew, garlic breads scattered, and a bottle of Sunkist exploded.

"For fuck sake!" a deep, raspy voice boomed.

Past the scattered feed big enough to actually feed a village, my eyes landed on what could only be described as one of the world's finest creations.

Holy sex-on-legs.

Wearing a skin-tight washed-out green shirt, now tie-dyed with Sunkist, he looked anything but. The shirt clung tightly to what was clearly a *very* ripped body. Chiselled shoulders fell into brawny biceps. Sculpted pecs lined up with what I could only assume was the beginning of a lickable set of abs. A head full of sandy blond hair sprawled around his neck and stretched halfway down that chest of his.

He looked up at me; the most beautiful set of ocean blue eyes gazing.

Nope, not gazing.

Glaring.

"Oh god, I'm so sor—" I started, bending down to gather the wholesale-worthy amount of food scattered across the floor.

"Watch where you're fucking going," he growled, tossing a pizza box into my lap.

Of course, he's an asshole. The hot ones always are.

I opened my mouth to respond when he reached down into the now-puddled Sunkist on the floor and fished his phone out of it. He grumbled another string of curses under his breath before furiously shaking his phone, trying his best to get the orange-flavoured liquid out.

I cringed. I wasn't a computer scientist or a phone technician, but phones weren't built to survive being dunked in a puddle of Sunkist.

He glanced at me and rolled his eyes, those stormy pools glistening with wrath. He clenched his jaw, once, twice, before tossing another nearby pizza box on my lap. This one had been sitting in the Sunkist puddle and had unfortunately turned victim to its crimes.

"Look, like I was trying to say before your rude ass interrupted me—"

That blue gaze narrowed, and I contemplated rolling *my* eyes and laughing at how little it took to upset this poor man. But I didn't, I narrowed my gaze right back.

Lifting my chin, I continued, "I'm sorry. I could barely see over this big pile of—"

Before I could even finish explaining, the man growled and stormed out.

"Need a hand, Mari?" Danny called from his office.

Restacking the mountain of food, minus a couple of pizzas and a Sunkist, I grumbled, "Little late for that."

CHAPTER 3

Mari

Monday rolled around a lot quicker than I had expected. JJ and I had spent the entire weekend cleaning up the gym for the 'new coach' to arrive.

What a pain in the ass that was.

JJ was good like that though. Whenever I'd call, he'd always answer. Anything that needed to be done, or if any of us needed help with, he was always the first to offer. It didn't surprise me anymore, being friends with him all of my life, but I would never stop being grateful for what he'd done for me and mine.

With a head of black curly hair, rich deep brown skin, and brown eyes similar to mine, JJ was not short of feminine attention. Being a strong, talented, heavyweight fighter only added to his resume with local women and passers-by of Soggla. But JJ was nothing more than a brother to me—which had been solidified the year we both got gastro together. Nothing, and I mean *nothing*, could ever attract me to JJ after *seeing* and *smelling* that.

Al and Nan had pitched in on the cleaning where they could too, which was usually providing snacks and beverages for us. Jobs that hardly ever get done, got done. Everything had been cleaned—gloves, shin pads, head gear, mitts, pads and mats no longer reeked of sweat and stale BO but instead of a very expensive, very thorough, lemon-smelling cleanser. Bathrooms had been scrubbed until we were all getting borderline high off of bleach fumes. The decades-old corner of the office that Al occupied, the one that was lovingly across from mine, had been cleared out. Pictures had been taken down, trophies packed away, old cigar butts tossed. I had tried to move all of his things back home for him, but found certain pictures kept making their way back onto the walls.

His own championship photo from back in the day.

My dad's collage of championship photos, all with Al by his side.

Countless all-stars that had passed through here to train alongside *The Allen Burke* over the years.

I forced him to keep the one of him holding pads for me for the first time when I was four—hung it up in his hallway myself.

Point is, the gym was cleaner than I had honestly ever seen it. Knock's isn't a dirty place by any means, but keeping a martial arts gym spotless is like selling wood to a lumberjack—requires a lot of patience and an ass that won't quit.

I zipped up the onyx black and burnt orange merch bag I had ready for the new coach and put it on top of what was soon to be his desk, a long shiny timber workspace Al had built himself. It had taken every last dollar of my dad's and Al's to get Knock's up and going in the beginning, so they'd taken a few shortcuts that they'd never bothered to have fixed.

It took a brave face and a solo tear session to acknowledge that all of the little things of Al's were no longer on his desk or scattered through the office. His dingy old radio wasn't spewing muffled music, leaving the room too quiet. A cigar wasn't smoking off in his colourful but faded ashtray that I'd painted for him when I was ten. Discarded coffee mugs weren't scattered about with half a sip left. Everything was just so fucking *clean*. Wiped free of one of the most important men, if not the most, in my life.

The office was a stretched out shared space between all of the coaches and staff. My father and Al set it up this way as they believed, down to the bone, no one was above another; a chain was only as strong as its weakest link.

I dumped the black manilla folders of paperwork on the bare desk, straightening the pile before checking they were in order. I nodded and gave myself a mental pat on the back for the colour-coordinated organisation.

"You're gonna give the poor lad a stroke with all of that crap." Nan's sudden voice startled me. I gaped at her. She was never crass, never used any sort of foul language. But an amused smirk sat on her face.

"It's everything he needs to know about our gym," I fumbled, fiddling with the corners on one of the piles.

"And more?" She raised a thin eyebrow at me, pursing her red-painted lips.

"No more than I would give to anyone else. He's got big shoes to fill, Nan. I'm just trying to give him the tools to fill them."

She nodded disbelievingly before walking out. I turned around and removed one of the smaller piles off the table and threw it in the rubbish bin.

***

I was refilling the sugar packets in the overcrowded, hexagon-shaped kitchen, as Nan had had nervously had three cuppas this morning. Not that I hadn't downed a couple myself. Welcoming someone new into the team was always stress-inducing and daunting. For Nan and me, it was almost as personal as welcoming someone into our own home.

That was the thing about Knock's; it was a special place to so many different people, everyone had their own history within the walls. Knock's was where Al and my dad had taken Nan in when she had nothing but her car and a daughter in the back. Knock's was where that same daughter had found love with my dad. Knock's was where I had been born and where I took my first steps. Knock's was where Nan and I had spent all of our time after Mum passed and Dad was in constant training camps for fights.

"He's here, dear." Nan poked her head in the door and gestured behind her. Her white hair was out from her usual high bun and flowed down her back. Sapphire-studded earrings glittered in her lobes and matched the colour of her glasses' frames today.

I sighed, ready to get this over and done with. There was no way whoever this guy was would last—they never did. There was a reason people came here for fight camps—because *camps* ended and they could get out of this town that was in the middle of butt-fuck nowhere.

I came around the corner to the open mat space to see the man of the hour. His muscly figure cast a tall shadow on the concrete floors as JJ squeezed him in a tight hug. His wavy, blond hair reached a few inches past his shoulders and was pushed off his face by a pair of sleek black sunglasses. The midmorning sunlight glistened on some of the strands, making his skin look even more the rich olive shade it was. Al was smiling ear to ear. Standing from the front desk chair, he opened his arms and embraced the god-like man in front of me.

My mouth fell open, unable to hide the irritation and shock that had just slapped me in the face.

It was him. The asshole from Lozza's.

"Chance, my boy! How was your trip? Hope the roads were good to ya'," Al said.

"Roads are always easy when you've got a great destination." A charming smile warmed his face as he and Al pulled apart. For an old man, Al was still pretty tall at six feet, but this guy had probably two or three inches on him. And definitely a *truckload* more muscle.

"That's the way!" Allen replied. "Chance this is Marilyn, part-owner of the gym."

Right before my very eyes, my seventy-year-old grandmother swooned over this man.

His straight teeth parted through his full lips into a heartbreaking smile as he bent down a little to address Nan.

Did he have to be so good looking? What's with the chivalry too?

There had certainly been no chivalry, no offering of hands or help when I'd run into him with a dozen pizzas on Friday night.

"Pleasure to meet you, Marilyn. I've heard so much about you," he told her gently.

Kiss ass.

A sliver of his long hair fell over one of his high cheekbones. A stark contrast to the tight-fitted black athletic shirt he was wearing above a set of navy blue jeans that had been worn in to the shapely figure of the obviously muscular legs he carried beneath them. And that *ass*? Could men really have a good ass? Apparently so.

I knew my grandmother had noticed too.

"Oh, dear, the pleasure is all mine!" she flirted.

I couldn't hold back a scoff, which landed his blue eyes on me.

Shit ... look at that blue.

Time somehow seemed to pause for a second, just a moment, when his stare locked onto mine. I was trapped in that gaze, the same vibrant colour of forget-me-nots. Ironic, since I could guarantee I would never forget the colour of those eyes. The lock I had on my jaw loosened, and his lips tilted up slightly. A rush of heat tingled in my chest before spreading up to my face.

Fuck, he noticed me staring.

"We meet again, Sunkist." He smirked an obnoxiously attractive smirk that made me wish I had that Sunkist bottle to pour on him all over again.

"You two have met?" Nan asked.

"No," I said.

"Yes," Chance said at the same time.

"Chance, this is Mari," Al stated, appearing at Nan's side. "Pretty much full owner of the gym."

Nan's eyes were darting between the both of us, and Al scratched his neck nervously. I knew why, of course. I wasn't exactly easy to impress, or all sunshine-and-rainbows towards the prospects making attempts to fill Al's shoes. They'd all come in, reciting the same things, until they read the letter.

"Elijah Trevino is my hero."

"I can't wait to continue his legacy here."

"This is an opportunity of a lifetime."

What a load of—

"Chance Riordan," he said, extending his hand towards me, that devious smirk still plastered on his face.

Is he puffing out his chest right now?

"Mari," I stated, grasping his hand. "Good to see no one shit on your Coco Pops this morning."

The briefest flicker of surprise washed through those blue eyes, but it vanished as quickly as it had appeared. We stood there, locked in a stare as I waited for his next move. To my surprise, his mouth tilted up into a smirk behind that undeniably sexy layer of mouse-brown stubble on his face.

I mean, seriously. *Why is it the hottest guys are* always *the assholes?*

Al cleared his throat. "Ease up on the young fella, Mari. He's only been here five minutes," he chirped.

I was preparing for an eye roll when Chance spoke up.

"Nah, don't stress it, Allen. Not the first time a woman has expected me to bow down to her."

My eyebrows flicked up of their own accord. His blue eyes bore into mine once again, a small dimple that popping on the left side of his mouth when his smirk deepened. He took a step closer to me, the smell of one of those annoyingly delicious-smelling colognes and coffee that was *oozing* out of him filling my nostrils.

"Wouldn't have thought any woman would give you the time of day with the attitude the colour of a shit stain," I scoffed.

"You'd be surprised." His smile was infuriatingly easy.

"I can assure you, I wouldn't be."

"They've definitely met before," JJ not-so-whisperingly whispered to Al and Nan.

"No, we haven't!" I snapped.

"What's the matter, Sunny? Don't want to tell your friends about our little run-in on Friday night?" That easy smile was gone, replaced with an arrogant, heated smirk.

"Friday night?" Nan asked, her eyebrows up expectantly.

"Didn't she tell you why she only came home with half of your pizza order?" His face softened to a gentle expression of amusement when he looked to Nan, before hardening right back up when he looked down to me. "Do you know how much of a hassle it was to undo the shit you caused me on Friday night?"

"Oh yeah. I'm sure washing orange soft drink out of your pretty green shirt was *such* a pain in the ass," I retorted.

"You *what*?!" Nan scolded.

"Nan—" I started.

"Marilyn Trevino, you better start talking." She put her hands on her hips. Somehow, even though she was half a foot shorter than me, she still managed to stand over me.

"None of this would have happened if your non-biological second grandchild hadn't ordered the entirety of Lozza's menu," I defended.

"It's really not a big deal, Marilyn," Chance crooned. "I have a new phone on order."

My jaw dropped.

You fucking—

"You did *what* to his phone?!" Nan shrieked.

A look of disguised triumph crawled up onto Chance's face. I spun around to Al for help, who simply raised his eyebrows, clearly unimpressed.

"It was an accident! He had his head up his ass and couldn't see I was walking through the door with the leaning Tower of Pisa in my hands!"

Nan shook her head and turned back to Chance. "The *gym* will compensate for your loss," she told him.

"I—"

"Thank you, Marilyn. But that's really not necessary," the asshole replied.

"Please, I insist." Her eyes flicked over to me, telling me we would be discussing the matter later.

I sighed. *Aw, shit.*

"Righto, now that we're done with the theatrics. Mari, show the lad to his office, will ya?" Al asked, nodding me along.

"Around the corner, past the mat spaces, first door on the left," I told him.

Nan lifted her chin and gave me a look that said, *'Pull your head in before I do it for you'.*

I rolled my eyes. "Right this way then."

***

I grumbled a string of colourful curses at my 4 o'clock alarm.

Chance-freaking-Riordan had already gotten to my head.

I'd lain awake for nearly half of the night, unable to get fucking comfortable after the day's events. He was so blasé and collected and laid back—with everyone but me *of course*. But he was somehow meant to step into Allen's shoes?

He was meant to forge the best fighters out of Knock's.

He was meant to continue the legacy that my father and Allen had fought for.

He was meant to *not* flirt with the staff members.

I cringed at the continuous replay of Chance's introduction to Liv, one of our Brazilian jiu-jitsu coaches.

"Oh, Chance. What a great name. I'm Liv, Liv Coleman. Pleasure to make your acquaintance," she purred, wrapping her hand in his.

"Trust me, the pleasure is all mine." He winked.

Of course he had been happy to meet her—she was a drop dead gorgeous black belt in BJJ. But did it have to be her? Of all people? I don't even know what I was thinking—perhaps that he would be repulsed by her forwardness?

You idiot, why would he be repulsed? She's stunning.

A girl could dream.

Whatever.

I took my time walking to Knock's, as I usually did in the mornings. The dawns around this time of year were always at their peak with the slightly cooler weather and consistently clear skies. The big, bright, burnt orange sign came into view, the beginning of the rising sun's heavenly rays shining from it. The streetlights began to flicker, almost at the time to turn off. But at the crest of the driveway, an unusual shadow fell under the tall figure's feet.

I would have preferred to have Gus with me but since the last time Nan got sick, he'd made it a part of his daily routine to wake her up in he mornings. He always used his patented, proven method of continuous love-licks to the face until she rolled over and put her glasses on. Nan would usually bring him in around lunchtime, and he would spend the rest of the day with me.

My hackles rose as I neared closer to the figure. Heart pounding, I pressed the outer button on my headphones to subtly turn them off and pushed my gait into walking on my toes in anticipation. I grabbed onto the blade I had hidden in my gym bag strap—a handy contraption JJ had helped me build after last year's drama. Being in a small town, outsiders were the only real risk of safety. In Soggla, everyone knew everyone, so there were never any break-ins when you'd probably recognise the person trying to heist your TV.

The dark figure turned around and met my eyes. That blue that had filled last night's thought-train bore into me like a laser.

"Morning, Sunny."

CHAPTER 4

Chance

It'd been a while since I was nervous. I'd retied my hair so many fucking times I had half a mind just to shave it all off. The shitty little prepaid phone buzzed in my hand, a text from my older brother.

Dylan: Stop messing with your hair and go eat something. Make sure your undies are clean too. No one likes a guy with skiddies. You got this, Chan Chan.

Even miles apart, I could still hear his voice as if he was right next to me. Talia's shitstorm had burned all of the photos of us that I had, bar one that I'd managed to save. The book was buried deep in the duffle bag I was currently living out of, the photo of us at my first UFL fight night pressed between pages.

JJ, being the good friend he was, had been gracious enough not to ask any questions about why I was here and where all of my stuff was. Not yet anyway.

"All in good time, dear JJ. All in good time," I said, blowing out the sweet weed smoke from deep in my lungs. "Thanks for having this ready, by the way."

"Figured you'd need it, trading up your noble existence 'round the Harbour for the Soggla life." JJ nodded, tossing me a cold bottle of water.

I grabbed one of the black and orange singlets from the Knock's gear bag and slipped it over my head. Gruffing in approval, I sifted through the rest of the merch. Surprisingly, it was all real quality shit. Merchandise was known to be the ultra money grab around gyms with the knock-on bonus of free advertising. So it was nothing short of surprising that a small-town gym had their own brand of top-grade gear.

A loud, haggard creak sounded from behind me. I turned, preparing for whatever the fuck I was about to take on. Nope—not a threat—just JJ. His snoring rattled the bloody house.

No wonder girls snuck out during the night on him. Not a chance you could get a wink of sleep when a fucking foghorn was going off next to you.

My hands rubbed at my face. The grown-out beard now trimmed to short stubble pricked at my palms but I welcomed the feeling. Anything to override the overwhelming shitty feeling of being utterly fucking pathetic. I was the number one contender for the light heavyweight title belt in the UFL and here I was, jumping out of my skin over a little noise?

Fuck that.

Never again, I mentally chanted the mantra I'd been repeating since I hit the highway a few days ago.

***

The streets were pitch black when I arrived at the gym. I checked my watch to ensure I wasn't too early.

4.30 am.

My first class of the day started at five-fifteen, but I mentally patted myself on the back for being the first one here.

Gold star, mate.

I dropped my bag between my legs and sat on the ledge of Knock's steep, gravel driveway. Staring at the view around me, I wondered just how many of the greats had sat where my ass currently was, looking at the same thing. Was I squashing some legacy's assprint at this very second?

Being farther out from the city lights, Soggla seemed to stay darker for longer. Somehow that wasn't disconcerting, the opposite actually. The start of the sun was beginning to rise over the dated brick houses lined up at the bottom of the driveway, but no one's lights were on.

Footsteps crunched on the gravel and a trim figure appeared. The slight gold coming from the horizon threw a small light onto the soft curls of her hair.

I stood, dusting myself off and slinging my bag over a shoulder. "Morning, Sunny."

Her steps faltered as she tried to cover the flinch. "You're awfully chipper for someone up at the asscrack of dawn," she grumbled, stifling a yawn with the back of her hand. The bottoms of her fingers, just below her nails, had small, lined designs inked on them. Two of them had three circles with a diamond in different formations, the other two had two overlapping squares.

"Not a morning person I take it?" I smirked at her early morning form.

"Ask me again once I've had a coffee."

Chapter 5

Chance

"Coffee?" Mari handed me a blue mug full of dark, hot coffee, her poor tired eyes barely open. Taking the mug from her hands, I flashed her an appreciative smile, struggling to remember the last time someone had made me a coffee I hadn't paid for. I groaned as I sculled the balmy cup of pure fucking joy.

Ah, I've missed you, old friend.

Her eyebrows were flicked up in surprise.

"What?" I asked.

She shook her head slightly and straightened up. Clearing her throat, she huffed out a laugh. "Nothing. Just didn't expect you to need coffee when you came in shitting rainbows this morning," she grumbled and stalked back towards the kitchen.

I followed, a smirk rising to my lips at how easy of a rise I could get out of her.

"Don't be jealous, Sunny. I'm sure you'll find one of my flaws some day."

She narrowed her brown eyes at me, and I stifled a laugh and tipped my chin up. Her eyes flared and she, in turn, lifted her own chin.

"Perhaps I already have. I personally wouldn't classify arrogance as a likeable trait, Riordan," she retorted, pulling her shoulders back and forcing her sizeable chest forward through her loose training singlet. "And stop calling me that!" she hurried to add.

"There's a fine line between arrogance and confidence," I stated, ignoring her latter request.

Mari clenched the mug in her hands, and I zoned in on her only inked hand. The patterns, the figurations of the diamonds and circles that decorated her fingertips were oddly familiar.

"And yet here you are, playing fucking jump rope with that line." A crease formed between her eyebrows, and she leaned her head down to guzzle further on her coffee. Though the steam that was coming from the rim was nothing compared to the steam coming from her ears.

"How very un-Sunny of you, being so grumpy so early in the morning."

A light red flush washed over her neck. A soft pop sounded as her loud mouth fell agape, words failing to come out.

"Sorry, but you're gonna have to try harder than that to get under my skin. No one talks shit like pro fighters and you, my dear, are not a pro. I've had the UFL's best and brightest talk shit to me, and I was the one left standing."

"T-the UFL?" Her eyes flared in recognition and widened so far I could see the whites around the tops of the honey browns.

"Do you even know who I am, Sunny?" My watch buzzed for 5.00 am.

"Should I?" she replied, scowling.

I laughed and downed the rest of my coffee, placing the empty mug on top of her half-full one.

"Google it and find out." I smirked at her, using my finger to shut her open mouth, and walked out with a wink.

***

Mari hit pads with a ferocity I'd never seen before. Her lips parted, barely a whisper of air floating past them, like these pops of goddamn lightning she'd been creating were barely taking a toll.

"One, two, one, slip, two, three," JJ ordered. Sweat was already starting to break across the back of his shirt.

BANG, BANG, BANG ... BANG, BANG.

I strained against every muscle in my jaw fighting to release in fucking shock. Those loud cracks of lightning sounded as if the pads had personally offended her. I watched her intently, picking up small errors here and there. Nothing wild enough to really require my assistance as of yet, but you know what they say—know thy enemy.

Somehow, in the twenty-four hours I'd formally known this woman, that was the category she'd subjected herself to. From her quippy greeting to her tempered introductions to the other coaches in the gym, I'd happily shoved Mari Trevino out of the 'friend' category. I was being given a second shot at this—this sport, this life, this world. There was no way in hell I was going to let a tiny lady—who just needed a weekend out and a good root—ruin that.

I inwardly cringed. As much as I hated to admit it, she was good. *Really fucking good.*

"You're dropping your left hand when you transition to southpaw." The words were out of my mouth before I could stop them.

Her head snapped towards me, a venomous glare in tow.

I laughed, lifting that smirk to my face I could already tell gained the appropriate reaction from her.

Game on, Trevino.

Not breaking eye contact, I threw my hand out, gesturing for JJ to swap out of pad holder with me.

"Throw the combo again," I ordered.

"It's—" JJ started.

"I got it, man," I replied, staring Mari down.

Her gaze narrowed briefly, then she raised her hands.

I snapped a hand into place to catch her flying fist as she threw a lead jab to initiate the combo. I caught all of her slick, skilful shots and bided my time. She threw her step-through two and I almost missed my shot when her sweaty, flushed, panting face filled my view.

But in this scenario, I shouldn't be able to *see* that sweaty, flushed, panting face. I pounced on the opportunity. After lifting the hand pad up, I snapped it down the middle. It landed true with a thud in the centre of her face, right on her nose.

She stumbled back in surprise; a blink was all she gave me before she threw again. Her rosy lips parted as an internal war clearly began inflicting itself upon her.

Go on, Sunny. Admit that I was right.

She closed distance as she neared the end of the sequence. She was standing so close I could smell the small beads of sweat starting to form on her brow. The scent, it was intoxicatingly sweet—almost like salty peaches.

She threw a calf kick onto the end, and I bit down on my tongue to distract from the fucking hollow pain bursting through my calf. Cursing myself for allowing the smell of *sweat* to distract me, I lifted that smirk onto my face and celebrated as her cheeks flushed with rage.

I handed the pads back to JJ. "If you're going to drop your left hand so obviously, you gotta have a plan that's better than just gettin' whacked."

A frown took place on her mouth as a crease formed between her brows.

I smirked. "Get back to it."

Chapter 6

Chance

I'd walked into Knock's with no expectations of how this all would go. Most gyms had the same sort of crowd, the same people in different bodies. But after teaching my first class, I could safely say I hadn't been expecting *this*.

From what I'd read of the gym's fighter profiles and schedules, *every single* professional and aspiring fighter signed to Knock's had shown up to this morning's class. Each had their own pre-training regime, as most of us did, some even offering help to the amateur fighters by wrapping their hands or touch sparring with them to warm up. It was quite a sight to see—an entire community coming together for *me*. Granted, I'd never lived anywhere outside the city before, but it was well out of the norm for all of the gyms I'd ever been in.

Then I saw them work.

I had to admit, I'd known Al was good, but I didn't know he was *this* good. The man was sixty-nine-years old and still managed to hold pads for anyone who showed up to class from what I'd heard. And after holding for some of those guys during my own class, I don't know how he wasn't crippled from it all.

We finished the session with some sparring and combined conditioning. No one complained, no one let out as much as a whimper. Not once. I've trained in bigger and better gyms than Knock's before, and yet somehow these people had the most grit and tenacity out of all of them. We were heading out of summer and into winter, but that sunlight still warmed the metal walls of the gym up into a fucking sauna. But no one complained, no one batted an eyelid at the heat burning from the tin walls.

Yeah ... people who thought martial arts were sexy were straight up wrong.

We're all stinking, sweaty messes.

Now, that particular statement certainly was not applicable to Mari. Female fighters have never particularly been my squeeze, but there was fucking *something* about her ...

Perhaps it was the fluidity in which she threw her strikes, or the malice that launched them. She moved like water, flowing and controlled. How could so much power come from such a tiny lady? Maybe it was the crease between her brows when she concentrated, or the blush of effort on her cheeks under her dusting of freckles. It could have been the curve of her waist, or that ass of hers that should require a license to carry—

Alright. That's enough there, big fella.

Point is, I've seen professional male fighters throw down with less destruction than Mari in a pads session. As much as I hated to admit it, it was, by far, the hottest thing I'd ever seen.

That echoing, booming voice could only belong to one lunatic. The same lunatic I called my best mate.

When he appeared moments later, Gus play-bowed at JJ and began doing gentle zoomies around the office area. JJ gasped and dramatically fell to the floor, not even trying to catch himself.

"What the—"

Marilyn held a hand up to me.

Those quick, tip-tap footsteps came pattering over, only stopping when Gus *launched* himself onto JJ. The grown-ass man on the floor laughed and giggled like a child as Gus, still with his ears pulled back, licked every inch of his face, pinning his chest to the ground.

"How long have you had him for?" I asked Marilyn. Looking at the size of her, her old and frail figure, there was no way she could handle a dog as big as Gus on her own.

"A few years now, though the public only know about the last two." She shot a look at JJ, who was now spooning with Gus.

"And why is that, Nana dearest?" My best friend smirked, looking like a mischievous cat who just *knows* he's been caught doing the wrong thing.

"No, no, Jaxon. I will let you tell that story." She winked at JJ's feigned shock at the usage of his first name.

I raised my eyebrows at him in amused question.

What did you do, you mad bastard?

"Mari and I may have heisted Gus from his previous shit-cunt owners," JJ grumbled, scratching Gus's belly.

"You two stole a dog?" I confirmed.

"Sure did, Chancey boy."

"And this didn't bother you?" I asked Marilyn.

She held her hands up in surrender. "You're crazy if you think I had any chance of somehow reversing what they did," Marilyn laughed and sat on the grey loveseat. Gus saw her seated and immediately abandoned JJ in favour of snuggling up on the couch with Marilyn.

"Pussy-whipped traitor," JJ sulked.

"Ah, I knew it would be this one she got rid of." Marilyn pulled a file out of the rubbish bin next to Mari's desk. "The most important one."

Reaching out in front of her, she nodded her head for me to take the file.

I opened it, finding a multi-page handwritten letter from none other than Elijah Trevino—my fucking *hero*.

"What is this?" I asked, lightly skimming through the pages.

JJ sat up, though his gaze stayed on the floor. "The last letter that the great Elijah Trevino wrote before he lost his damn mind."

Any breath in my lungs whooshed out as my entire world slowed. *Lost his mind?*

"No need to be so crass, JJ dear." Marilyn frowned. "Though he is right about it being the last letter he wrote." She began softly stroking Gus's fur, avoiding anyone's gaze but his.

"I thought he just retired?" I could remember the day clear as ever. The commentators on UFL 430 had announced it during the break between fights. The tribute highlight reel they had played was incredible. All of the people in the pub I was in had been out of their seats, applauding, cheering, whistling, crying. Elijah Trevino had made history.

"He did, just not voluntarily." Marilyn sighed, pushing her glasses up her slim nose. "Did you watch UFL 425?"

I nodded. UFL 425 had turned out to be Elijah's last fight. The main event had been Elijah Trevino vs Dustin Spades. They'd beaten the absolute *brakes* off each other. Dustin Spades had come out with the decision, and Elijah Trevino could barely stand when they were announcing it. I remember one of his coaches, who I now recognise as Al, had been standing behind him to hold him upright.

"The damage he took in that fight sped up the process of something that was a long time coming," she said cryptically.

I raised an eyebrow, urging her to continue.

"His team of doctors put him into a medically-induced coma for four days to allow his brain uninterrupted time to heal. The public doesn't know about this, as Mari forged his signature for the procedure to go ahead."

JJ loosed a breath, stood, and closed the office door.

"He wasn't the same when he woke up—"

"But he wouldn't be alive right now if they hadn't put him under," JJ interrupted, casting a pointed look Marilyn's way.

"*Anyways* ..." She returned the favour. "His decline happened quickly over a few months after he woke up. In his mind, he was still ready and *willing* to continue fighting. But he just wasn't the same after it took over."

"After what took over exactly?" I asked softly, noting the tone of the room.

"The CTE," JJ filled in after a moment of silence. "He'd have good days and bad days. Some days he would realise what was coming for him, and some days he would do training sessions as if he was in fight camp again." He sighed, rubbing a hand over his face and leaning back on my desk. He solemnly looked at me, the grief written all over him. The grief over a loved one who hadn't passed but was no longer themselves. "We collectively put together a retirement statement after Mari and I found him trying to do a water cut in the sauna at two-thirty in the morning. Congratulations, you're in on the secret now. A secret bigger than Santa Claus. Because this isn't some magical story that makes children giddy and full of joy—this is reality here at Knock's, man."

"On one of his *good* days, before he went away, he had his will changed. When he was no longer deemed clinically stable, Mari was to inherit the business. There was one condition—each staff member, both current and future, was to be given a letter. He called it his legacy letter; and it's the reason why we still have so many of the staff left after a period of ... financial struggle."

My eyes shot up to Marilyn's. "Are you guys still strapped for cash?"

A string of plans began to unfold in my mind. I would have to head into Darlington Harbour early, but skim past the old Lakehouse Brewery so no one would spot me. Then I would hit the bank branch on the outskirts and—

She chuckled softly. "No, dear. We found a way."

She patted Gus's rear, signalling for him to hop down from the couch. Marilyn stood up slowly, Gus carefully watching her every move.

"Come on, boys. Let's leave him to it." She put a hand to JJ's shoulder and turned him towards the door. "I want to hear all about the young lady you had coffee with this morning."

"Well ..."

I could practically hear JJ's smirk.

"There wasn't much coffee drinking, if you're pickin' up what I'm puttin' down."

Their voices faded away as I started reading my hero's 'legacy letter'.

"Welcome to the beating heart of my soul. Great to have you here ..."

"Knock's has always and will always be a place of healing and serenity. Ironic due to the nature of what we do to each other on those mats ..."

"My beautiful daughter, Mari, is as fiercely protective of this place as I was. If you can't see it as anything but that, then Knock's isn't the place for you ..."

I read on and on and on.

Then I read it again.

And again.

And again.

I read it until I could practically hear Elijah Trevino's voice in my head. He detailed how *The Elijah Trevino* came to be. How he met Al, when the coach-of-a-lifetime saved his ass in a bar fight one night, and how he might've wound up dead in a gutter if Al hadn't been there. He spoke of Leah, the love of his life, whom he dedicated every inkling of his success too. He described her as 'who Knock's would be if it were a person'. And finally, for the last page and a half, I read about his one and only daughter—Mari. It was so fucking surreal to read about the true love a father had for his child. Heaven knew I'd never experienced that. It felt like he was in my corner, telling me, 'She'll be a challenge to win over but once you do, you'll have her for life'.

I never was one to back down from a challenge.

***

"Trevino!" I called, lowering my voice to that steely level so people knew I wasn't fucking around. "Bag work. Five rounds. Start with 20 kicks a side."

"Pardon?" Fury burned hot in those eyes. Their sweet honey colour turned to dark cocoa brown almost instantly.

I smirked as she stormed over.

"Who do you think you're talking to?"

"Who do *you* think *you're* talking to?" I countered. Gloriously amused at the look on her face, I lifted my chin and sure as shit kept my eyes on hers. "Last I checked, this is my class. Play by my rules, start pulling your goddamn punches, or get out."

She glared at her sparring partner, a shorter, bearded fighter who was now wiping away a bloody nose. "You—" she started.

"What's it gonna be, Sunny?" I cut her off, taking a step closer into her space.

She was puffing, panting lightly through her nose, lips tightening into an angry frown.

"You gonna hit the bag or the bricks?"

"Fuck you, Riordan," she spat. Her face was flushed red with rage and those dark eyes blazed back at me. She tore her thick black gloves off and threw them towards her gear bag—identical to mine but with an elegant *MT* embroidered in white stitching on the front pocket.

I set my posture, standing tall as I turned around to find everyone milling around watching us. The timer blaringly sounded, signalling a new round, and my thoughts broke free.

"Everybody hit the ground for push-ups! Since you would all rather stand around and gossip like a bunch of schoolgirls instead of workin'!"

I could hear JJ's mocking laughter as he lapped everyone in push-ups. How? I had no idea. The man switched between salads and KFC every five hours. But, I had to give it to him, it appeared to be working for him considering he was the biggest and strongest in the class. JJ stood at six-five and filled his frame with 125 kilos of pure muscle. He was bigger than me, sure—but he and I both knew he would *never* beat me.

"You want more, Jones?!" I boomed in response to JJ's laughter.

"You know I do, Rio!"

Everyone else in the class groaned in unison.

"Push-ups through the next two bells! No rest!"

Chapter 7

Chance

I fist-bumped the last person in the line and began to walk off the mat when a wet, slimy body pressed itself up against me.

"JJ. You're a real pal for letting me stay at your house and for ensuring I don't starve to death or freeze out on the streets." I sighed. "But for the love of god, will you get your sweaty ass the fuck off of my back?"

"Shh!" he snapped. "The lioness is still out of her cage."

I followed his line of sight, straight over to … Mari.

She was grumbling to herself as she packed her bag. Sweat glistened on her skin, outlining each and every line of the spectacular muscle map of a back she carried. I wasn't surprised she was in a foul mood or absolutely *soaking* after the brutal rounds of bag work, followed by intense sparring where I strategically placed her against quick and agile partners. It was enough of a punishment to leave a mark. A string of curses sounded from that mouth, and she quickly scurried off into the office, leaving her phone behind and slamming the door shut.

"Don't even think about touching that," JJ said, letting a dramatic breath loose. "With what just happened in there, you'll lose a hand if you go near her or her toys."

"Toys?"

"Yeah, the big cats like to play. Some in captivity will play with toys."

"Since when did you become David Attenborough?" I filtered through my bag, placing a hand on the book. A small sigh of relief escaped me. It did every time I confirmed it was still in my possession.

"The only non-fictional animal I could ever describe Mari is as a lioness. Anyone who calls her anything else is just wrong." He shrugged, pulling a fresh shirt from his bag. I cringed.

Dear god, that bag needs a wash.

"Non-fictional? What about fictional?"

"A fire-breathing, gigantic, human-eating dragon," he answered swiftly, digging around for more clothes in his duffle.

"Graphic. Point made," I replied.

"Come on, Chancey boy. Come hose me down." He winked and strutted off towards the open showers.

***

It was midmorning by the time JJ and I had washed off the class and headed out for breakfast. Quickly, might I add, as JJ was 'worried about staying too long in the lioness's den'.

"Class was good this morning, man," JJ said, making a left turn down a quiet street with well-maintained gardens lining either side. "Push-ups and all."

"It's kind of weird how much you like doing push-ups." I returned the smile a local old man gave me with a curt nod.

"There's no way I'm gonna let something as trivial as push-ups make me their bitch."

I stared at him.

"What?"

"This is coming from the guy who cried when Monica proposed to Chandler on *Friends*."

He stared right back, his face utterly blank. "What's your point?"

"You let a TV show make you its bitch but—" I cut myself off. "You know what? Never mind."

We continued walking and talking shit for what felt like hours, but in reality was probably around twenty minutes. The walk was flat and lined with old but well-kept houses. Most were made of bricks; most were surrounded by various greenery and flowers. Some had older women, who very clearly took pride in their yards, out the front with wide-brimmed hats on while they watered and trimmed their plants. Many of them gave JJ cheerful 'hellos', to which he responded to with flirtatious remarks.

"You're like a celebrity around here." I was already starting to sweat from the walk in the sun to wherever JJ was taking me for brekky.

"Jealous? Don't be, Chancey boy. I'll take you out on the town, give you a few good sightings."

"Yeah, because that's what I want. More attention on me." I rolled my eyes. "So, are we going to eat in the next 24 hours?"

"Of course we are. We're going to breakfast," JJ replied with an innocent shrug of his wide shoulders.

"Where the fuck are you taking me?"

"Relax, hangry. The Rustic Roo is just up here."

"Sorry, what? *Where* are you taking me?"

"The Rustic Roo. They do a bangin' eggs benny, bro. You've gotta try it."

***

The Rustic Roo, or 'The Rusty' as locals apparently called it, was bumping—well as much as a small-town cafe could when we arrived. Just over a dozen people sat at the outdoor seating. Most were dolled-up retirees who spared JJ and I a fair few glances as we approached. The outdoor metal seats were old and 'rustic' as the name would have it, but each had a thick cushion with a wildly bright pattern on it. The tables were well looked after and appeared to be custom made, seeing as each one was different. A slice of a tree trunk had been treated, stained, and attached to a matte black stand. A few chipped windchimes softly whistled as we neared, and the smell of bacon wafted out like that of a pie on a windowsill in a cartoon.

My mouth instantly watered.

"Hi, JJ!" an older bird chirped at JJ, waving her ring-clad hand that jingled all of the bangles on her wrist.

"G'day, Hilly. How you goin'?" JJ lathered it on thick, waving back and sending a wink her way.

The old lady blushed and giggled before waving a hand in dismissal.

Several other older women and even a couple of their husbands said their hellos to JJ, who gracefully moved through the small cafe with waves and nods—asking questions here, checking in on people's relatives and pets there.

"You should start charging for your affections," I joked to him as he led us up to the counter made of metal roofing sheets and a narrow strip of timber.

"My affections are invaluable," he cooed. "You'll be famous around here before you know it—known as '*JJ's single friend*'."

I caught the sneaky eye he sent me when referring to my relationship status. I ignored it, letting that say everything that need to be said.

"I'm already known as something that's not '*your single friend*'," I stated, reminding him of my status in the UFL.

"Not here you're not. Most of these people don't watch anything on TV other than the news and *Jeopardy*, and that's because they're both on the same channel."

I glanced at the people around us—the crowd was full of hearing aids, canes, walkers, glasses and receding hairlines. Not a single person here, outside the two of us, looked like they would even know, nor care, about what the UFL was.

"Look what the cat dragged in." An occa accent came from the round, tall lady that waddled up to the other side of the counter. As if on cue, a ginger cat leapt up in front of us, tail swaying in what seemed to be annoyance.

"Mornin', Nancy," JJ hummed before leaning over the counter and dropping a kiss on the woman's puffy cheek.

She rolled her eyes, but her lips quirked up into the smallest of smiles.

"Where's Patty?"

"Patricia's out back cookin' today, since we got a full house." She threw a thumb behind her at the open kitchen window. A thick gold wedding band sat on her ring finger, along with similar ink to Mari's. "Who you brought with you?"

"This is Chance. He's a bit of an angry bastard when he's hungry so I'd save the pleasantries until after he's eaten."

I smacked him upside the head.

"Dick," I muttered.

"Ow! Point proven," he whined.

Nancy smirked at me and shot me a subtle thumbs up before wiping her hands on her already-dirty-probably-never-clean white apron.

"What can I get for youse?"

"A coffee. Black. In your biggest cup, preferably bucket-sized," I ordered.

"Ugh, even your coffee order is soulless. I'll have my usual, Nancy," JJ said.

"What you gonna eat?" she asked me, lifting a dark brow at me. Her dark cocoa skin was glimmering with sweat. I thought about the collective seventeen dollars I had until Knock's started paying me on Friday.

"Nothin'. Just the coffee."

"Pfft. He'll have the same as me," JJ told her and handed over a crisp fifty-dollar bill. The register dinged and the cash drawer popped. Nancy handed JJ back his change, which he dropped straight into the cracked plastic jar that had a piece of masking tape with 'TIPS' written on it. The older woman's face softened as she shot my friend an appreciative look.

"You really didn't have to, man," I said lowly, a twang of shame following. JJ had known I couldn't afford to buy a fucking breakfast—not with every damn cent I had tucked away in an account no one could get to. Not me, *or anyone.*

Idiot. Should have fought to take more.

"You're the one who left the big town life to move out to little ole' Soggla. Least I can do is buy you a decent brekky." He shrugged, though he didn't meet my eyes.

"I'll get you back for it," I promised.

JJ was about to respond when two young girls, no older than thirteen, approached the table.

"H-hi, JJ," the shorter one with the long blonde braids stammered. The taller one, a gangly brunette with a grown-out buzzed haircut, waved shyly and fiddled with her glasses.

"Hi girls," JJ greeted, flashing an award-winning smile at the very clearly swooning girls.

"W-we just wanted to say hi a-and invite you to the next show we're putting on." The blonde girl's face flushed pink under her freckles. "We've already reserved you two front row seats b-but no pressure if you can't make it! We know how busy you are and there will be another three shows this year so—"

"I'll be there," JJ interrupted softly, taking the flyer from the taller girl's hands and placing it under his phone and wallet to stop it from flying away.

"O-okay, great! We'll see you there! T-thanks again!" She grinned a smile full of purple and pink braces and tugged her star-struck friend away to the next table.

"What was that all about?" I asked when they were far enough from earshot. The flyer under JJ's belongings was bright orange with bold black writing on it and lots of exclamation marks. Punctuation aside, the aesthetic reminded me of Knock's.

"Just local celebrity things." JJ waved a hand. "Maybe I should start wearing a disguise. How do you think I'd look in a fake moustache?"

"You do realise you're a man and you have the ability to grow a real moustache?"

"Pfft, rookie. Everyone will know it's me then," he replied.

"Not gonna lie to you, mate, but you don't exactly travel incognito." I gestured to the people around us, who were taking up significantly less space in their chairs than JJ and I were. Then I waved a hand up and down his right arm sleeve tattoo.

"Long black in a tub." Nancy appeared at my side, holding the biggest cup of coffee I'd ever seen with a foamy, precise layer of crema on top. I immediately took a sip, ignoring the burn from the temperature, and almost moaned in relief. Real, non-instant coffee, made by a competent barista.

Coffee snob.

"And your iced chocolate coffee." She plunked down what could only be described as an oversized chocolate sundae.

"Christ, JJ," I chastised.

"What?" he asked innocently, slurping on the diabetes-in-a-glass. "I trained this morning."

"Yeah, for an hour. Not a *month*."

He shrugged and used the long spoon to start breaking off pieces of the almost raw brownie surrounded by whipped cream.

"Don't be jealous that I don't have to cut weight for my fights." He slurped obnoxiously at a spot in the glass where the liquid hadn't quite replenished.

"Just because you don't *have* to doesn't mean you *shouldn't*," I replied, taking a deep gulp of what could only be described as sex in a mug.

We sat, guzzling away at our drinks and spitting shit, when Nancy dropped a bomb in front of the both of us. A literal bomb. I don't think I'd ever seen an eggs benedict so loaded up. My mouth watered at the half a dozen eggs on my plate stacked on top of what appeared to be thick as fuck potato rosti and crispy bacon. A profuse amount of creamy hollandaise sauce was drowning everything underneath it, but it had parsley and chives floating on the top, making the dish look somewhat healthy with the pop of green.

"Enjoy," Nancy said over a shoulder before waddling away, crocs squeaking underneath her. The woman smelled of cigarettes, coffee, and bacon. I'm assuming at least one of those was stashed in her apron.

There was absolutely no time for talking as JJ and I dug in to the masterpieces we'd been served. Reality TV had *nothing* on this amazing race. The flavours, textures—everything was incredible. If my coffee was sex in a mug, this was an orgasm on a plate.

CHAPTER 8

Mari

*F*ucking Chance Riordan. Having Jayden around was hard enough, let alone when I got paired up with him for sparring rounds.

The taunting.

The teasing.

The sneaky little threats.

Fucking pricks. Both of them.

It drove me up the goddamn wall.

Then, *Mr Superhero Chance* comes along and punishes me?! If he's gonna punish me, he can at least have the decency to get me naked—

Don't even go there, you absolute degenerate.

I huffed as I slammed the microwave door shut and pressed *start* on my lunch. After two morning classes, I was already starving. After two morning classes *and* dealing with a stupidly hot asshole coach who not only got on my nerves but spiked my goddamn sex drive—I was intolerably ragey.

"Pissed off with the microwave? Or pretending you're locking someone in there?" a taunting voice said.

I tipped my head back, looking to whoever was up there in the sky, asking them the simple question, '*Are you fucking kidding me?*'.

"What do you want, Jayden?" *Still another ninety seconds on my food.*

"Just wanted to see if you'd learned your lesson."

I could *hear* the smirk on his face. My throat began to vibrate with what I could only describe as the growl of a rabid dog working its way up.

"I could ask the same thing of you," I snarled. "How's that bloody nose I gave you?"

"Pretty good, since I didn't have one of the UFL's top fighters telling me I'm a shit training partner."

Forty-five seconds left on my food. I kept my back towards him and gritted my teeth. I knew better than to play his intolerable migraine-inducing games. I shouldn't have bitten on the stupid bait he lured me in with.

"Tell me, what's it like to be ordered around in your own gym?" He was closer now. His volume was lowering, which I knew from the past meant some *heinous* shit was about to be spat at me.

"It must feel pretty demeaning. I mean—" He laughed, and the sound was anything but warm. His breath was so close I could feel my hair parting around it.

Shouldn't have worn your hair down, Mari. That was one of the very first things Dad taught you.

"You try to act like this badass boss lady that no one can touch or order around." He stepped closer.

Fifteen seconds left on the microwave. This brekky bowl Nan cooked up better be worth it.

"But you're just a soft little girl, aren't you? You and I both know just how *soft* you are."

"Everything okay in here?" An icy-cool voice came from behind us, and Jayden sprung back as if someone had put hot coals under his feet.

My traitorous body let out a breath I'd been holding at the loss of contact, and I dropped my hands onto the counter to regather myself.

"Everything's fine, Coach. Just came to clear the air with Mari here. We both got a bit heated in sparring, didn't we, Mari?" He placed a hand on my shoulder and squeezed my trap.

I didn't respond. *Fuck the last five seconds on my food.*

"Trevino?"

I yanked the container from the microwave, ignoring the burn on my fingertips. The anger I felt in the pit of my stomach was much hotter.

I ignored both of them, until my ego got the best of me and I flipped them both off.

Sighing when my ass hit my desk chair, I stabbed a piece of chicken and forced some egg, bacon, and potato onto my fork.

"That pig still alive? Or are you pretending that it's my eyeball?"

I heard the smirk on Chance's face before I saw it. His blue eyes studied me, an ocean-worth of depth swirling in a mixture of boredom and ... *concern?*

"Depends, are you here to berate me about this morning's class?"

A flicker of surprise lashed through his eyes. He blinked and it was gone. "Not at all."

I barely swallowed before I shoved another forkful into my mouth. The simmering pit of rage in my stomach started to fade.

Note to self, hunger and assface ex-boyfriend do not mix well. Add Chance Riordan into the mix—straight up shitshow.

"Surprised you're not berating me for it though."

"And why would I do that?" I said with a disgustingly full mouthful. Heat moved into my cheeks when I realised just how un-ladylike I was currently being.

"You tell me." He cocked his head to the side and studied me.

My chest felt a kilometre deep when the gentle thudding of my heart turned into a brash sledge-hammering.

"It's your class, Riordan." I swallowed and clenched the fork in my fist to stop from taking another mouthful. I ran my tongue over my lips, and I could have sworn he tracked the movement. "You're the coach here now, not me. If I'm not meeting expectations, I expect you to tell me, just as I would expect you to tell *others*." Like that asshole who got the blame pinned on me earlier.

"Anyone in particular I should keep in mind?" He folded his arms over his chest. Any trace of boredom on his face was gone, replaced with an intensity of something I couldn't read.

I shrugged, giving in and eating the last of the food in my container.

"Interesting."

I flicked my eyebrows up at him.

"Figured you would have told me about the little rat I just found you in the kitchen with." Something even darker than before crossed his face.

The vein bulging on his bicep screamed at me to stare—to run my eyes up, down, and *all* around him. I stared at the empty container in my hands to take the slack off my eyes.

"I'm a big girl. I'm not weak. I can handle myself." I scowled at the fact that Jayden had made me feel this way again. He'd made me feel like I needed to justify myself, physically announce that I was strong and capable and not fucking *soft*.

"Just because you can, doesn't mean you should have to." Chance unfolded his arms and bumped his fist against the wall. "Let me know if you ever feel like *not* having to." With a wink and a flick of that cocky smirk, he left.

***

"Let me know if you ever feel like not having to."

Chance's words ran through my head all afternoon. Surely, he was just being polite? He wasn't offering to be my own goddamn security detail ... *was he*? How could a professional UFL fighter possibly care about people giving me a hard time?

Questions upon questions spun around and around in my head, all as I watched him from the side of his evening class. I couldn't even tell if what Chance was teaching was any good. Why? Because he was teaching in a scrap of material you could call a singlet. The evening was unusually warmer than the last few, meaning his singlet was *saturated* with sweat, along with his delicious frame. He looked like every twenty-something-year-old girl's pin-up man.

Was I still intent on maintaining my zero-fighters rule? Absolutely. But a girl can window shop without buying anything.

Chance picked JJ up and threw him to the ground. He casually stood, continuing his explanation of how to perform the throw and why it was useful in MMA. As if I'd screamed his name myself, his gaze whipped to mine. When the corners of his mouth tugged upwards, I realised my jaw was slack.

Yup, caught with a slack jaw.

I was almost positive, from the way he was looking at me, he could *see* the patch of wetness that was forming under my spat shorts.

"Get a drink. Three-minute rounds, running in between."

While everyone began making their way off to the side of the mat to prepare for sparring, Chance and JJ walked straight towards me. JJ was chewing Chance's ear off about god knows what, but his stare stayed on me.

"Happy with the class, boss?" Chance asked, interrupting something JJ was saying. JJ pouted and swatted his arm. Chance completely ignored him.

"Absolutely," I replied, sliding a blank mask over my face, trying desperately to hide the fact that I knew he'd caught me ogling him.

"What did you think of the footsweep? Pretty effective right?" His hint of a smirk widened across his face.

"Looked great. I'm a big fan of footsweeps myself," I replied as coolly as I could.

Chance laughed, *fucking* winked at me again, and strode off towards the sparring timer.

"You absolute horndog," JJ scolded.

"What?" I gaped.

"We didn't learn a fucking footsweep, Lynnie. We've been doing major throws the *whole* time."

Some sort of weird telepathic connection between JJ and Chance pricked, and that cocky, sexy, infuriating smirk erupted onto the latter's face.

"God, you two," JJ grumbled. "At least try to keep it in your pants."

CHAPTER 9

Mari

My foot slammed on the ground to catch my fall.

God, I'm so tired I'm tripping over my own fucking feet.

The sun, only just beginning to rise, warmed my stiff body. That dawn sunshine was something I loved most about walking to the gym each morning. But on a morning like this, where I was unbearably tired, that warm sun felt a little too similar to the comforts of my own bed. Meaning instead of my usual cuppa when I arrived at the gym, I'd need a double ... or quadruple.

The rocks crackled underneath my feet as I stopped in front of the gym—all of the doors were open, but none of the lights seemed to be on? I thumbed the hidden blade I keep in my bag strap, sucked in a breath to hold, and silently crept around the corner.

My knife hit the ground with a clatter. There was someone in the gym.

Not just anyone.

Chance.

"Mornin' boss!" he chirped, curling the dumbbell up his arm with a slight grunt.

There's a man in my gym, at the asscrack of dawn, doing bicep curls.

Correction—there's a very hot, very shirtless, professional UFL fighter in my gym, at the asscrack of dawn, doing bicep curls.

"Sorry, didn't mean to scare you," he said, racking the dumbbells and grabbing his towel from the bench. Sweat greedily dripped down his chest, in between every crevice of his carved stomach. "Just wanted to get a workout in before the crowds came." He smiled, and if that didn't just make me melt even more.

"Are you alright?" he asked, concern knitting his brows together.

"Perfectly fine," I replied, unable to stop my eyes from openly wandering over his frame. The built, muscled body of a fighter—a warrior.

Fuck, was it getting hot in here?

"Something on your mind?" Like the moment before the storm hits, the sudden snap in temperature, his gaze turned heated as he watched me drink him in.

"A thing or two." My fingers reached for him; a warmth spread through me at the feel of his sweaty, blood-filled chest.

"Anything I can help with?" Chance took a step closer. He towered over me. He was so much bigger that I couldn't not get lost in him—he was everywhere.

He reached his own fingers out and brushed the backs of them across my cheek, skimming them further until they were tangled in my hair. Thank god I left it out this morning.

"A thing or two," I repeated, breathless.

His skin felt incredible on mine. The fingers that were gently tugging on my hair released and traced an invisible line down my side all the way to my waist. He palmed my hip, pulling me closer in one quick motion while his other hand fed back into my hair, weaving easily through the curly strands.

Yes.

Yes, yes, yes.

"You know where to find me, Trevino."

My curtains were wide open with the sun blazing in—but it was blindingly obvious that wasn't the reason I felt so *hot*: unbearably turned on, a hand between my legs, and absolutely soaked through my pyjama pants.

No.

No—I refuse to feel good from this.

No. He's a fighter. He's an employee—

He's a sex icon.

Nowhere was safe from this man—not even my subconscious. I cursed the world for not recognising the effort I'd been making. After the slip I had in his wrestling class two weeks ago, I'd been making a point of avoiding him at all costs. I trained every day but showed up a second before class started and left as soon as it ended. I partnered up with someone other than JJ, not wanting to give Chance a reason to come my way. I even ignored Jayden and all of the hush, hush comments he'd fire at me. All to avoid the unavoidable—Chance's attention.

Though I hid like an absolute child, he still found me. Whenever I was doing well, he was always there telling me. Whenever I wasn't, he was there too.

The worst part about it all—I didn't hate it.

I didn't hate the fact that he always watched me.

I didn't hate the fact that he taught most of his higher intensity classes *without* a shirt on.

What I *did* hate was the fact that I couldn't bring myself to hate these things.

I should have loathed all of these things—my vow against dating fighters required me to do so. But I couldn't help but *notice* things. Like the fact he always watched me do the techniques before he watched anyone else. Or that he hadn't partnered me up with Jayden since that day in the kitchen. Or that he always glanced my way before stripping off at the end of class, usually for a heartbeat longer when I was also shedding my clothes. He usually cast a glance over the room, to see what everyone else was doing during the latter too.

My inconvenient dream did a fantastic job at kicking my ass into gear, and I got dressed and to the gym in record time.

I opened up the gym, sighing in relief that I was the first one in, and headed straight for the kitchen. I filled and flicked the kettle on boil, a soft squealing starting to sing from the old machine. Needing to keep moving and fight the goddamn *itch* in my hands, I strode over to the offices quickly. It was dark and I couldn't see shit, so I flung my bags in the general direction of the couch. Instead of landing with a *thud*, a soft groan sounded, followed by my bags hitting the floor.

"Ah, fuck."

That voice.

I ran my hand along the wall until I hit the light switch. "Jesus! Riordan! What the hell are you doing in here?!" I gawked at his once-again shirtless torso, along with the sleepy expression he was wearing.

Yep, my subconscious was right on the money with that image.

His long, golden locks were messy and some were starting to fall over his face.

How he still looked so delectable first thing in the morning was just plain unfair. After sleeping, when our hair is wild, eyebrows muffled, and with sleep in our eyes—as humans we're meant to wake up out of shape. Wake up gross, with dried drool on our faces.

But Chance Riordan appeared to not fall into the category of human.

"Well, I *was* sleeping." He groaned again, rubbing his hands slowly over his face and grumbling a few more curses.

"A-are you ..." I could barely get the words out.

He raised his eyebrows in question, those blue eyes looking a little grey, matching the circles under his eyes. Had he always been this worn-out? Or was I only just noticing?

"Are you living in my gym, Riordan?" I whispered. My chest twinged uncomfortably at the thought.

"Relax, Sunny. I'm not squatting in your gym." He sat up, tossing the blanket aside to reveal the pair of baggy tie-dyed shorts he was wearing underneath. The shorts nearly reached his knees, but the lines that sculpted his torso cut in deep as he moved to stand.

My breath stuttered at those lines—how dangerously low his shorts were hanging.

"JJ had company last night ... and happens to snore like a fucking foghorn."

"You're more than welcome to come and use our spare room." Nan's sweet voice filled the room, and my eyes bulged.

I turned to face her at the door as Gus trotted to my side.

She smiled a closed-mouth smile, her telltale sign of mischief. "We're well aware of just how badly JJ snores. Aren't we, Mari?"

I narrowed my eyes at her and hummed in response. Chance chuckled from behind me.

"Thank you, Marilyn, but I don't want to intrude." He smirked. "Besides, wouldn't want to make Sunny here feel ... *uncomfortable*."

The exhausted grey that his eyes wore before vanished as amusement lit the way. The tension in his forehead relaxed, as well as the crease between his brows. For a moment, he smiled, a true smile, as he and Nan laughed together. I almost forgot about what they were insinuating.

"Me? Uncomfortable?" I scoffed. "Please."

"You sure you'd be okay with it?" Nan poked.

"Yes, I'm sure," I snapped, folding my arms.

"Great. Chance, be at the table for dinner at seven. I trust you to shower before coming over." Nan settled, the tone of her voice leaving no room for bailing out on the plan she'd made. I looked over and Chance's blues flared ever so slightly in surprise. Those eyes scanned my face before he smiled at Nan.

"A gentleman doesn't show up unwashed now, does he?"

"I'd confirm that statement with that friend of yours," Nan replied.

"Who? Sunny?" Chance asked, pointing a thumb towards me.

"No!" I scowled. "I do not smell!"

Any ounce of amusement left Chance's face.

"No, you definitely do not." Raw, fiery heat filled his gaze. His eyes ran over my figure, spending a generous amount of time along the curve where my waist met my thighs.

"I—" I sputtered. "Whatever!"

Chance and Nan laughed as I stalked out, Gus trotting alongside me all the way back to the kitchen.

"At least you wouldn't rat me out," I muttered to my sweet boy.

"And I suppose you think I did?" Nan asked, her ruby red lips pursed.

"Oh yeah. Big time, Nan," I huffed. "You totally threw me under the bus back there!"

"What makes you say that, dear?" She took her usual seat at the table.

I levelled a look on her, and she laughed.

"I was just being polite, Mari," she said, clicking her now emerald green nails on the table. She must have gone to the salon yesterday. "I thought I raised you to do the same."

"I—"

"If that man needs somewhere to get a peaceful night's rest, he is *more than welcome* to come and stay in our guest room."

She raised her eyebrows at me. "You were raised better than to let your libido get in the way of being a good person."

I gawked at my grandmother talking about my libido of all things. Gus moved and lay at Nan's feet, as if even he could smell the burn she'd just delivered.

I sighed, running a hand over my face. "The fact that I find him attractive"—*extremely* attractive— "has nothing to do with me not wanting him to stay at my house. What would the others think? It's unprofessional."

"I believe you have offered *our* house to others before, dear." She emphasised that I was not the only one in ownership of the house, scolding me with my mother's eyes. "Like when Liv was in-between houses? Or before JJ's parents moved out and were having all kinds of troubles? What about when Wazza needed—"

"Those were different!"

"Why? Because it wasn't Chance asking to stay? Because there was no opportunity for anything in your life to *change* from that occurring?" She tilted her head at me, and I should have just agreed with her from the start. She was in no mood to argue today. "I know change is scary for you, but sometimes we have to put that aside and help the people who need it. It's exactly what your father would have done."

I discreetly rolled my eyes at the mention of his name.

"Fine. I'm not offering though—it's your offer," I huffed.

Nan patted my shoulder and walked out. Gus trailed along behind her, worshipping the ground she walked on.

Chapter 10

Mari

"Get a drink!" Chance squirted water into his mouth, a few droplets falling loose onto his grey shirt.

Oh, for fuck's sake.

"Timer's on!" He pointed the long, slim remote at the clock to start the countdown. "Grab a partner!"

Glancing around the room, my stomach dropped and filled with butterflies at the same time.

Everyone else had a partner, except ...

"Trevino," Chance called, that cocky smirk lifting his lips as he beckoned me forward with two fingers, "you're with me."

My wrestling boots pattered as I walked over to the middle mats he was occupying. His arms fell relaxed by his sides, his face that fusion of arrogance and superiority. The smirk on his lips was long gone, his head dipped slightly to the side.

He reached a hand to slap and bump, signalling an unofficial beginning. I immediately reached one back but locked it in a tight grasp around his extended wrist instead. Pushing my opposite arm behind his tricep, I drove my weight through and moved around so we were standing parallel.

Too parallel.

Chance pummelled his arm through to an overhook, and in half a second I was flying. Rolling over his hip, I threw my arm out at the very last second to catch the momentum of my fall. The impact knocked the air out of me, but I refused to stop. I pushed my foot onto his thigh and spun myself to square with him. Hooking my feet behind his knees, I used my hands as a wedge and drove my hips up and over, forcing him to fall on his ass. The second he hit the mat, I knew he'd let me have it. He sprung up so fast— sliding a hand over my inner thigh and cupping my hip, setting enough pressure on it that I couldn't move. He caught my counter before I struck, taking an undergrasp grip on my opposing wrist and pinning my arm down with his weight. I struggled against him, fighting for any inch of movement. But he'd *completely* disarmed me. The corners of his lips tipped up in satisfaction.

"What next, Sunny?" he asked, cockiness and victory lacing every word.

With a very unladylike growl, I shoved my top wrestling boot into the gap next to his inner thigh, freeing my bottom leg and pushing the other foot on his knee. Using his undergrasp grip against him, I laced my top arm over his in a semi-tight overhook. Semi-tight because his arms were gigantic, and I could barely get one of mine over his. Mustering a push-pull motion with my legs, Chance landed flat on his back as I straddled him, holding on to the arm I'd isolated in as much of a death grip as I could muster.

A low rumble skittered through Chance's chest, and I was being rolled over the overhook I'd grabbed to sweep him, the arm now trapped and leaving me unable to post out on it. It was my turn to land flat on my back, and Chance rolled directly between my legs, hips higher than mine and pinning them down once again.

"You need to use moves less predictable than that if you have an *opponent* coming after you," he said lowly, his face so close to mine a bead of sweat dripped from his forehead onto my chest. It smelled of everything Chance—salt, fresh air, and authority.

He must have caught onto my confusion,

"Don't think I haven't noticed the little *rat* we have in here," he hissed, completely bypassing the heat I knew was burning in my eyes from his proximity.

Stupid flaring libido.

I froze. The only person he'd called *rat* was Jayden.

"I don't know what you're talking about." I feigned innocence, trying to force it into my face, though my heart was pounding so hard I was sure he could hear it.

Chance let out a laugh that was anything but happy.

"If that's how you want to play it, Trevino, then so be it." He stood and the timer beeped loudly.

People around the room scattered apart and started to run along the edges of the mat space.

"I'll play cat and mouse for a little while longer."

I waited for that smirk to dance on his lips, for some sort of amusement to flash over his face. It never came. His face as he joined JJ in the running line reflected one thing—death's grace. This wasn't Coach Chance on the mats for rounds tonight—it was light heavyweight fighter Chance Riordan.

Chapter 11

Chance

"Get a drink, guys," I ordered, clicking the series of buttons on the remote to turn the digital timer on. "Sparring rounds in two minutes."

JJ strode to my side and began talking about ... who knows? Something caught my attention. Not something—*someone*.

Sunny had been quiet during classes today. No witty banter with JJ. No laughing jokes with members.

No fiery remarks with me.

The quiet wasn't her—but neither was the rock she was currently resembling in my MMA class. Rigid and completely un-*Sunny*. Not an ember of fire from her, not a single ray of that hot, burning sunshine.

There was no swift but frazzled dash to try and dodge me. She wasn't on edge, or antsy. She wasn't itching to be moving. She wasn't fidgeting every five seconds.

No—this was something new. And I couldn't work out why there was this stupid twang in my chest over it. It was uncomfortable.

And inconvenient.

Sparring rounds had started exactly twelve minutes ago, and I was over helping a couple of guys with a particular kick they had been trying to work on. My ears had pricked at the sound of JJ's whistle. It was how we had communicated in bustling areas when we were kids—whistling to each other like dogs. I met his stare and he turned and nodded towards the back corner of the mats.

Mari and that short, bearded guy were sparring. Jason? Jake? Jack? He was the one person who's name I couldn't seem to remember. Though, after finding him and Sunny in the kitchen that day, I'd self-referred to him as one thing—*rat*.

I stepped away from the blokes I had been helping and walked along the edge of the mats slowly, trying not to draw suspicion at my sudden interest in the back corner.

Sunny's face was pale and yet flushed with rage. She swung at him, hard, lobby punches that were never going to land. That was the problem when you got angry; you got sloppy.

Rat caught onto that too—a grin breaking out on his face that had me wary before he swung back. I was already moving for them when his fist connected with her nose. She slipped, falling backwards onto the floor. Rat followed her down, pouncing on her as he forced his way to mount and began a vicious ground and pound.

"Jayden!" JJ yelled.

Jayden, then.

"What the fuck is this?!" I yelled when I arrived, yanking Rat off Sunny and tossing him behind me. The guy wouldn't have been bigger than a featherweight.

Jayden pulled a sharp intake of breath to start throwing words instead, but Sunny got there first.

"Nothing," she said, pushing up from her elbows to stand. "It's nothing. We were just sparring."

The blood in my veins cooled, simmering down to an icy frost that felt much worse. I stared at Sunny, waiting for it. Waiting for the truth. Waiting for the fiery remark.

But it didn't come.

She stood there, hands by her side, face void of emotion. Blood trickled from her nose, the swelling had long since started, and she still didn't flinch. Those brown eyes weren't glowing with honey and weren't that cocoa brown filled with anger. They were a soft hazel, nothing shining or glimmering about them. They were shaded in something *I couldn't fucking decipher*.

For fuck's sake!

"There shouldn't be blood in sparring," I growled. Again, Rat opened his mouth to speak, but Sunny beat him there.

"Accidents happen." She shrugged.

"So do beatdowns," JJ countered.

Sunny shot him a look, strong enough to make him hold his hands up in surrender.

"Time's up," I told her as the loud beep went off. "Start running."

***

"C'mon, Lynnie! Just let me pound on him a little bit? Please?" JJ begged.

I stood in the office doorway, arms folded tightly over my chest as I stared at Sunny, sitting on the couch between our desks. Her curly hair was pulled into a knot on top of her head, with loose stray curls dropping all around her face, and her white training shirt had red blotches pattered all down it. And her face? She'd refused to let me or JJ assess the damage, but she held firm a wad of paper towel and an ice pack to her fat nose.

Yeah, that one is gonna be sore in the morning.

"No need, JJ," she mumbled, sucking a breath in past her teeth as she readjusted the ice pack. "It was an accident. No punishment necessary."

"Bullshit," I growled, stalking over to where she and JJ were on the couch. "Let me look."

"I'm fine, Riordan—"

"Let. Me. Look. Sunny."

She hesitated, and I contemplated just ripping the damn thing off her if I didn't know how much it would hurt. Her brown eyes met mine, still clouded over with that hazel that left me with nothing but unease. Sighing in defeat, she dropped both hands away from her face.

It was an effort not to grind down on my teeth at the sight of her. Bruising was already starting to form over her nose and between her eyes, meaning it would be ten times worse tomorrow. Her cheekbones had a slight puff to them too, where Jayden must have landed some of those ground-and-pound shots.

My back teeth burned, a raging ache that demanded I fix this. Not the responsible way— with words and warnings. But the *irresponsible* way—with fists and blood. Lots of it.

"You'll have one hell of a headache tomorrow," I managed to grind out. "Feel like telling the truth yet?"

She scowled at me, immediately cringing at how the expression hurt her face. "I don't know what you're talking about. I've told you the truth four times now. I got my ass beat in sparring. *No biggie.*"

"C'mon, Lynnie. Spill your guts. This isn't the first time Jayden's roughed you up in sparring."

My eyebrows flew to the ceiling.

This isn't the first time? He's hurt her before? He put hands on her before?

"And I've roughed him up plenty. We're even."

"This, compared to the blood nose you gave him the other week, is not '*even*'." I don't know how I could even get the words out; I was clenching my jaw so tight. "I'm kicking him out. I'm not having men who hurt women in my classes."

"No! You can't kick him out!" Those hazel-filled eyes were wild, frantic, panicked.

My blood stilled for a beat.

What does she know that I don't?

"Why the hell can't I?"

Another conflicted sigh, another internal argument she was having with herself.

Her hand rose to pinch the bridge of her nose before she thought better of it and ran it over her hair instead. "Because"—she sighed a shaky breath—"if we lose Jayden, we lose the gym."

Chapter 12

Mari

Silence filled the office. Unbearable, uncomfortable silence. The kind of quiet that came after you say something you shouldn't have. After you spill a secret that shouldn't have been told.

"What?" JJ's eyes were just about to fall out of his head.

"What do you mean *we lose the gym*?" Chance asked, much, much softer this time.

I looked back to JJ, knowing he would understand the context of what I was about to say next.

"Camden McLarry is the founder of DiplomatGen."

"Yeah? What does that have to do with anything?" JJ asked.

"DiplomatGen is also the founder of lots of smaller, minor companies. Presumably to … make *business* easier, you could say."

"You sure could. That's why Jayden, Camden, and the rest of their soul-sucking, pocket-filling family are a bunch of obnoxious fucktards who stick their nose up at everyone. What's your point here?" JJ hurried me along.

"One of those smaller companies goes by the name of Pepper Tides."

"Fuckkk," he groaned, running his hand over his dark curls. "Pepper Tides as in—"

"Yep. That's the one."

"What's Pepper Tides?" Chance asked.

After glancing at JJ, who shot me a look telling me I had some explaining to do, I dipped my head towards the door. "Shut it?" I requested.

He dramatically huffed before getting up, closing it, and flicking the flimsy lock into place.

"Pepper Tides is the company that saved us from going under three years back." I ran my thumb and pointer fingers over my eyebrows, smoothing the tension from between them. "We did fundraisers, so many goddamn fundraisers. We went into the city to meet with investors at sleazy clubs and restaurants. JJ and I took on some local fights in some of the towns nearby to make up some extra cash. But ... it just wasn't *enough*.

"One day I received an email from a company called Pepper Tides, offering a buy-in for stakes in the gym. The offer was ludicrous, looking back on it—far more than what the business was worth. But it would keep us afloat for a long while and allow us to put measures in place to move in an upwards direction. It gave us a budget for a social media team, some advertisements, and marketing to bring people into this butt-fuck nowhere town."

"How long have you known Pepper Tides was a Camden Company?" JJ asked, that blankness on his dark face anything but calm.

He was *pissed*.

"I found out the day before we moved Dad into his ... home." I took a shaky breath in. The truth had to come out. There was no hiding it now. I needed them to understand how catastrophically fucked we were if they kicked Jayden out. "I signed the papers the next day. Camden has been feeding me *requests* for changes ever since."

I decided *not* to reveal that Jayden was the one who had convinced me to sign the papers. That was a ghost that could stay in the closet, come out another day.

"Lynnie." JJ's icy voice chilled the room.

Even Chance had tensed in his desk chair opposite me. He hadn't said anything, just sat with curious, watching eyes.

"Why the *fuck* didn't you say anything sooner?"

"Because, JJ, there was no other way—"

"Of course there was! There's always another way—you were just too chickenshit to find it!"

"I'd just moved my dad into a respite home and was trying to keep the only thing he, and I, have ever loved afloat. What the fuck did you expect me to do?!" I snapped.

"Camden's into some dodgy shit, Mari. It's not just about knowing some people you don't want to know. All of those little companies of his are *money-laundering schemes*. They all clean his money for him since it's all tainted. *Tainted!*" JJ stood and began pacing in front of us.

I looked to Chance, who still said nothing, just followed JJ with his eyes.

"You don't know them like I do, Lynnie. Why do you think Jayden always refused to hang around if I was there?"

I didn't know what to say. JJ and I had both kept things from one another.

I opened my mouth to speak, taking a breath to start, but nothing came out. No words, no snappy comeback—*nothing*.

Which, apparently, didn't matter since JJ continued to ramble.

My mind began to whirl, spinning around and around in a grey cloud of *mess*.

Mess.

That's what I'd made of all of this. My need for independence, to not ask for help, had fucked us all over. And now? Now we were in debt to a man who JJ was *angry* at me for involving us with. JJ. Cool, calm, charismatic JJ—was rambling on and on about how colossal of a fuck up this was—

"I think she gets the message, mate."

I shot Chance a grateful look, only to find him already looking at me. Understanding shone in his eyes as he sent a subtle nod my way. Warmth, comforting and easy, spread through my chest.

"Rio—"

"We get it—this Camden guy is bad news," Chance interrupted, standing from his chair and opting to lean on his desk instead. He folded his arms over his chest and subtly rolled his shoulders back.

I guess Chance had decided JJ's ramblings were over then.

"What can we *do* about it?" he pointedly asked JJ.

"Nothing," I rasped, my voice coming out thick and wavering.

Chance raised his eyebrows at me in question.

"The amount it would cost to buy Camden out is completely out of reach."

"Is that so?"

"Forget the money, Lynnie." JJ ran both of his hands through his hair, his dark skin disappearing in the overgrown curls. He stopped pacing and sat down on the couch next to me. "Forget about all of the money and contracts and how dangerous that already is. Think about the fact that Camden's fuckface of a son gets to come in here and *put hands on you*, and you're telling me there's nothing we can do about it?"

JJ's gaze burned me, full of disappointment, worry, and anger. Anger at me for keeping this from him. Anger at Jayden for throwing down with me today. Anger at himself for not being able to do anything.

I reached a hand across and squeezed his.

"I'm okay. We're all gonna be okay. I can handle my own." I urged him to listen, urged him to believe I wasn't the same woman as last summer. The same woman who let Jayden walk all over her; push and cross boundaries with her; torment her.

JJ squeezed back. "We'll find a way out of this, Lynnie. I'm sure of it."

CHAPTER 13

Mari

"I still can't believe you invited him for dinner," I grumbled, setting the knives and forks next to the plates on the table. I leaned over Al, being careful not to knock over his cold beer.

"Chance is a part of the Knock's family now, Mari," Nan snapped, the wooden spatula clattering on the edge of the pot as she turned to face me. "It's about time you started acting like it."

"She's right, darlin'," Al chimed, drumming his fingernails against his stubby.

"Stay out of this, Al," I groaned, letting my head fall back on the cabinets above the bench I was leaning on.

"Chance is a nice young fella," he replied, completely ignoring my protest. "And is now an integral part of the team, serving as my replacement. I expect you and everyone else to give him the same courtesy and respect as you did me."

Nan and Al shared a knowing look and I sighed.

So this conversation has already been had outside my presence. Game over.

"Respect is earned, not given." I crossed my arms.

"Then let the poor lad earn it, Marilyn," Al growled, thunking his beer can on the table. "Not everyone has been surrounded by people who love them for their whole lives. It's not up to you to decide who deserves it and who doesn't."

I opened my mouth to protest but he held a hand up at me.

"You don't have to *love* him, but you need to find a way to get along with him because he's sure as hell been trying to find a way to get along with everyone—including you."

A knock rattled the door as Al finished.

My face flushed when I remembered exactly how he'd proven Al right with what he'd said just a few hours ago.

"Don't think I haven't noticed the little rat."

Al sipped down the last of his beer and put it on top of the pyramid of cans he'd started. "I mean this in the most loving way possible, Mari. Pull your head in and step up to be the leader I know you are." With a pat on my cheek, he headed for the door.

I huffed, turning to find Nan smiling over her delicious-smelling pot.

"Did you and Al scheme against me again?"

"Of course not, dear," she laughed and her eyes softened. "But sometimes I need a little help getting through to you."

"Getting through to her about what?" JJ bounced into the room, crossing straight towards Nan. "Getting a sauna in the gym?"

He planted a kiss on Nan's cheek, to which she patted his in return, before heading straight to the fridge.

"For the last fucking time, JJ—"

"Definitely not, Jaxon," Nan politely interrupted. "We can't trust your history with public nudity."

"Exactly and—" My eyes narrowed. "What the fuck are you wearing?" I gestured to the casual white button up he had on and the jeans that followed.

"Language, Marilyn," Nan scolded.

I held my hands up in surrender and quirked a brow at JJ, question still unanswered.

"Ask that little shit out there—"

"Ask me about what?" A deep, rasped voice came from over my shoulder. I turned, finding those blue eyes already on me.

"Ask him about why I'm wearing this dumb shit to family dinner!" JJ whined, though I could barely hear him in the face of what was in front of me. A forest green linen button up hung off Chance's *divine* frame. The arm cuffs hugged his strong biceps, and the top three buttons were undone, revealing a smooth column of his upper chest. Light-wash denim fell from his waist, loose but tight in all the right spots.

"I think you both look lovely," Nan crooned.

Chance's eyes were still on me when the corners of his mouth tipped upwards slightly. "Back at you, Marilyn," he replied, though he wasn't looking at Nan.

With heat starting to creep up my neck, I returned to the conversation.

"I'm just surprised you got him to wear actual clothes." Al patted Chance on the shoulder before moving past us.

"Hey! I wear actual clothes!" JJ cried.

"When was the last time?" Al asked.

JJ drew breath to speak when Nan spoke first.

"When you *weren't* trying to bed some poor girl." She raised her eyebrows for emphasis.

A burning sensation tickled my neck and I turned to find Chance's eyes still on me.

"Sunny." He flicked his chin up. "Nice shorts."

I frowned down at my satin red pyjama shorts—shorts that were way too *short* for the dinner everyone was apparently dressed to attend.

"Riordan." I rolled my eyes. "Nice ass-kissing 'fit'."

He tipped his head back in a laugh, the column of his throat moving with the sound. Extending a hand out, his large palm was wrapped around the side of a tray I hadn't even noticed. "If you like the *fit*, you're sure to love my ass-kissing brownies." He smirked and pushed the tray into my hands.

Gently sidestepping me, he made his way to Nan and planted a kiss on her cheek, and she tenderly squeezed his arm in return.

"It smells fantastic in here." He inhaled deeply over Nan's steaming pot, the rising heat pushing more colour into his lips. "Is there anything I can help you with, Marilyn?"

"Don't be silly." She shooed him out of the kitchen and steered him towards the set table. "I've got it, dear."

"You let me know," he said, smiling up at her as he sat in the chair next to JJ's.

I scoffed and Chance winked at me.

Ass-kissing indeed.

"Ignore her. She's always been hopeless in the kitchen," Nan said, glaring over her shoulder at me with a look that said, '*We just talked about this, Marilyn, and if you don't do something about it, we'll be talking about it later too*'.

"You got that right," JJ said, getting up to grab another beer from the fridge.

Nan whirled up the towel and whipped his ass with it.

"Ow! What was that for?!"

"Manners! We have company!" she scolded, finger pointing and everything.

I swallowed a laugh.

"Ugh! Fine!" He threw his hands up in the air. "Would any of you like a drink?"

"Actually—" Chance started.

"Not you. I'm wearing this shit because of you—that's enough for one day," JJ cut in, pulling his singular beer out of the fridge, followed by a sparkling water can.

"You held up your end of the bargain, I'll hold up mine. Stop whining," Chance replied, catching the can JJ threw him.

"Not having a beer?" I asked, sliding into the only available chair that wasn't next to him but across from him.

"Teaching tomorrow morning—remember?"

"Of course. How could I forget?"

Al cleared his throat. "So, how're you finding things at the gym, mate? Anything we can help you with?"

Those blue eyes flickered to mine for a beat before returning to Al's. "Nah, everything's great." His eyes bounced back to mine again. "Everyone's real welcoming and patient with me."

"I'd hardly think they'd need to be patient with someone of your expertise," Al replied.

"You'd be surprised," JJ snorted.

Though Chance rolled his eyes, his face was soft and content. Gone was the man I saw on the mats today during class—tucked away for another time was the fighter inside of him.

"You're the only one we have to be patient with around here, JJ," I retorted.

All eyes snapped up to me, Al's expression gleaming with approval. That familiar burning sensation trickled up my neck and I didn't have to look to know Chance's gaze was on me. I dared a glance, just one, and lost myself instantly in those ocean blues.

How is this even happening?

They were brighter—maybe it was the colour of his shirt? That blue roamed shamelessly over my face, studying me with blatant curiosity.

JJ grumbled something about everyone coming after him when Nan slipped off her apron. Pushing out of my chair and away from the conversation, I grabbed the oven mitts and put my hands through them.

"I got it, Nan," I said, picking up the hefty pot of goodness she'd been cooking.

"Thank you, dear." She patted my shoulder before heading to the fridge for what I assumed would be her bottle of wine.

"Any fights coming up?" Al nodded his thanks at Nan, who had a beer for him in one hand, her wine in the other.

Chance pursed his lips. "Potentially. Things are in talks at the moment," he replied, sipping from his water.

"Pfft," JJ scoffed. "Tell them the truth, man."

"What truth?" I asked.

Chance shot our friend a look that had *thanks asshole* written all over it.

"My next fight should be a title shot," he said casually—as if it wasn't a big fucking deal.

"A title shot? Against Randy Rager?" I asked.

After Chance had taunted me with his little 'google it' comment, I'd made myself pretty fucking aware of who was what in that world—his world. Randy Rager was the current champion in the light heavyweight division with an impressive record to match it. He was known for playing dirty, both in and out of the cage, and turning MMA cage fights into bar fights—using any and every rule possible to his advantage and brutalising his opponents. Not to mention, outside of the cage, he appeared to have been caught in some *really* sketchy shit.

"The one and only," Chance grumbled, unimpressed.

"God, I'd love to watch that asshole cop a fucking flog—"

"Watch your mouth, Jaxon," Nan warned, slipping into her usual seat at head of the table.

"It's quite well-warranted, Marilyn. Rager isn't a very nice person," Al cut in.

"Understatement of the century," Chance retorted, shaking his head slightly before setting his eyes on Nan. "What's for dinner, Marilyn?"

***

"I feel like a stuffed pig," JJ moaned, leaning back in his chair. "Your cooking never fails me, Nana Maz."

Nan waved him off, though I saw the compliment sink in. If there was one thing she was unconditionally proud of—it was her cooking. Rightfully so.

"Anytime, dear. You know you're always welcome at our table." She pressed a kiss to JJ's cheek as she stood and began clearing plates.

"I got it, Marilyn." Chance stood, towering over the table, and extended a hand. "You sit down."

Nan's cheeks blushed at the act of kindness before her eyes found mine. Her eyebrows flicked up above her glasses. *Help him.*

Mine scrunched. *No, I did the dishes last week.*

Her eyes narrowed on me—I had zero chance of winning this argument.

"You wash, I'll dry, Riordan," I sighed as Nan grinned triumphantly. Al laughed, having caught the whole exchange.

"I'd really like to go over the details of the anniversary party with you while I'm here, Marilyn." Al smirked my way before gesturing for Nan to follow him. Gus greedily sniffed around the table. Deeming the floor clean from scraps, he skittered off to follow the oldies.

"Right, well I have places to be," JJ said, tucking his chair in, head buried in his phone, no doubt in talks of a booty call with some poor woman.

Chance put the dishes in the sink, turning the hot water on and pushing the plug into the drain. He turned to our friend, hand extended while the other squirted soap into the sink.

"Keys," he demanded.

"Wha—no way. I need to get myself to the other side of Soggla. You can walk your lazy ass home, thank you."

"Keys," Chance said again, flicking his fingers upwards.

"No! No way am I giving up this call over just because you don't want to walk the two kays home," he grouched, sending pleading glances my way.

I held my hands up, tea towel in one—no way was I getting involved in that.

He pointed a dark finger at me, evil gleaming across his previously panicked face. "You owe me."

"You owe me more," I countered. Chance snickered.

"Come on, Lynnie. Look at all those times I've played innocent wingman for you over the years, all the dick I've gotten y—"

"For fuck's sake! Fine! I'll drive him home just *stop talking*," I growled.

I swear he squeaked in excitement before running over and planting a fat, sloppy kiss on *both* of our cheeks before racing out the door.

"That poor girl," Chance mumbled.

Chapter 14

Chance

How I ended up in this house, washing dishes alongside the only woman able to simultaneously make me both hot *and* bothered, was beyond me. How we'd managed to get through nearly the entire stack of dishes without saying a word to each other was the less surprising of the two.

"Is there a reason why you're here, Riordan?" she asked, breaking the long stretch of silence. The tightness in her voice showed how she was forcing the claws away to ask.

"Well, I was invited. And usually when someone invites you some-where, you go—"

"Not in my house. I'm well aware of why you're here. My grand-mother has a thing for stray puppies. I meant why are you here, in Soggla?" She eyed me suspiciously as she wiped the tea towel over the last bowl I'd handed her.

I released the water in the drain and started on wiping away the excess. "I was given an opportunity that was too good to pass up," I replied with a shrug.

Technically, it wasn't a lie.

She scoffed. "That's what they all say."

"Who?"

"Anyone who has even attempted to fill Al's shoes, or any other coach's for that matter," she replied, rolling those honey brown eyes.

"Ah, so that's why you've been avoiding me like the plague." I threw her a smirk I just *knew* drove her crazy. "You think I won't last."

She shrugged but immediately dropped her gaze from mine.

Interesting.

"Something like that," she replied. Her eyebrows pinched gently as she pushed the towel into the edges of the bowl.

"Why are *you* here?" I dared ask.

Rosey lips tightened to the point where I was sure she wouldn't answer. Irritation took over her face, creases forming at the edges of her mouth and in between her arched eyebrows.

"Where else would I be?" she asked quietly.

Looking down to her, her eyes were already waiting. Pools of swirling honey met a delicate core of cocoa.

I shrugged, tossing the washcloth over the tap. "I don't know, somewhere outside of a small town I'm assuming you've spent your entire life in," I replied smoothly.

"Like I said, where else would I be? I've been here forever; my life, my family, my identity—is here." She folded up the towel before placing it on the counter beside her. "There's nowhere else I'd rather be."

A soft, small smile picked up on her face.

Her lips, blooming and pink and shapely, started a domino effect across her face. I have no fucking idea how, but her freckles sparkled. The dusting across her nose and cheekbones shone. Her eyes shone too, glistening with some sort of contentment, peace, and love in Soggla that clearly ran deep for her. It was like the small smile she showed me had been the start of all other things shining.

"Have to admit, Sunny"—she shot me a look to tread careful-ly—"That's pretty fuckin' cool."

"You reckon?"

"I've never had a place like that."

"Like what?"

"Home."

Chapter 15

Chance

Three am. JJ's sea-siren of a snore echoed through the house. Still a little buzz from the half a joint I'd had to get to sleep.

Yep, perfect conditions for this.

I stared at myself in the mirror of the small bathroom. My shoulders were wider than what the mirror could show, and the single light was hospital-white. JJ's *many* skin products littered the vanity, though he claimed it was because he had no space since he had generously given me half of the storage. A whole drawer to myself.

I'd shaved the grossly overgrown stubble down to an appropriate length before dinner tonight, making me look less stray. I snorted at the irony of it. I was trying to look the opposite when that was exactly what I was—*a stray*. Hell, even Sunny had picked up on it.

I shared the colour of my hair with my siblings, as well as the shade of my eyes with my sister. A gracious gift from the piss-poor excuse of a man we all shared as a father. The strands stretched to about mid-chest, and it was the same blond the man himself had had back in the day. It had somehow thickened out in the last few weeks, quicker than I ever knew hair even *could*. It didn't look so frail and like it was two seconds away from falling out. It looked like the beginning of strong, healthy hair.

I stared at the reflection staring back at me. The man in the mirror. The hair that I'd had for the last few years. The hair that had thinned from stress and anxiety. The hair that was such an identifying feature and that tied me to what I was so fucking desperate to run from.

I laughed and picked up the electric shaver.

CHAPTER 16

Chance

J J stared at me as I walked into the gym kitchen.

And stared.

And stared.

And kept on *fucking staring*.

"Can I help you?" I grumbled.

"Where the fuck did your hair go?" he asked, eyes so wide I could see the whites at both the top and bottom.

"I dunno, man. I just woke up like this," I replied, rubbing my hands over my face as I walked over to the pot of coffee.

"... really?"

"No, dickhead, of course not. I shaved it last night." After pouring milk over my Weet-Bix, I pulled the foil off of the yoghurt container and began dumping heaped spoonfuls into the bowl.

"Why? Your hair was so majestic," he whined.

I turned back to make some snarky comment in reply, but stopped short when genuine concern rippled across JJ's face. He ran a hand over his head of dark curls, and wrinkles creased his forehead from his raised eyebrows.

I sighed, putting the lid back on the yoghurt. "I'm okay, man. Really," I started. "I'm just figuring things out."

He nodded. He lightly shrugged his shoulders, telling me he wouldn't push me on the subject, and dug back into his own breakfast. "Next time you want to shave all of your hair off, at least wake me up so I can do the honours. I always saved you from those stupid eyebrow and hair shaving pranks when we were younger."

***

After dumping my duffle on my desk, I quickly rolled the curtains down to block out all of the goddamn wandering eyes.

"I told you all of the old birds would be disappointed," JJ said, flopping on the couch next to Mari's desk.

It was true. Marilyn was running some sort of morning tea for some of the oldies in town, and they'd all but gasped when I'd stopped in at the kitchen to use the fridge.

"Well, your new 'do looks lovely, dear," she'd said.

Though I definitely hadn't missed her analysing gaze, as if she could see straight through me. Something told me it was impossible to lie to the woman.

"Hate to disappoint the fans," I replied, pulling the book out of my bag along with my keys to unlock the filing cabinet. My chest cramped as I forced steady breaths through it, hunkering down on the inevitable internal shake.

In.

Out.

In.

Out.

It's a fucking filing cabinet.

In.

Out.

"You lose your key?" JJ asked, the faintest trace of concern wavering his voice.

I cleared my throat. "Nah, man. Just not all there this morning." I shoved the red key into the lock and turned. The drawer sprung open at me, along with that box in the back of my mind that I tried so fucking hard to keep closed.

The smell.

The sickeningly sweet smell of what was in here—

A hand squeezed gently on my shoulder, a black and silver ring shining on the index finger. Seeing the book that was still in my hand, he tugged it from my grip. Releasing my shoulder, my best friend tucked my most prized possession in the back of the filing cabinet, shut the drawer, and turned the lock.

"I dunno what happened back in Darlington Harbour, mate," he started, running a hand through his hair. "But I know that my best friend is going through some shit right now ... and I have a sneaking suspicion he's busting his own balls to deal with it alone. Would I be correct?"

I stared at him—

My oldest friend.

The person I trusted most in this world.

The person I owed my fucking life to.

Biting on my tongue so hard I could taste blood, I shoved every instinct of denial down. Down farther, away from that box in the back of my mind. Away from me, away from JJ.

I nodded.

He let out what seemed to be a breath of relief, and something cracked inside me. He'd seen me. Of course he'd seen me. He knew me better than anyone else. He knew who I was, inside and out.

"I'm here, Chance." He put his hand on my shoulder again. "You're not alone."

"I—" I scrubbed my face with my hands, not having a single fucking clue of where to start. That box in the back of my mind had stopped rattling about, but I could still feel how fucking full it was. That was the thing about ghosts—when you went to point one out, say 'Look! The grim fucking reaper is chasing me!'—they vanished into thin air. But a cold presence always lingered, an icy hand on the shoulder with a promise to return later.

JJ turned and sat back on the couch next to Sunny's desk, splaying himself out in the most casual manner, but I caught the message from it.

Nothing is ever too big that you can't tell me.

"Take your time. I've got plenty." He smiled, dipping his chin in a gesture for me to sit.

I paced in front of him before finally joining him on the couch.

We sat in silence for a long minute while I sorted through the bowl of fucking spaghetti in my brain. Tangled and knotted, no beginning or end. JJ, to his credit, didn't make any jokes or try to urge me on. He waited, patient and calm, as if he didn't have anywhere else in the world he'd rather be.

"Shit got pretty bad before I left Darlington Harbour, man," I started ... and finished.

All the words cluttered up in my throat.

"Everything had kind of reached its tipping point the day you called me," I croaked.

His eyes flared, and I let out a self-pitying laugh.

"I mean, for fuck sake, I was sitting up at Fuller's Point when you called, about ten seconds away from ending it—"

"Morning team," Mari's voice sounded from outside.

A cluster of responses followed before the office door opened.

That woman—that *fucking beautiful* woman—stopped dead in her tracks. A light shimmer of sweat coated her skin, slightly tugging parts of her white singlet closer to her hips; she must have walked here. Torn up denim shorts sat at the tops of those legs that ran a mile long. Alluring lines wrapped themselves around the slender curves of her thighs, showcasing just how beautifully capable she was.

And she was staring at me.

"Mornin', Sunny." I lifted a smirk onto my face, catching the flare in her honey brown eyes when they met mine.

"Riordan." She nodded at me, eyes flickering over my newly buzzed head, before moving over to her desk. "Aren't you supposed to be working today, JJ?"

A sudden wave of coolness swept over me when her gaze left mine. No fucking clue why, but I didn't like it.

"Nah, they're just getting ready for the big dance tonight. Apparently my services aren't required later on."

"Shit," she cursed. "I forgot about that."

She padded over to the couch JJ was on and signalled for him to shuffle aside.

"I have to make an appearance, don't I?" She folded her hands over her face and sighed, her elbows pressing together her alarmingly noticeable cleavage.

Fuck sake.

"To one of the gym's biggest sponsors? Yeah, Lynnie, you should probably make an appearance," JJ replied. "You can join Cassie and I."

"Cassie?" I asked.

"My date for the evening," He waggled his eyebrows. "Or maybe it's Casey. I should probably figure that out."

"Sorry, JJ, there's about a million other people I would rather go with than you and your hook up for the night. One of which includes a wasp nest."

"Rude." He gaped, placing a hand over his chest.

"I've done it before," she groaned. "Never again."

"Do I bother asking?" I interrupted.

"No—" Sunny started.

"Yes," JJ finished.

I looked to Sunny—a scowl scrunching up her pretty face—trying to plant innocence over the top of my burning curiosity. She rolled her eyes.

"She's just mad because I got some that night and she didn't," JJ tried.

"Yeah, you got some! When you were *supposed* to be driving me home!" she shrieked. "We stopped for fuel for five minutes, JJ. Five minutes! I went in to pay for the fuel in *your* car—I come out, and you guys are getting it on! In the car!"

"You didn't." I couldn't hold in the laugh that burst out.

"Sure did, Chancey boy. I saw an opportunity, and I took it." He shrugged.

"We were thirty minutes out of town. You couldn't have waited *thirty* minutes?!" Sunny yelled. "*I* had to wait outside for nearly an hour!"

"An hour? That's a long while for you, J," I said. I could practically see the steam coming out of Sunny's ears as she glared at me.

"She was a nice girl. I was just trying to look after her," he replied.

"Ugh!" Mari threw her arms up and stomped out.

"You seriously do that?" I asked.

"Hah, yeah. Not one of my prouder moments, but I bought her breakfast the next day." He waved it off.

"Mari? Or the chick?"

"Mari, of course. One of the three women I'd ever buy food for willingly."

"Who're the other two?"

"Marilyn and your sister," he teased, smiling like a Cheshire cat.

"Jackass."

Chapter 17

Mari

"G'day, Mari!" Rocco shot me a beaming smile from behind the bar where he was simultaneously pouring someone's beer and making what looked to be a gin and tonic.

"Rocco!" I squealed, stepping up on one of the nearby bar stools and hopping over the old, sticky wood.

He put the drinks down in front of two patrons before waving them off when they tried to pay. I recognised them instantly as Gina and Bobby, parents of little Jacko—a short, stocky kid who trained in one of our junior classes a few days a week.

Rocco was good like that—generous but fair and fiercely loyal. The old man had owned Rock-It's for over half my life. He'd been behind the bar for even longer. He had never been the owner or manager who sat out in the back room, tapping away on his computer. In fact, he'd hired Nan for a while to do that for him.

Rocco was a Soggla original, someone who loved the town as much as the people in it. Despite missing two front teeth from one of the countless games of footy he'd played, he was always pouring drinks with a smile and a good laugh.

Though his hair was now wispy and grey, he used to have the town's most renowned dark, long, curly mullet. It was iconic to the pub that was known as the Soggla Hotel.

Though half of the sign's lights had rarely worked, I could still remember the place clear as day. Dad would take me in with him every Friday after a hard night's training. We'd sit with Rocco at the bar, who would pretty much abandon his other patrons to have a beer with Dad and me with a fire engine. Even before my mother passed, that tradition had always belonged to just the two of us.

I had been about nine when Rocco took over the old pub and turned it into Rock-It's. The grand opening party was one of the last things we did together as a family before Mum's accident. The pub was in shambles when he bought it, *literally*. Holes in the walls, pool tables missing half the turf, tables surviving on only three legs. He threw everything he had into Rock-It's, and all his hard work and dedication had paid off.

The now-old man pulled me into a warm hug, just as he always did. Same as he had the day JJ and I admitted my father into an assisted living facility. He'd been here for everything, right behind this counter.

"Good to see you, kid," he said, beaming proudly down at me.

He turned and pulled a glass from the rack behind him, filling it with half a scoop of ice. I hopped back over to the other side of the bar while he made my usual, with the fingers on his right hand tipped in the same inked patterns of my own.

"I'm sorry it's been so long," I replied, a rush of guilt hitting me like a brick wall.

He waved a hand in dismissal. "Don't apologise. I know just how busy you are these days." He smiled, putting a double version of my usual on the bar in front of me.

I raised my eyebrows in question.

"There's a certain *someone* and their rich, *fucknob father* out back in the big corporate room. Figured you might need this," he said, picking up my glass and gently shaking it so the ice hit the sides with a gentle tinkling.

"You're a lifesaver," I replied, guzzling the drink quickly as Rocco got to work on another. I downed the next just as fast.

"How's your old man doing? He coming tonight?" he asked the questions smooth and casual, but the longing in his overshadowed eyes was enough for my heart to crack in sympathy. He missed his friend.

"He's doing good. Nan spoke to his nurses this morning and today wasn't a good day, so ..." I trailed off.

"There's always next year." He smiled softly, though it was impossible to miss the disappointment in his drooping his expression.

"I'll take you out there one day soon," I promised. "He'd love that, I reckon."

"I would too." Reaching over the counter, he put my next drink in front of me and squeezing my hand gently. He nodded his head towards the corporate rooms. "Sing out if you need me. I care about havin' you in here more than those snobby pricks in there."

I chuckled — he truly meant it. I'd seen the lengths he'd gone to for my family and I before, and I didn't doubt it for a second. But I could suck it up, play nice, dumb girl for twenty minutes while Camden McLarry used me as a pedestal to stand on in front of his little-dicked, suck-up friends. I could deal with Jayden and the actions his insecurity brought down on me for twenty minutes. I could do it for Rocco, and I could certainly do it for Knock's.

Leaving Rocco with a mock salute and a deep gulp of my perfectly made old fashioned, I made my way over to the corporate rooms. The rumble of male laughter got louder as I got closer, could practically smell the *money* in that room. I straightened my spine, pulled my shoulders back, and lifted my chin. My sleek black heels clicked on the floor, contrasting with the red Nan had insisted on painting my toenails earlier this afternoon. Using my free hand to pull down my crimson miniskirt, I ensured it was at a respectable length before reaching the door.

"Evenin', Mari." The security guard, who's name I couldn't remember for the life of me, smiled sympathetically down at me. He'd been working for the McLarrys for a short time now, but that was enough to know how they treated the women around them.

I smiled in thanks as he opened the door for me. The laughter stopped, but it wasn't because I had walked into the snake pit full of sleazy rich men. No, their attention was elsewhere. Everyone crowded around the middle of the room, listening avidly to the speaker.

"It's been a wonderful … *opportunity*," they said.

Wait.

I knew that voice.

"I have to say, I'm surprised you're here. Your last win against Doug Speddlehimer was nothing short of incredible," Camden said.

I clicked around the edge of the room, regretting wearing heels. But no one seemed to notice, or care, about the sudden female presence.

I stood on the opposite side of their little huddle from Jayden, who also hadn't noticed me yet.

And there he was. All six-foot-three of him, a metric fuckload of muscle, crammed into the velvet green chair, it's high back facing towards me. His newly buzzed hair was shining off the dim lighting, as if he had his own personal spotlight. He went back and forth with Camden, brushing off any compliments the short, tubby business-man paid him as if they were of little importance. Even from here, it was obvious the way Camden grappled verbally with him, trying to imprint some sort of significance through his opinions. But Chance, swiftly and politely, brushed each and every attempt away as if it was a speck of lint on his navy blue shirt.

Camden's eyes met mine and lit up wickedly.

"And I'm sure you've had *ever the welcome* from Knock's owner, Mari?" He plastered a mask of pleasantry over his always flushed face.

"Mari has been nothing short of fantastic to work with," Chance surprised me by saying. "As the daughter of Elijah Trevino, I'd already had high expectations for her. But what she's done for Knock's since his retirement is extraordinary."

Thank the heavens and all of the angels above for makeup and dim lighting. I prayed they hid my flaming face from Camden's watchful gaze. He narrowed his eyes on Chance, searching for a flaw, a lie, a bone to pick at. But Chance didn't flinch. His shoulders didn't tense. He just sipped from a glass that looked oddly similar to mine.

Surprise flashed over Camden's face, and I wondered what Chance had done to cause it. Staring at the back of his head, I couldn't make out anything different.

Camden looked up to me, feigning pleasant delight at my 'sudden' appearance. "Ah, Mari. We were just talking about you."

Chance's shoulders tensed under that dim, yellow lighting.

I stepped forward and extended a hand to Camden, who stood to meet me. In my heels, I was taller than him by about an inch. My tongue burned from sinking my teeth into it, swallowing the smirk that would kiss my gym goodbye. My eyes involuntarily found Jayden's. It had always annoyed him when we were dating that I was taller than him in heels. There was no doubt in my mind that it was a genetic pet peeve.

"All good things, I would hope," I replied.

Camden's hand was clammy and firm when he finally shook mine. His expression faltered for a beat, telling me whatever he was about to say should be taken as inflammatory.

"It would appear so," he grumbled before planting a fake smile on his face and gesturing for me to sit. "Please, join us."

Whether it were true, or it was the two drinks I'd just downed, Chance's gaze burned me as I sat down.

"Sunny." He nodded.

"Riordan."

His eyes lazily roamed up my bare legs. He swallowed the last of his drink before standing and walking to the bar—something people in these rooms didn't have to do. Bar staff were typically *summoned*.

"I trust you're taking good care of my little investment." Camden gave his nearby associates a devious grin.

The crowd began to disperse, the men returning to their conversations.

My teeth ground together. '*My little investment*'.

"Of course." I smiled sweetly.

"Good. Then we have some changes I need to inform you of."

CHAPTER 18

Mari

To say JJ was the life of the party would have been an understatement.

He *was* the party.

At least half of the room was over there, listening to him babble on about some story of how he'd nearly died when a non-venomous snake bit his left testicle. Though, as per usual, he'd failed to mention the 'non-venomous' part. I chuckled to myself as I scanned his audience, so captivated and in awe of the idiot. I forced myself to swallow my laughter with a swig of my whiskey. The group started laughing and clapping—I assumed they'd gotten to the point where he'd run around his poor grandmother's house butt-ass naked, screeching for someone to help him.

The rest of the *'pleasantries'* I was forced to exchange with Camden had been sent by Satan himself. Though this time, I hadn't broken.

I'd sat through each and every one of his idiotic suggestions, every one of his unwarranted criticisms. I'd thought of Nan and Al, how much effort and love they'd put into Knock's over the years. I'd ordered another drink. I'd thought of JJ and the difficult task he'd completed of getting people to come and find the home in Knock's that the rest of us had. I'd ordered another drink. I'd thought about all of the kids I'd taught over the last few years, all of the report cards that had changed to reflect positive news rather than dreary. I'd ordered yet another drink.

And I'd continued ordering drinks at the back corner of the bar since I'd walked out of the room that reeked exclusively with little-dick testosterone.

Well, not completely.

My gaze found Chance and I scanned over that face of his. His eyes were alight with amusement in a way that confirmed he'd picked up on the slip of certain details in JJ's story. He smiled at my best friend—*our best friend*—so at ease and relaxed.

That fucking smile.

Since Jayden, I'd sworn not to get involved with fighters. I always have been and always will be surrounded by fighters. But I refused to ever be treated as being below them, ever be treated as a punching bag myself.

And yet here I was, gawking at him like a schoolgirl with a crush.

You just can't help yourself, can you?

This niggling, almost itching part of me yearned to reconsider—baiting me with thoughts of '*He doesn't seem to be like the others*' and '*What if he's different and he's everything you've been looking for?*'.

I doubted it.

So, I shut down each of those thoughts as they came. Which, apparently, was rather quickly and frequently when I'd been drinking.

These crinkles showed right below his eyes as he laughed at something JJ had said. I'd never known I could see value in the lines on someone's face—their lines of happiness.

Those particular creases told me he was in fact smiling true.

Chance boggled my mind in ways I hadn't even known were possible. He drove me to a state of pure anger one second, pure libido the next. He sprinted circles in my head, not to mention he put on one hell of a guns-show when he was teaching.

Fucking nowhere is safe from this man and his orgasmic, god-like existence.

Chance's creases deepened even further, and I startled when it became obvious he'd caught me staring.

Shit.

Shit. Shit. Shit.

I downed another drink.

Fuck. My. Life.

Chance snickered and stood, patting JJ on the back before moving over towards the bar. Moving? No—gliding.

Yes, this man glided.

Jesus, Mari. How many drinks have you had?

He picked up a bottle of whiskey—my favourite kind, in fact—and nodded his head towards the door, his blue eyes boring into mine.

Not enough.

I broke.

I was up and out the door before he was, sprinting down the back exit hallway.

His laugh was behind me; such a delightful sound, running its way down to my bones.

I couldn't even hold back the laugh that tumbled out of me.

A bright flash blinded me momentarily. Paige, our town's customary artistic photographer, stepped aside as she lowered her camera. A big smile with a crooked gap between her two front teeth beamed back at us as we slowed our pace slightly. She flashed me a double thumbs up, and we were off again.

I ran over to the pub's mailbox and slipped two crisp pineapples into it for the whiskey Chance was currently holding.

"You don't think someone'll wanna grab that?" he asked me.

I laughed again. A jolt of excitement going straight to my chest at the sparkle in his eye when I made such a noise.

Or maybe it is just the alcohol.

"People don't steal shit in Soggla, Chance," I replied. "At least not the locals." I winked at him and gestured to the bottle of whiskey.

He laughed before taking a swig and handing me the slightly cool glass. I took two long gulps before we moved along and started walking up the road.

Gym-ward. *Where else?*

"So ... did you know this is my favourite brand of whiskey or is it a happy coincidence?"

He gently pulled the bottle out of my hands and gulped again before looking down at the bottle and smiling. "This is actually my favourite whiskey as well," he replied. "I haven't been able to drink it for a few years now. Wasn't going to pass up the opportunity."

I chuckled. "What, were you in prison or something?"

He smiled down at the bottle again.

"Something like that." He lifted the whiskey and took *four* long gulps as if it were orange juice. "So, tell me," he offered the drink my way. "What's it like being the daughter of the great Elijah Trevino?"

I groaned. "We're actually having a really nice time together, for once, and you choose to throw a nuke at it?" I tossed back another swig.

"You're not close, I take it?" He gave me a sidelong glance, wariness lining his gaze.

"Nope." *Not anymore*, that little voice said. I took another gulp, the whiskey starting to lose its burn going down my throat. "One day, I'll stand at his grave and be filled with the regret of the times we didn't have. But today isn't that day."

Chance stared at me for a long moment, those blue eyes scattering across my face as if he was reading a book.

"Righto, my turn," I said.

"Uh-oh."

"Tell me how a big-time UFC fighter, impeccable record, thousands of adoring fans ... ended up here."

"What's so strange about here?"

I gave him a long look. "Come on. You're from the city. *Mr Darlington Harbour*. You can't possibly mean to tell me that small-town Soggla is better than that."

"I don't know what to tell you, Sunny." A playful smirk broke out across his pink lips. "I love it here."

There was not a single part of me that could ignore the warm feeling inside my chest that sprouted from hearing those words.

CHAPTER 19

Mari

We reached the gym in what somehow felt like both hours and minutes. We had taken many, *many* accidental reroutes. Chance, I learned, could hold his whiskey much better than I could. He was still walking perfectly, catching me swiftly whenever I stumbled. Only the slight slur in his voice gave him away.

"What now, Sunny?"

I grinned and held up a finger for him to wait while I whisked over to the radio. The switch flickered when I pushed it into full blast. Turning back towards him, I found his eyes quickly snapping up to mine.

Sneaky, Chance. Very sneaky.

"Come on." I waved a hand towards him, gesturing him forward. His brows ticked up in silent question.

"Dance with me, Chance."

His blue eyes darkened, and he stiffened.

After a moment, I asked, "What's wrong?"

He cleared his throat. "You've never called me that before."

We stared at each other for a long moment, until the song changed. "Tennessee Whiskey" by Chris Stapleton filled the room.

"I love this song." The alcohol coursing through my veins fused with the music. I hadn't even felt myself slip into a sway until strong arms swept me up.

We fell easily into a thankfully simple slow dance, my left hand curling and brushing over his scarred knuckles and calloused fingers.

"Such a pretty dancer, Sunny baby," he murmured.

His face was so close to mine, the dim light shining off his lips.

"I could say the same thing about you, *Twinkle Toes*," I teased.

He bowed his head in laughter and the warmth of his breath caught on my lips.

"Wanna know a secret?"

"Mmm." I nodded my head.

That glorious fusion of music and whiskey found a third friend—those forget-me-not blue eyes staring down at me.

"I took dance lessons when I was first starting out in boxing."

"Really?"

"Yeah, helped me with my footwork."

I smiled—beamed, I'm sure. "Why does that not surprise me?"

His gaze slowly snaked its way up my face, and it dawned on me that he'd been staring at my mouth.

"You're far too smart to be surprised by things as trivial as that," he replied.

Feeling an uncomfortable weight from the compliment he'd just paid me, my eyes fell to our hands.

"Don't do that." His hand left my waist and tenderly pulled my chin up, my face much closer than a moment ago.

"Don't do what?" I whispered as his tongue swiftly coated his lips slick, the bottom falling between his teeth for a split second.

"Don't turn away from a compliment, Sunny. You of all people deserve them." His drunken slur was lost, those last few words clear and as bright as day.

His fingers moved up to trace the line of my jaw, and I *groaned* when they tangled in my hair.

"Congratulations, you've found something I'm bad at."

My eyes fluttered shut as his fingers lightly tugged on the strands of hair, his face inching closer.

"Don't tell anyone." My pulse skittered and my breathing hitched. The smell of him, mint and cologne, was more intoxicating than the alcohol I'd drunk tonight. This second, this moment, this *man*—that was all that mattered. I was utterly lost in him.

Him.

Gorgeous, glorious *him*. The man who had driven me up the fucking walls since he'd gotten here. The man who was so gorgeous it hurt. The man who poked at me, challenged me to be better.

"Let's practice, shall we?" he mumbled in my ear. "Your mind, Trevino." His lips brushed against my earlobe. "Seeing that brilliant mind of yours in action ... You're a *real* martial artist. You move like water, smooth and flowy with the fluidity of power that so many could only *dream* of."

A gentle pressure from his mouth tugged at my earlobe. A hot breath followed, sending a shiver shooting up my spine.

"You're sharp and strong and capable," he murmured.

That pressure moved to his lips as they fell to the middle of my neck. Chance inhaled deeply, the action ripping gooseflesh to the surface of my skin.

"And fuck if that doesn't drive me insane." After growling the last word, he nipped at the base of my neck, catching the delicate skin just above my collarbone. He pulled those remarkable lips away, the cool air finding my neck instantly. His fingers gave my hair a gentle tug again, asking me to open my eyes.

"*And ...*"

His lips were so close to mine, his taste already overwhelming my senses.

"You're sexy as hell, Sunny baby."

He began moving us to the music once more, never retreating an inch from my face but staying in time with that chorus that felt oh-so-fitting for this moment.

And with every chorus, every verse, he kissed me.

One kiss.

Two kisses.

Three kisses.

Four.

CHAPTER 20

Mari

"**A**h! Shit!"

I cringed at the searing pain that ripped through my skull. Turning my head in towards the pillow, I felt something behind me. Not something ... *someone*. The smell of mint and Chance's cologne flooded my nose, surprisingly easing the nausea that was churning in my stomach.

A warm, calloused hand was wrapped around my waist, and another *something* was pressed into my lower back. I strained my memory to last night, coming up blurry and spearing further into my current headache. My skin warmed along every inch that touched him, as if to say, *Don't be alarmed—we're okay here.*

Traitor.

I gently pried his hand from around my waist using my own. As I was about to lift his heavy, muscular arm farther, his fingers laced with mine. That wild beating in my chest fluttered. It gnawed at me over and over.

Lie back down.

Wrap yourself in his arms.

Enjoy the warmth.

"Oh, shit ... shit, shit, shit, SHIT, SHIT!" JJ's sudden screeching cursing broke my trance.

The aching muscles between my legs confirmed it was a post-sex trance.

That's all it was. Just a post-sex trance. No feelings. That stupid fluttering in my chest and excessive warmth from Chance's insanely smooth skin was just post-orgasm brain fog.

I used our linked hands to manoeuvre myself out from underneath that gloriously muscled arm. I ignored every second of exposed air that hadn't come from his warm skin, making me feel cold in the midst of spring.

I pulled my top on over my shoulders and my miniskirt up my bare legs. It took me an embarrassing amount of time to find *both* of my shoes—one under the bed and one thrown into a corner. Jumping between creaks in the floor, I paced around the room searching for my underwear.

Great. Nice going, Mari. Now you're going to have to sneak out past JJ whilst going commando.

Huffing and grabbing my phone from his nightstand, I allowed myself to look.

I allowed myself to drink in the Greek god-like man laying sprawled underneath the sheets. At his now buzzed hair that still somehow appeared ruffled from last night's activities. At the grown-out stubble around his mouth and across his face, forming that short beard. Those full, devilish lips were slightly parted as his breathing got shallower and shallower.

He's waking up.

Praying to anyone in the skies that could be listening, I opened Chance's bedroom door slowly and carefully. The groaning of the door started just as I'd slipped through. I could faintly hear JJ singing to ... *was that Shakira?*

I moved along, quickly and quietly, remembering where all of the creaks in the floor were and bouncing around them. I'd spent so many nights sneaking in and out of this house with JJ, I knew it better than my own home. All I had left was to clear the kitchen door and it was straight hallway from there.

"Gooooood morning, Chancey-boyyy—OH SHIT!" A clang louder than JJ's shouting rattled the house as he dropped the metal pan onto the gas stovetop.

My eyes were as wide as saucers, I'm sure, as I glanced back to Chance's closed bedroom door. "Jeez, JJ. Way to wake the whole neighbourhood up!" I whisper-scolded, hugging my heels to my chest. Just the thought of wearing them right now had my legs wobbling.

Come on, Mari. We both know that's not the reason why your legs are wobbling.

JJ's mouth opened and closed like a fish out of water.

I was loading up on my back foot to leave when his smile turned.

Feline, mischievous, rascal.

"Don't say a word," I growled, spinning on my foot and stomping out towards the front door.

"You sure you want to do that?" JJ drawled from the kitchen door, flinging a tea towel around in circles.

"Do what?" I narrowed my eyes at his tone.

"Leave, before he even wakes up." He nodded back down the hallway at Chance's still closed door.

"Why shouldn't I?"

"I just don't think he'd be very happy to wake up and find you'd snuck out in the early hours of the morning." He shrugged, still wearing that mischievous look. But his eyes were still studying me.

"Don't be such a drama queen. He knows the score." The words burned on my tongue as I said them. "Riordan isn't the cuddly type." A lie, considering the position I'd awoken to just minutes ago.

"Your doom." He held his hands up in surrender.

I rolled my eyes at his theatrics and left.

CHAPTER 21

Mari

"There she is!" one of the older guys, Wazza, called out when I walked through the gym doors.

I'd taken half an hour in the bath. Half an hour was all I'd allowed myself to think on the events of last night that still had my legs shaky and my mind hazy.

Chance's lips trailed down my neck, across my collarbone, all the way to my fingertips.

With his teeth pressing slightly against the delicate skin on my fingers, he murmured, "God, Mari, you taste every bit of incredible I'd imagined you to."

I groaned.

The strain contained in his jeans brushed briefly up against my spread legs. I subtly spread them wider, using my fingertips in between his teeth to bring his mouth to mine. His hand cupped my neck, tilting my head back as my lips parted for him. His tongue swept through as I willingly, so eagerly, flavoured the taste of him.

Clearly half an hour was not enough.

The gym was buzzing with people, some hungover, some utterly wrecked, but everyone with huge grins on their faces.

"How you going, Wazza?" I bumped him as I passed him to go dump my bag in the office.

"Absolutely fantastic after that banger of a party you threw last night!" He beamed.

I nodded my thanks and continued on my path to quiet.

Where I can process the sex scenes of last night currently playing on loop in my mind.

I shut the door behind me and dumped my bag beside my desk, not bothering to hide the loud *thunk* it made.

Blinds closed, lights off, I slumped on the coffee-stained couch in-between mine and Chance's desks. Resting the crook of my elbow over my eyes, I let out a hot, traitorous breath. Every part of me felt tingly, glittering with warmth.

Chance had awoken something inside of me, a part of me that had predominantly lain dormant. He'd awoken it to a hot, oozing fire that had me wanting to jump his bones—

Pull yourself together, horn-dog.

I breathed slowly, deeply, trying to settle the spike in desire that somehow hadn't been fulfilled by last night's activities. I just wanted *more*. Each breath brought a new memory back.

Inhale.

Chance's tongue traced intricate patterns up the lines between the muscles of my inner thighs.

Exhale.

He nipped lightly, almost teasingly at the skin beside my wine-red G-string, as if teasing himself with the proximity of what sat so close, so slick and eager.

Inhale.

A skittering electric sensation filled my nerves in anticipation at the slowness of his goddamn teeth *as they removed the delicate fabric.*

Exhale.

Nothing could have ever warned me—ever prepared me for the other-worldly sensation of Chance Riordan devouring me as if I were his own personal feast.

The door opening dumped cold water all over me. I could practically feel steam coming off me when the man himself entered the room, all six-feet-three-inches of sex-on-legs.

He looked at me; a burning gaze that I was sure was actually about to set the office on fire. Two lines formed between his eyebrows as a mask slid over his face. A perfect facade of boredom and indifference, as if I was nothing but some shit he'd accidentally stepped on. He held eye contact with me, those blue eyes as hot as the centre of a flame, as he dropped his duffel bag on his desk before he turned and strode out.

The hell?

"Five minutes! Wrap your hands. No excuse to miss warm-ups!" The authority in Chance's voice, sexy as it was, had me up and out of the office. I grabbed a set of my favourite blue wraps from the shelf, not missing the way my brain instantly recognised them as the same colour as Chance's eyes.

The gym had almost silenced itself at Chance's sudden reveal of his bad mood. A few people were muttering, talking quietly and avoiding looking anywhere near where he stood. I tucked one wrap in my bra as I unfurled the other. A few guys—JJ, Franko, Jonesy—had already started shadowboxing.

I tried to catch Chance's eyes as he watched them warm up. Dread found a new home and pitted itself in the bottom of my stomach.

Does he regret last night?

More and more questions and imaginary scenarios were spinning around my head in a whirlwind by the time I finished wrapping my first hand. I hadn't taken my eyes off Chance. My fingers tingled slightly, telling me I'd wrapped my hand too tightly.

"Two minutes!" he shouted, not taking his eyes off the now extended group of people shadowboxing. The increasing stiffness of his body, of those sculpted muscles, told me he *knew* I was watching him.

"Time's up! Everybody on the wall!"

My jaw dropped. *Two minutes my ass ...*

I fumbled with my last wrap to get it down, pulling it tighter than the last without thinking.

Thirty of us stood on the wall. The tension was palpable.

These were my people. I knew them so well I could *feel* their exhaustion, the alcohol their bodies were still processing.

"Shoes on. Run down to the Murray and back. For every thirty seconds you miss the time limit, it's twenty burpees for the team."

"What's the time limit?" I asked, the apprehension now rippling like a wave through the group.

Chance clenched his jaw but still didn't meet my eyes. "Ten minutes."

You could hear the crickets. To get there and back in ten minutes would be hauling ass on nearly a full sprint.

"But that's—" I started.

Chance's eyes finally snapped to mine.

"For every word of bitchin', the burpee tally starts," he said coolly. None of that warmth from last night in his eyes. None of that tension-based mocking we'd been teasing each other with for the past few weeks. Nothing but pure ice.

I narrowed my eyes at him.

You wanna play, Riordan? I can play. Game on.

"Go," he said, almost sounding bored.

With a shared mutter of curses, people scrambled to get their shoes on.

JJ ran past Chance, smacking his ass on the way through. Chance scowled, that annoyingly beautiful face scrunching.

"Fifty burpees on your tally, Jones!" he shouted.

"I look forward to it, Coach!" JJ saluted and caught up with Wazza to lead the group.

I found one of the quieter dads who trained with us and buddied up with him for the run of doom, knowing he would at least leave me to my own thoughts for the duration of it.

"Nine minutes, ten seconds, Trevino," Chance interrupted, staring out at everyone leaving. Though, through that mask of stone and faux boredom, something was locked up tight beneath a swirling storm.

"The hell is your problem, Riordan?"

His eyes flickered down to mine for a beat, as if I was nothing but a goddamn fly buzzing by. "That's 'Coach' to you, Trevino," he growled. "Now get moving."

Chapter 22

Mari

"Would you look at that! Jayden dropped a knee! Time resets!" Everyone groaned in unison at the torture of the timer reset.

Much to our chagrin, we did not make it back from the run in ten minutes. Or twelve. The last of us rolled in at fourteen minutes. The back end of the burpees had a few out the front, throwing up the leftover drinks from last night.

Then we had Cejudo drills.

Then push-ups.

Then sprints.

Then wall sits.

Then skipping.

Then sprawl call-outs.

Until we'd gotten here. The final leg of this class of sadism.

A plank—simple, right? All we had to do was hold it until Chance called 'time'.

'Time' never came. We'd reset the clock three times now, with Jayden being responsible for two of them.

"Fuck sake, Jayden," I muttered, my core violently shaking.

"Shut the *fuck* up, Mari!" Jayden roared, his body trembling from fatigue.

If I hadn't been so quick to look, I would have missed Chance landing a kick into his ribs, making him clatter to the floor once again.

"Uh-oh! Jayden dropped again!" Chance called.

No one said anything that time, except for the daggers Jayden glared my way.

"Told you," JJ muttered beside me, solid as a rock but dripping sweat all over the floor. The Japanese warrior he had tattooed on his left delt stared at me as my muscles began to tremble with fatigue.

"Told me what?" I forced out.

"Told you it wasn't a good idea to leave before he woke up," he replied coolly, fumbling with his fingers to distract himself from the lactic acid burn. That same lactic acid burn seared my muscles, but I stopped hearing the screams from my body at his revelation.

He shrugged at my gaping expression. "He's pissed, borderline on a sadistic rampage—"

"Borderline?" Franko asked from nearby.

"All because I left when he was asleep this morning?" I asked quietly. The guilt hit me like an explosion in my chest, followed by a strange seeping sensation as it spread across my tired, aching body.

"I warned you it would be your doom."

Malicious, gross laughter found its way into my ears.

"I'd be pissed too if I got dumped by a frigid bitch with piss-poor pussy."

I didn't have time to spit back a retort before I glimpsed the thunderous expression on Chance's face.

"Oh, shit. You've fucked it now," JJ muttered.

The room went silent, and it was anything but tranquil.

The only noise being Chance's phone bouncing across nearby mats where he'd thrown it aside. His footsteps had a calm grace to them, something I had learned was a common trait of only the deadliest of fighters.

'Death's Grace' they called it.

Chance made it to Jayden's side and single-handedly *snatched* him up by the back of his sweaty shirt. Jayden began to sputter, clearly shocked and in fear of what was about to happen. Chance held him in front of him, facing the open roller door as he walked him outside, using only *one hand*, as if he was taking out a smelly bag of rubbish.

"Chance—" I started, getting up and going after him. JJ was instantly at my side. Distantly, the sound of people dropping from their planking positions echoed, their footsteps following ours.

"Chance! Chance ... bro ... please ... What are you doing?" Jayden continued.

Chance stayed alarmingly silent as he walked him out into the middle of the carpark. He shoved Jayden forward, out of his grip.

Jayden turned around, confusion and panic written all across his face.

Then ... *THWACK!*

Chance's lead hand connected with Jayden's jaw fast enough that I wondered if I'd imagined it, loud enough to know I hadn't.

"Chance!" I lunged for them, but a sweaty arm wrapped around my stomach and pulled me back.

"No way in hell you're getting in the middle of that," JJ snarled.

"What?! JJ, you know what happens if we don't stop this!" I panicked.

"Just … trust him. He's got this."

Chance landed another left hand to Jayden, this time cracking onto his cheekbone. Before he could recover, the right hand was already following through.

Jayden's body landed with a thunk on the ground, groaning and whimpering in pain.

Chance stood over him and wrapped one of his large, calloused hands around Jayden's bleeding throat. "In case you hadn't realised, you're no longer welcome in this gym." Chance spoke with a calmness that rattled even *me*. An icy, frosty tune of promised pain. Almost animalistic, the protective rage cascaded off him.

"That's … not your call," Jayden said between groans.

"Oh, I think you'll find it is." Chance yanked his hand away and turned to Jonesy, standing a few people to my left. He reached out and took the obnoxiously gold duffel bag from Jonesy before throwing it roughly against Jayden's chest.

"You can't kick me out!" he roared, blood spraying from his nose and over his mouth. His hazel eyes found me and darkened. Not in that heated, raw way that Chance's had, but in true hatred. "My dad will *end* this place and all of you in it."

Chance's brows flicked up in response. "You might want to go home, Jayden," Chance said. "Seems like I've been there more than you have lately."

Jayden's face paled, making the crimson blood pouring over it look even darker.

Chance let out a breathy chuckle before stepping in close once again. "One more thing," he breathed. "If you ever say *anything* about her again, next time I won't *let* you get back up. Got it?"

Jayden refused to meet Chance's wrathful gaze. His stare remained on the blood that stained the ground nearby.

Chance's pointer finger pushed his chin up to meet his. "*Got it?*" he snarled softly.

Jayden nodded, seemingly frozen to the spot.

Chance patted him on the chest. "Good boy."

He turned and swept his gaze over the rest of the group before finally holding my stare. "Everyone back inside. Circle up."

***

"Are you insane?!"

Chance was hunched over his desk in the office. Those ripped muscles in his back were flexed, tense with every slightly panted breath he took.

"Lynnie—" JJ started.

"No, JJ!" I cut him off. "Do neither of you understand that his little temper tantrum will *ruin* us?!"

They didn't respond, so I took it upon myself to continue a little temper tantrum of my own. "I had it handled! I've been handling Jayden and his bullshit for nearly a year now. I didn't need you guys to go all alpha-male on me! I didn't need saving! He's a little fucking rat who doesn't get enough attention from *daddy* so comes in here to stir shit!"

Chance finally turned to meet my gaze, his face *still* in that perfect mask of calm. I was about to speak when he blew out a breath and pushed himself away from the desk.

He moved over to his stack of filing cabinets. After rifling through his pockets, he pulled out a navy blue keyring, a matching star dangling next to a small red key. The key fit the lock that was at the corner of the cabinet, and he yanked the top drawer open. He found the file in a matter of seconds before slamming the drawer shut.

"What is that?" I asked.

He turned and swaggered over to me. That cool, calm, collected face never left mine as he opened the file on my desk.

"Read it." He nodded at the stack of paperwork, arms folded over his chest. The paperwork was littered with coloured pointers with minimal handwriting, multiple series of dot points, and Chance's name written everywhere.

My mouth fell open. "Thi— You're part-owner of the gym?"

"Unofficially, yes," he said, still stone-faced as ever. "Jayden's old man accepted my offer. I signed the paperwork last night."

"Wh—why didn't you tell me?" I asked.

"I didn't want it to come across as something it wasn't." He shrugged.

Shrugged. As if he hadn't just dropped an absolute bomb.

As if he hadn't just changed the course of Knock's' history.

"Wait. You said unofficially?"

Chance closed the gap between us.

That intoxicating scent of his crashed over me in waves. I felt dizzy.

The corners of his mouth lightly twitched upwards, as if he knew exactly what his presence was doing to me. "See here? And here, here, and here?" He pointed at various empty dotted lines. "They're all that stands between me being part-owner of Knock's."

"Your signature seals the deal, Lynnie." JJ put a hand on my shoulder and squeezed. I could feel the apology in it, saying, *I'm sorry I knew and didn't tell you.*

I reached into my top desk drawer and pulled out my father's thick, golden swirled pen from the bottom of the pile. I scribbled my signature over each empty dotted line and put the old pen back in its spot.

"Welcome to the business." I took a chance on smiling up at those stormy eyes. Whether it was the midday sunlight that was shining hot rays into the gym or because some kind of puzzle piece had moved across the board, the clouds parted and a rich blue peeked out.

Chance's lips twitched up into a smile and he held his hand out for me to shake.

I wrapped my clammy hand in his.

JJ's hand piled on top, squeezing our fingers. "Woooo! You're stuck with us now, Chancey boy!" JJ hollered, breaking all of our hands when he pulled Chance into what could only be described as a bone-crushing hug.

Chance stared straight into my eyes over JJ's shoulder. "Nowhere else I'd rather be."

CHAPTER 23

Chance

"So, you're telling me that you're now part-owner of one of, if not the most, influential MMA gyms currently standing in the world?" my brother asked.

"Yeah, man."

And I drained nearly everything from that handy little secret bank account.

I yawned, stepping off the curb to cross the road into the driveway of the gym.

It had been over a week since I'd thrown Jayden out of Knock's, and he was yet to test my threat. JJ had done some sleuthing and found out when Rat was planning to come and get his things. So when he'd come to collect his gear a few days later, I'd made *sure* I was conveniently sorting through paperwork and study tape at the time.

The coward hadn't even looked in her direction.

Good.

"I'm assuming the owner came around to you and your charm then?"

I sighed.

It had also been just over a week since Mari and I had slept together. A week of her avoiding me—

Okay, maybe we are avoiding each other.

Switching and swerving in every over-the-top fucking way. A week of awkwardness and tension that had been all too graciously pointed out by JJ in quiet moments. A week of *my* subconscious putting on a goddamn show about her almost every night.

"You could say that," I replied.

Every night was like a new memory surfacing from that drunken night we'd shared.

I pressed my lips into the slope where her neck met her shoulder, lightly running my tongue over the taste of her skin. A moan slipped from her, a fucking delightful sound.

Every muscle in my body was rigid with anticipation, but I'd never felt more relaxed. My fingers skimmed the red thong, a patch of moisture visible right above where I knew her tender slickness was waiting for me. Pain flickered in the back of my jaw under my teeth, desire for the woman below me bursting to the point of agony. I relished in it, in her. Using my teeth to sooth that ache, I bit down on her thong and dragged it lower, lower, lower.

Hard to the point of self-combustion, I decided I would happily die in this moment. The taste of her—her own personal flavour of salty peaches—was blinding. One lick of her, one flick of my tongue on her soft, wet clit, and I knew I would never taste anything better than this. The vibration of her moans rattled through my tongue as I swirled and curled it around her tight, dripping hole.

Her lips parted in a pant as she lowered herself down onto my cock. I gritted my teeth. So fucking tight. So fucking wet. So fucking perfect. Her small hands splayed on my chest as she levered up and down.

"You look so fucking good riding me, dripping all over me," I groaned. "Fuck, Sunny, you're soaked."

"Y-you … fuck." She gushed all over me, picking up her pace. The breath whooshed out of me in a frantic pant. Her pussy … fuck, she felt like home. *This was light. This was warmth. This was fucking life in its most extraordinary form.*

I was drowning in her. Constantly. She was everywhere.

Fucking inconvenient.

How was I meant to think about anything, anything at all, when I had memories as good as *that* rattling around in my brain?

"She still giving you a hard time, bro?" Dylan asked, the phone connection going fuzzy for a second.

"Nah, she's fine. Just got some things to think over in the next few days, and my brother decides to call me at half-past four in the morning when I'm on my way to work," I grumble. Between working, training, and waking up multiple times from dreams of a certain curly-haired brunette, I felt like my fucking wheels were falling off.

"Your classes start at the asscrack of dawn. I figured you wouldn't be a cranky bastard," he replied with a laugh. "What's on your mind?"

"Baltis gave me an offer."

There was silence for a moment.

"And?"

"It's everything I've ever fucking dreamed of. Main event fight. Title shot. Home arena."

"Holy shit, Chance. That's amazing! Congrats, brother!"

I sighed, the weight of the offer feeling like boulders hovering above me. With spikes. Dripping in acid.

"It's pretty unbelievable," I grumbled, pulling my keys out of my pocket to unlock the gym's doors.

"You don't sound stoked."

"I'm wrapped about it, man. I'm over the fucking moon that I'm being given the opportunity to fight for the championship title, particularly in my home arena." I let out another loose breath. "But it's in my home arena, Dylan ... and I—"

"Don't have the bandwidth to plan for running into the past?" he interrupted, seeing where I was going before I'd even gotten there.

"... no. No, I don't. I left that shit there for a reason, Dyl. Because it was *fucking shit*. No one, me or others, needs to visit that steaming pile of it," I admitted quietly.

Shame burned like a thousand candles had just been lit inside of me. I didn't want people to know what had happened back in Darlington Harbour—why I'd been so quick to jump into a new life. I'm sure the press and the public had questions; I was Chance fucking Riordan. People were bound to have questions as to why voted 'Mr Violence' of this year had up and left his home city in a matter of hours.

"Don't you think that's up to them to decide?" he asked softly.

There was a silent, underlying question in it; *are you ever going to tell me what the hell went down in Darlington Harbour?*

"Not when it comes to this," I replied, shutting down the hidden question.

"You can't give everything up on a '*what if*', Chance. You're way too talented and have worked way too fucking hard to let whatever this is stop you." Agitation flowed through the phone, and I could practically see the scowl on his face.

Dylan was the oldest of us three and lived up to the fierce protective nature that older siblings usually had. He had taught me to fight when he left for high school, so I could take care of Milah. He'd been there, at my back, through every up and down I'd had growing up.

I knew it would be killing him to not be able to know, not be able to help me now. But I was a man now—it was my problem. There was no reason to force anyone else down into the trenches with me. Not when I'd just started to get a foothold out of them.

"Yeah, I know," I sighed. "I'm about to walk into the gym, Dyl. I gotta run."

"Chance—"

"I love you, mate," I said, ending the call the same way I always did.

"I love you too, Chance."

I rolled my shoulders out, fighting the inevitable tremor that came from hearing those words.

CHAPTER 24

Chance

BANG. BANG. BANG.

BANG. BANG.

I slammed my fists into the bag time after time after time. Finding therapy in the bag was as easy as breathing. It was music to my ears, the pounding booms I made.

Bag work let me be alone—let me be wherever I needed to be. Let me lose myself in the constant movement, slip into a world where everyone and everything dissipated into the dark void.

Most times I went without gloves, my hands usually wrapped or bare-knuckle. Any pain only drove me further, harder, faster.

Movement flickered out of the void to my right, so I pushed harder—shoved everything that was and ever had been into the black hole and threw *everything* I fucking had into the heavy leather bag. My knuckles grazed; small droplets of blood surfaced. The beacon of motion to my right refused to fade into the void, beaming blatantly.

With the force of my entire rotation, I slammed a cutting elbow into the bag before turning over my shoulder.

Sunny stood in denim shorts and a Knock's tank, stacking gloves into the racks. She rose up on her toes to shove a pair of shiny golden gloves back into place on the top shelf. Even the gloves weren't as bright as her. Her tank shifted just a smidge away from the thick waist of her shorts.

My legs moved of their own accord, like a moth to a flame, when she stumbled backwards from trying to put Jayden's stupid fucking gloves away. Her skin was a little moist when my hands found her smooth, still exposed waist. She let out a breathy gasp at the contact before finding her feet.

"T-Thanks," she croaked.

"I've got you," I replied, withdrawing my hands. My skin, as well as her shoulders, slumped slightly at the loss of contact.

What the fuck is happening to me?

Pussy-whipped, that's what.

I turned to walk away when her hand gripped mine. She plucked it up towards her and inspected the open wounds I had on my knuckles. Her lips pursed and a crease formed between her eyebrows in concentration.

"Let's get these cleaned up," she said quietly and tugged on my hand in request to follow her. I slipped it from her grasp, feeling the cool air replace her warmth immediately.

"I'm fine. I was just finishing up," I replied, snatching my water bottle from the edge of the mat. I made a show of tipping some of the water over my knuckles and then shut my eyes as I poured it over my head.

Sunny stared at me with those big brown eyes swirling like hot pools of the richest chocolate. With her lips slightly parted, she scanned my shirtless torso before bringing her stare to mine.

"It wasn't a request," she stated, stepping forward to grab my hand once again. The softness and politeness in her grip was gone, replaced with a firmness leaving no room to argue as she dragged me to the bathrooms.

After pushing me to sit on the closed toilet, she opened the larger of the vanity drawers and pulled out a fluffy white washcloth and a bottle of antiseptic. Wordlessly, she ran the tap as hot as it would go before shoving the washcloth under it. She wrung it out and crossed the room to me.

"I would have done this myself," I lied. I knew how to, of course. I'd been doing this for so long, dressing cuts was something I could teach even a blind man to do. But I found that when it came to dressing your own wounds, it was easier to go with the 'it'll be right' approach.

"No, you wouldn't have," she said, wiping the hot fabric over the top of my right hand. "Besides, I like to protect my investments. Who'll take class tomorrow if you get staph or whatever from punching a filthy bag *bare-knuckled*?"

She shot me a pointed look.

"Careful, Sunny. You almost sound like you care." I smirked up at her. She was bending down slightly to address my left hand now, her magnificent cleavage well on display and directly in my line of sight.

Torture.

This was *torture*.

This strong, sexy woman was all I could see. She was light and warmth and fire. *Fire*. Everything about her was heat, a burning flame I was fucking drawn to.

"Don't get your hopes up, Riordan. I'm purely taking care of an asset."

"Mmm, I love it when you talk dirty," I mused.

She snickered.

A zapping rush filled the open cuts as she poured antiseptic over them. The brown liquid ran off the sides of my hands, dripping to the floor. The bleeding had stopped, so I declined the need for bandages.

"Don't come crying if they get infected," Sunny said, shoving the bandages back in the drawer and the washcloth in the laundry basket.

"Not one to cry over a split knuckle, Sunny," I joked.

"What's the deal with going bare-knuckle?" she asked, wetting a paper towel under the tap.

"What's it to you?"

She rolled her eyes. "I'm just curious, jackass. Relax." She crouched down and wiped up the antiseptic on the floor that was probably minutes away from staining.

"Sometimes it's just what I need. It's not that deep," I replied, that mask of boredom slipping over my face, urging her not to ask any more fucking questions. "Thanks for giving my hands a clean."

I sidestepped her and pulled the door open before heading back towards where my gear was. The sound of the bathroom bin squeaking open and slamming shut became muffled as I strode away.

"Seriously, Riordan?" she complained loudly. "I extend the olive branch and make an effort, and that's all I get?"

I turned, finding her standing in front of the bathroom block, arms crossed. A gentle crease had formed, no doubt from frustration, between her brows. Those full, rosy lips were pulled down into a scowl, her cheeks flushing the same colour.

"What's that supposed to mean?" I snapped, folding my arms right back.

She rolled her eyes and stormed over to me. "You haven't spoken to me since we ... you know. It's childish and I won't have this *petty shit* in my gym." She lifted her chin, but there was uncertainty in those brown eyes.

I scoffed.

Fucking women.

"So, let me get this straight." I ran a hand through my damp hair and let my hands fall to my hips. "We sleep together, I give you *several* mind-blowing orgasms—" I held up a hand when she opened her mouth to speak. "You leave the next morning without a note or a goddamn text. *I*, being able to read between the fucking lines, take that as my cue to move that night into the '*drunken splendour*' category—"

"That's why you haven't been speaking to me?" she interrupted, honey eyes widening. "Because I left without saying goodbye? That's what this is about?"

"It's not *about* anything," I snapped, the lie tasting as foul as it was. "It's about the fact that you think I owe you, just because we slept together. News flash, Sunny baby, you're not the be-all-and-end-all of orgasms"—*Watch yourself, mate. You're about to dig yourself a hole here*—"I can find myself a good orgasm, just as easy as I found yours."

Her eyes flared, and my stomach knotted.

She nailed her walls back in place. Gone was any banter between us, any kind of flirtatious tension.

"You're a real asshole, you know that?" she said through gritted teeth.

"And you're a pain in it, Sunny baby," I snarled.

"Stop calling me that!" She stepped into my space, glaring up at me. A droplet of sweat ran down the side of her temple, and my nostrils were instantly filled with that fucking intoxicating smell of salty peaches.

"For fuck sake," I growled. Her lips parted and blew out a hot breath that had saliva filling my mouth. "That fucking mouth of yours."

"Right back at you, big guy," she growled, though neither of us made a move to step away.

My fingers brushed hers, teasingly testing the scalding waters we were surrounded by. Her slender fingers startled at the contact but warmed very fucking quickly. Gladly allowing my own to thread through hers, I yanked her in flush against me.

Sunny let out a small breath before meeting my gaze, still fiery as ever.

"You're such a—"

I cut her off by slamming my mouth on hers.

CHAPTER 25

Mari

All thoughts floated away from me when his mouth landed on mine. The kiss was rough, needy, and torturous. My hands roamed Chance's chest, his shoulders, his arms—anywhere I could reach. He bent down slightly, dropping his hands from my face. One wrapped around my waist and tugged me closer. A second later, the other tangled in my hair. With a teasing tug, I opened my mouth for him. His tongue swept inside, lashing and ravishing mine. A traitorous groan slipped from the back of my throat, which was met with a gruff moan of his own. Then we were moving.

He pushed us back into the nearby wall, avoiding the heavy leather bags hanging nearby. The hand that was in my hair caught the wall before my head could with a thud, the other hand trapping my hip as he leaned over me. I couldn't see anything outside of his towering, muscular frame. That hot mouth found my neck and peppered it with frantic kisses. His usual cologne and mint flooded every sense, mixed with the salt lingering on his sweat-slicked skin.

"This doesn't change that you were a total ... *Oh*." Any train of thought went off the rails when his teeth skimmed my skin, sucking and nibbling along my jaw.

"You were saying, Sunny baby?" he murmured in my ear before taking the lobe in between his teeth.

"Don't call me ... that," I struggled.

Abandoning my hip, his hand found my breast. He palmed it, my nipple instantly pebbling at the touch.

"Don't call you what?" He smirked before flicking a finger over the sensitive tip.

Do not tell me this man is going to make me come without even taking my clothes off.

"T-that," I tried, already panting.

"Tell me what, Sunny baby, and I'll stop." Another teasing flick, another breathy moan.

"I ... I ..." I tried, desperately tried. Any chance of success went out the fucking window when he exposed my aching, heavy breasts with one swift tug of my tank top.

"Fuck," Chance groaned, driving his hips into me and sealing his mouth over mine again. "This is all that's been on my mind the last two goddamn weeks."

"Are you gonna do something about it then?" I demanded, barely.

It was more like a pathetic excuse of a demand.

That cocky, arrogant, *sexy as fuck* smirk lifted onto his face. "My, my, Sunny baby. Do *you* want me to do something about it?" That teasing finger traced a line up the side of my neck before the whole hand wrapped around my throat. "Look at me."

I dragged my eyes up from where our bodies met to find his.

I knew how to swim—almost every Australian child learned. But I was fucking drowning in the ocean in his eyes. A frenzied storm swirled, both hot and cold, both night and day, both lust and need.

"Tell me, Sunny baby." The thumb that was pressed into the side of my neck moved, tracing over my bottom lip. "Tell me what you want."

There was a warm, electrifying touch between my legs before the button of my shorts was jerking open. A mocking finger probed the top of my underwear, running along the smooth fabric. I mentally pat two-hours-ago Mari on the back for deciding she needed to wear nice panties today.

"Do you want me on my knees? I'll gladly make you come using just my tongue, right here on these mats."

I swear I stopped breathing. Every single cell on and in my body ached in anticipation as he continued to tease and tug at my underwear.

"Do you want to be on your knees, Sunny baby?" he teased. "Do you want to be on your knees, so I can take your mouth before I take *all* of you?"

A breathy chuckle fanned my face as he gently snapped back the underwear elastic he had been toying with.

"Should we move this to the office? I'd bend you over the couch, take you hard and fast for being so eager." Just as he finished his sentence, he dipped a finger between my folds. My knees buckled, but he was already there, holding me upright.

"You call the shots though, Sunny baby. Because once I start, I don't give a fuck who walks through those doors. I won't stop."

As if on cue, the most cold-shower-voice to ever exist called out through the gym. "Yo, Yo! Lynnie?! Rio?! Where you at?"

Chance sighed in annoyance. Shoulders as rigid as rocks, he reluctantly stepped away from me. He brought his finger, the one that had been so fucking close to being inside of me, to his lips and sucked it from bottom to top.

"Cover up, will you?" he growled, pointedly glancing at my still exposed chest and undone shorts.

"Shit!" I hissed before tucking the girls back away. *How the hell did he free them in one tug?*

"Ah! My friends!" JJ sang as he walked around the corner, just in time for me to do my shorts up. I folded my arms over my chest, knowing my face was still flushed. I could still feel Chance's lips on mine, the swelling he'd left behind.

"How are we?" he asked, slinging an arm around Chance's shoulder with a big, dopey grin on his face.

"Sunny was just yelling at me about hitting the bag bare-knuckle." Chance threw me straight under the bus.

"I was not—"

Chance silenced me with a look that said, '*Do you want JJ to know I was ten seconds away from fucking you against said bag?*'.

"I was just ... protecting an asset."

"Aw, Lynnie. You big softie." JJ waved a hand and let go of Chance, moving over to ruffle my hair. I swatted his hand away before turning on my heel to leave.

"So, did you give Baltis your answer?" JJ asked hesitantly.

It was that hesitation and my blatant curiosity, that had me stopping in my tracks. "Who's Baltis?" I asked.

"My manager," Chance replied, shooting JJ a look that had him wincing.

"What was the answer for?"

"He offered me a fight." Chance shrugged his shoulders.

"Pfft, not just '*a fight*'," JJ mimicked. "The fight. The fight of all fights. A real history-maker."

"Dude, shut up," Chance scolded.

"I don't understand what there is to shut up about, man. It's *the dream*. Home stadium. Title shot. What have you got to lose?" JJ rambled.

Those forget-me-not eyes scanned my face, then my body. He huffed an apparently bored breath before shaking his head.

"You're right. I have nothing to lose," he replied, turning away from us and heading towards his gear bag.

"So you're gonna call him?!" JJ squeaked, trying his best to contain the excitement that was clearly vibrating inside of him.

"Yeah, mate," he said, picking up his phone.

JJ bounced from foot to foot in anticipation as Chance pressed his phone to his ear.

I couldn't for the life of me understand what all of this hesitation and tension was about. A title shot? In his home stadium? That was the best circumstances possible. No travel days, no jet lag, no paying for the flights of your entire team.

"Baltis, it's Chance." He stared at the heavy bag that was still stained with his blood as he said, "I'm in."

CHAPTER 26

Mari

The news hit the media in a flash. The top contender in the light heavyweight division of the UFL, Chance Riordan, would take on the current champion, Randy Rager, in eight weeks.

'I'm itching for it. It wouldn't take me eight weeks to get ready for Rager, but he'd need a year to get ready for me,' Riordan says.

'This one'll be more than a main event. I'm coming for blood and bones, Riordan,' Rager responds.

I snapped my laptop shut quickly when the office door burst open. A very sweaty Chance strolled in, kicking the door shut behind him wearing nothing but a white, fluffy towel.

Guess that isn't sweat…

"Aren't you meant to have a session with Al and JJ?" I asked, fidgeting with a pair of prototype boxing gloves on my desk, desperate to find a distraction from that valiant white towel that was hiding this man's magic orgasm stick. The kind that puts a spell on you, leaving you lusting, pent-up and having dirty dreams for weeks.

It took a second to catch onto the fact that Chance was levelling me with a look. He cleared his throat before unzipping the duffel bag on his desk, a small smirk playing on his lips.

"That finished about an hour ago, Sunny," he replied, stacking up a change of clothes.

An unwanted frown tugged at my lips. Of course, what happened earlier had been a heat of the moment thing.

Don't overthink it, Mari. He can get orgasms elsewhere, as he very asshole-ily informed you.

"They head off already?" I squeaked, avoiding watching the glorious muscles in his back work as he moved.

"Yup." He paused. "That a problem?"

"W-why would it be a problem?" Curse my inconveniently timed voice cracks. Apparently, I was hitting puberty again—at least that would explain my sudden spike in libido.

"Just wasn't sure if you needed more time to ... *cool off*," he replied, though his tone told me he knew I'd need another century to be able to cool off.

"I'm plenty cooled off, thank you." *Fake it 'til you make it, right?* "Cool as a cucumber."

"That so?"

"Sure is. Sorry if your ego was expecting me to be a puddle on the floor after your little performance earlier."

His ego had been right on the money with that one. I'd hidden out in the office trying to think about anything but jumping Chance Riordan's bones for ... well, three hours now.

"Pity," was all he said.

"Pity?"

"Yeah. Pity." He turned to face me, that bored tone no match for the heat burning in his gaze. "Was happy to offer some help ... *cooling off*. But it appears my services are not required."

Every thought in my brain was alight with a fire I had no control over.

"It seems I'm not the one in need of services, Riordan," I said, standing from my chair and folding my arms over my chest. His eyes flickered to the movement. "It seems *you're* the one still standing in my office in nothing but a towel."

"*Our* office," he corrected, closing distance towards me.

I scrambled backwards until I was halfway leaning over my desk.

"Get dressed, Riordan. JJ brings enough unwanted nudity into this place." Every word came out breathier than the last.

He was close to me; I could feel his warmth. Like a burning fire in the yard on a cold winter night. It irked me how homely, how *safe* it felt.

He's a fighter — he's anything but safe.

"Stop staring at the towel around my waist. Look me in the eyes and tell me to back down and I will, Mari."

Hearing his deep voice say my name was another form of heaven. Or torture because I knew I couldn't have this man.

He's a fighter.

"Come on, Sunny. Look at me." He pushed.

I looked up.

Rookie mistake.

I was swimming, or floating, or drowning. Which one? I had no idea. I was surrounded by that eternal expanse of balmy blue liquid. It was too warm to be a pool, and too calm to be an ocean.

It was *him*.

It was passion and lust and *him*.

"Well?" he asked, brows raised, hands loosely by his sides.

"Huh?"

The corners of his lips rose, and he stepped in a touch farther. "I'm waiting for you to tell me to back down, Sunny." His fingers brushed my cheek as he tucked a stray curl out of my face. "Say the word and I'll stop."

"And what if I don't want you to stop?" I breathed.

A wicked, feral grin erupted across his face one second. The next, my backside was in his hands and my feet off the floor.

He set me down on the edge of my desk, swiping the contents away like those criminally hot men do in movies. Except this wasn't a movie, this was *real*. Chance Riordan had cleared my desk for me, so he could do lord knows what with me on it. The thought was invigorating. I trembled, shook in anticipation.

Hands on either sides of my hips, he caged me in. His nose skimmed up my neck as he breathed me in. My pulse skittered, the rhythm of an entire bag of M&M'S being poured on the floor. He loosed a chesty, devilish rumble. A sound of satisfaction and delight.

Hot lips and breath found my neck. Slowly, so fucking slowly it was agonising, they moved. Up, down, and around. As if he was trying to taste every inch of my skin, leave nothing untouched. A hurried shiver shot up my spine and a shaky breath tumbled out.

"Mmmm," he mumbled into my neck. "Wherever shall I start with you?"

Somehow, without me noticing, he'd gotten the button of my shorts undone followed by my zipper. His pointer finger ran tauntingly up and down my exposed panties.

Once again, fantastic choice, past-Mari, on the underwear.

"Maybe here?" he said, though it sounded more like a plan than question.

Without warning, his finger slipped through the open zipper, immediately meeting the soaked fabric. I hissed a breath through clenched teeth. I urged, begged, pleaded with my legs to stop shaking.

I know it's been a while for you, Mari. But please don't embarrass yourself by coming before he's actually touched you.

"Just a taste." He dipped a finger behind the wet thong. Using that painfully slow touch, he slid up my folds. Bursts and jolts of electricity came to life in my body.

He removed the finger, only to suck it deeply.

"Tease," I panted.

His eyes darkened on my face. "Darling, you haven't even seen teasing yet."

"Prove it," I dared.

"Not tonight," he replied, freezing my blood over momentarily. "Tonight I want you hard and fast, coming so hard you can't see straight. That alright with you?"

"You can try," I attempted, tongue-tied.. I really did my best to sound like his words didn't have every cell in my body vibrating with excitement.

His eyes didn't leave my mouth. "Last chance to say 'no', Sunny baby. I want you too damn bad to stop."

He leaned in, and I braced for the impact of his ferocious mouth that I'd been dreaming about.

"I don't care who sees us. Who hears us. I don't fucking care if the building collapses around us. So long as I get to be inside you again."

My panties may as well have slipped right onto the floor then and there.

"So, I'll ask you once again, Sunny baby," he purred. "Are you gonna tell me to back down?"

"No," I breathed.

CHAPTER 27

Chance

I dove for her mouth.

That fucking mouth.

I'd been fantasising about kissing hers for over a week now. A week of remembering what those lips felt like, what it could do. A week of being *without* that mouth.

The kiss was anything but romantic. It was full of need and eagerness. I ran my tongue over her bottom lip, demanding her to open, but spiralling when she did. Her taste, her breath, her lips; all mine for the taking. Every block that had been put together to make this sweet, sweet mouth *hers* was a fucking divine feast on the senses.

Her fingers sprawled through my hair and tugged, urging me on. Her legs wrapped around my waist, seemingly unbothered by the erection that had made its appearance almost as soon as I'd seen her in here. She gasped into my mouth when the end of me hit her, annoyingly covered by those shorts that showed off her mile-long legs. In a burst of frustration—frustration over having to use my fucking hand so often these last two weeks, frustration that it was *her* I was struggling over, frustration that once hadn't been enough with her—I shoved my hands in the back pockets of her shorts, fisted the fabric, and yanked them apart. A loud tear filled the room, overriding our heavy breathing. She pushed on my chest, separating her swollen mouth from mine.

I was honestly expecting her to yell at me, berate me for tearing her shorts in half. But her eyes were dark, almost black. It was a deadly, enticing heat. Like touching a stove when you didn't realise how hot it was until you get burned. I couldn't not touch the heat; I couldn't walk away. Not yet.

She latched onto my shoulders and lifted her ass up, waiting for me to clear the torn-up fabric. It hit the bin with a *swish*, but I was already on her mouth again.

Fuck, *this mouth*. How could I ever use my own to breathe again when tasting hers was better than air?

My hand wrapped gently around her throat as I dove deeper with my tongue, lashing and ravishing hers. I lay her on her back, and she so eagerly, so willingly obliged. Her brown curls spread around her, and I paused.

She was so beautiful.

She was fucking divine.

She was mine, just for right now.

Between her folds and her upper thighs glistened. Saliva filled my mouth, begging to relive that taste again. Though her sexy as fuck thong was sleek and black, it failed to hide that soaking patch of desire.

I dropped to my knees at the end of the desk and smirked when her breathing picked up. Those damn panties, sexy as they were, were still in my goddamn way.

To shreds, I say.

And did.

They fell apart easier than her shorts but followed the same path. That deep, cocoa fire in her eyes exploded. She sent blood straight to my cock by scooting that full, muscular ass closer to my mouth.

Taking the hint, and refusing to take my time, I dove in—licking and swirling around that sensitive bud, her pussy the most beautiful shade of pink.

Don't get all sappy there, mate. Focus on the task at hand.

I flicked and twirled her clit with my tongue, and when those breathy little moans started, I slipped a finger inside her. She was so wet my cock ached. She was so willing, so ready for me to fuck her.

"F-fuck, fuck, Chance!" she moaned.

I curled the tip of my finger in a different direction each pump until I found it. This tight, soft spot inside of her that seemed to almost grab on when I brushed up on it. Within a couple of pumps over it, that sweet pussy was tightening down on my finger and her cries filled my ears.

"Chance!" The sound of my name falling from her lips was like a crack of thunder—demanding and heated.

Pulses of pleasure rippled through her as I tasted every second of her climax. Salty and yet sweet, I wasn't sure if I would ever get enough of this taste. Of tasting her—

Enough of that now.

I stood from the end of the desk and wrapped an arm under her back. Her climax still on my face and on the desk, my balls ached as they wound up tight. Limply and full of post-orgasm bliss, she wrapped her legs around me as I used one arm to move us to the couch and the other to drop my towel. Her wetness slid perfectly over my cock, sending that familiar flame into spiral.

Oh, mate. We know this is only just the beginning.

As soon as her back hit the couch I lined myself up to her. Taking her mouth once again, I thrust inside her. She was so wet, and so goddamn tight.

I pushed a breath out my nose, my mouth still on hers. The taste of *her* flooded my senses, so impossibly indescribable. And with her wrapped so tightly around the top of my cock; fuck it felt incredible. I'd promised hard and fast, but I couldn't let it be *that* fast. Reluctantly, I pulled away.

"C'mon, Sunny baby. Make some more room for me." I dropped my mouth to hers again briefly. "I need you to make some room for me, sweetheart."

Those brown eyes opened on me, desire and bliss and pleasure swirling around in a heated mixture. Those pools of honey were sticky, but I felt no urge to get 'un-stuck'. A soft pink flush coated her upper cheeks, making her freckles seem darker. Those brown eyes had pupils inflated with oxytocin. Her lips were a deeper rosy pink, swollen from mine. Those brown eyes stared and stared.

Those eyes.

Those eyes.

Those eyes.

I couldn't look away, didn't even bother to as soon as I felt her walls slacken around me. I pushed farther inside her, her pleasure driving me closer and closer to a climax of my own. Taking her hand, I pinned it above her head by threading my own through it.

"Fuckkk," I groaned. "Fuck ... fuck, Sunny. I need a little more room, baby."

I rocked slowly back and forth, savouring the slickness on my cock. Her walls slackened once more, and I drove home. As I picked up the pace, her walls tightened and slackened, tightened and slackened, over and over again.

My whole body was shot with pleasure. She gasped at the same time I groaned. I could feel that spot inside of her grabbing on, begging me to run my cock over it. Hard and fast.

Pinned to the couch, Sunny moaned over and over as I rocked in and out of her. Somehow, she got wetter. I was sure she was actively dehydrating. Was I complaining? Fuck no.

Pushing into her harder and harder, driving us both towards an explosive release. The office filled with the sounds of us—skin on skin, her pants and moans, and my constant cursing.

Chapter 28

Chance

"We should probably clean all of this up before we go," I groggily mumbled in her ear. My eyes were straining to stay open, but after what we'd just done and where we currently lay—staying awake felt impossible.

Her curly-haired head was laying on my arm, warm body pressed in close to mine.

Did I mention she was still naked?

Her skin was soft and silky, laying over a body full of muscle, strength, and capability.

Did I mention she was still naked?

She let out a breathy laugh before rolling back to face me. The long, fluffy, black threads from the rug below us made her skin glow a deeper olive. It could have also been the post-sex afterglow she was wearing.

Her fantastic set of breasts crammed together, practically begging me to go back and give them the attention they'd greedily taken not an hour ago.

Did I mention that she was *still* naked?

"You mean *you're* cleaning that up before we go? You're the one who made the mess."

I pinched her ass and she squealed, possibly along with a small, childish part of me as well.

"What?! You're the one who made the mess!" she whined, pushing herself to sit up on an elbow

"Up time, Sunny baby. I think I've earned myself a helping hand."

Her face flushed pink, and my hands jumped to cup her cheeks. After internally swatting them away, I stood from the rug. I turned back and reached for her hands.

"I may need a minute to get my legs working again." She yawned, a sleepy haze taking over her face.

CHAPTER 29

Mari

"You need a ride into Koresvale tonight?" Chance asked, finally putting on his clean, post-shower shirt.

It had taken ... longer than expected to clean up the mess we'd made in the office. What started as picking things up from the floor, had very quickly turned into round two.

I patted the desk, silently thanking it for not breaking under what we'd just done ... twice.

"I ... had totally forgotten about that."

Nan and Al had insisted on throwing a party for Chance once they'd found out about the 'fight of a lifetime' that he had accepted. Koresvale was a town about an hour over from Soggla, best known for its nightlife. It was the only town with more than one place to drink.

With three clubs, Koresvale was always popping off on a Friday and Saturday night. The clubs—Oasis, Moonies, and Karly's—had only recently implemented the legal rule of smoking to be carried on outside. Inside each club still reeked of stale cigarettes, but at least now there was a dimmed, coloured lighting that made the space feel somewhat new and refreshed.

Excitement rushed through my body at the thought of him and I showing up together, possibly hand in hand. Possibly dancing up on one another. Possibly getting it on in one of the outdated bathrooms.

But then, the excitement stopped. My eyes landed on the prototype gloves that Camden had had sent to the gym. The same obnoxious, golden gloves that Jayden had paraded around.

That was what happened when I got involved with fighters.

And I was still living with the damage.

"Look, Chance." My heart thumped in my chest, nerves short-circuiting all over my body. "I think you're really great, but—"

"Relax, Trevino. I was asking if you needed a lift in tonight, not for your hand in marriage."

Post-sex bliss, over.

"Oh, uh … I—"

"Assumed I'd fall head over heels in love with you after having sober sex with you?"

I fumbled with the navy blue shirt in my hands, avoiding his heavy gaze.

"No," I snapped, temper flaring when I met his darkened gaze. "Just wanted to make sure we're on the same page. I'm not interested in you."

Stupid, stupid liar. You know this will come back to bite you in the ass.

"Glad we have an understanding." He slung his duffle over his shoulder, that mask of boredom strapped into place over his no-longer-glowing face. "See you 'round, Trevino."

CHAPTER 30

Mari

I barely wanted to be here at this party, celebrating, let alone seeing my boyf—whatever we were off having a *fantastic fucking time* over in his corner booth.

The corner booth that was surrounded by women.

Beautiful.

Gorgeous.

Model-like.

Women.

JJ wasn't here tonight, which meant I had no *get out of jail free* card when it came to awkwardly standing by the bar by myself.

"Long time no see, Trevvy," a raspy voice said from beside me, suddenly but gently breaking me from my blank stare with a childhood nickname I hadn't heard in years.

I immediately knew who the owner was from the use of it.

Beau Beckett was a country boy gone city man. He'd graduated dux of our high school and left Soggla without a second thought. Last I'd heard, he was big in the finance world over in the United States. With a head of shaved, dark hair, high cheekbones and striking green eyes, he'd been the darling of Soggla when he was around. His family owned one of the larger farms on the outskirts of town that provided most of our dairy products. Loveliest people anyone could ever meet, as well as the hardest working. But Beau knew humble beginnings. With parents living a busy, bustling farm life, they'd refused to feed their only son everything life had to offer on a silver platter. When Beau turned fourteen, his dad had told him to get his backside down to the main square and find himself a job.

And so, he had. And that first job had led him all the way to the big leagues.

I plastered a bright smile on my face for my old friend. From the look he gave in return he wasn't buying it—but he simply pulled me in for a hug. I hadn't seen Beau in so long that we both knew it wasn't his place to question it.

"Always too long, the time between visits," I replied. I signalled to the bartender to pour Beau the same as what I was currently drinking. The bartender was young, new, and *very* intimidated by the sheer size of the crowd in his workplace. I slipped him a five-dollar-note in tip and turned my back on him before he could try and give it back.

"The big city is like a minefield, Mari," Beau replied with a grin, clinking his glass against mine. "You step out at the wrong point and your fuckin' leg blows off."

I laughed, taking a deep swig from the glass in my hand. "At some point you've gotta learn to outrun the blast," I teased. A familiar warmth spread across my chest and along my arms, alerting me that I had gathered the attention of another person in this bar.

I downed the rest and signalled for another. On either side of me, the bar was completely overwhelmed—people throwing their hands up in frustration as they watched the person beside them get served. Within half a thought, my boots were up on my chair and I was jumping the bar.

With a deep breath, a good steadying of the slight sway in my boots, I put on a fake-as-hell bright smile and started pouring drinks left, right and centre for the wave of community we'd brought in with us. Laughing with friends, old and new. Downing shots with one or two.

I grabbed the wad of cash that had been thrown in the tip jar and thrusted it out to the young bartender, who I now knew to be Noah. "Word from the wise, crack a joke with a smile or two and both you and the patrons will feel a lot better."

His bright eyes shone as he nodded frantically.

"You're doing great, don't stress." I patted his chest and poured Beau and I another whiskey each. Then, with a wink Noah's way, I climbed back over the bar and plonked down beside my old teenage fling in the fancy suit.

"Awfully kind of you." Beau tapped his glass against mine.

"I'm just an awfully kind person," I replied, downing my drink quickly and signalling another.

"I remember you lecturing me that this was a *sipping* whiskey all those years ago," he teased, eyebrows flicked up in curiosity.

"I sipped." I nodded to Noah as he placed another drink in front of me. "Just didn't take many of them."

Beau laughed. "Ah, I forgot how much fun you are."

"A two-year absence will do that." I swirled the large cubic ice in my drink.

"I missed you, Trevvy," he mumbled, taking another deep swig from his glass.

"I missed you too, Beckett."

CHAPTER 31

Mari

I'd meant it when I told Beau I'd missed him. We sat together, talking and laughing as if we'd seen each other just the other day.

"I shit you not, Trevvy, people do some weird stuff to avoid paying taxes."

He told me stories about the finance firm he worked for in the U.S, and I filled him in on the shockingly low amount of news in Soggla.

"So, when were you going to bring up the fact that you have one of the UFL's top up and coming fighters not only training with Al but *coaching* out of your very gym?" he demanded, shocked that I wasn't deeming this big news.

"Must everything be about *him*?" I groaned, nearly tripping on the slip of my tongue.

His eyebrows flicked up in surprise and it was clear as day I'd fucked up.

"Hmm ... I don't know, Trevvy. Must it?" he asked mockingly.

"Ugh!" I threw my head into my hands and groaned again. "No, it mustn't."

I glanced over to the beautiful women who were inching closer and closer to Chance. One had wiggled her way in-between him and one of the bigger guys from the gym, Hogs, and was currently twirling circles on his chest. My very blood boiled at the sight of it, a wave of unnecessary possessiveness crashing into me.

Chance's blue eyes met mine, bored and blank.

Light-bulb moment.

"Come dance with me!"

"What?" Beau gaped, nearly choking on his drink.

"Come dance with me," I repeated, hopping down from my stool. "Come on, Beckett. We haven't dance together in *ages*!" I began swaying my hips in the fashion of the way we'd used to dance together in clubs. Mind you, we had been sleeping together in some weird friends-with-benefits arrangement back then.

"Alright! Alright! Calm your tits. I'm coming."

I laughed and pulled him onto the dance floor.

I jogged over to the DJ set and hit a song. The flow of a sexy beat bounced out of the speakers and thrummed through the room. My hips tipped up and down as I danced my way through the crowd.

He held out a hand and pulled me into him and we fell straight into sync, just like old times. But somehow, for some reason, we were moving in sync and yet we felt *off*. I struggled hard to ignore the fact that Beau's body felt cold compared to Chance's.

Chance.

Where is he? I can barely see off the dance floor with all these people moving around us.

I stalled the spin Beau twirled me into and pushed myself lightly up against him.

Light enough for Beau to know I wasn't serious.

Heavy enough for Chance to not.

"Does this have anything to do with the angry UFL fighter looking at me *very* murderously from the booths?" Beau asked in my ear.

I smirked, the asshole side of me *wanting* him to notice.

Wanting him to hate it.

Wanting Beau off me.

Wanting him to be on me.

Chance straightened, the agitated tick in his jaw flaring. His eyes had blackened to dark, flat steel. A frosty iciness in them as they bore into me and the hands gently on my upper waist.

Beau was great, and a very dear friend. We had great dance chemistry and our senses of humour gelled together wonderfully.

But he wasn't Chance. And for whatever crazy twist of fate, I didn't hate that. He didn't ignite me like Chance did. His hands on my waist felt cold and all *wrong*.

Wrong.

Wrong. Wrong. Wrong.

"I'm just gonna go freshen up—back soon," I said loudly in his ear and headed off to the back-door bathrooms. They were typically only used by staff, but I knew on a busy night like this they would have to use the patrons' toilets.

The sexy, Latin beat still purred through the tiled walls as I leaned over the sink. I looked up, meeting glassy eyes that had a scalding storm brewing beneath them.

Beau and I always had great fun together whenever he was in town, but I'd never felt so *illicit* being close to him like that. Everything about him was so wrong, and not in the *sexy, forbidden* way. It felt like trying to fill a hole that wasn't his to fill. A gaping space inside of me that was waiting, yearning for the presence of another. Not just any other; Chance.

You didn't want him, Mari. Except I did.

You made that clear to him. Except I shouldn't have.

You don't get to be mad if he moves on. Except I was.

The bathroom door opening and slamming shut made me jump, turning immediately into a defensive stance. My legs were heavy and wobbled as I faced those blue eyes behind me.

"What the *fuck* was that, Sunny?" Chance growled.

His short-sleeved khaki shirt brought out the olive in his glowing skin. It tightly stretched across his pecs and at the beginning of his biceps. Those muscles, those glorious muscles, were taut with tension and fury.

"I don't know what you're talking about," I mumbled, turning back to the mirror. I brushed a slightly shaking finger under my eyelashes, pretending to check my makeup.

"Oh, you know *exactly* what I'm talking about." He seethed. "You tell me you don't want to be with me, then get all green-eyed fucking monster jealous when I'm sitting in a booth surrounded by women."

My mouth opened to respond, to fire some snarky comment back his way. But even the thought of those women on him—

I dropped my hands on the basin and squeezed. I squeezed all of the tension in my body through my fingers at the *thought* of those women around him, touching him.

Chance slowly stalked towards me, as if pursuing prey. He was the lion; I was the fawn. Difference was, it wasn't fear my legs were beginning to tremble with.

"You got all jealous about the dozens of women *surrounding* me, *touching* me, *pushing* up on me."

I began to grind my teeth, needing some more goddamn relief from the unfiltered rage pumping through my veins.

"You got mad, enraged about the fact that they're *beautiful*, *sexy*, *stunning* women who were *fawning* over me." He was behind me, so close I could smell his cologne and the faint scent of my favourite whiskey. *Our* favourite whiskey.

I was already well and truly on my way to getting sloshed, the shots and whiskey buzzing through my system. But here I was, with someone more intoxicating than any booze.

Him.

"You got so mad ..." His chest pressed against my back as his lips found the shell of my ear. "That you didn't even notice that I wasn't paying them *any* attention."

His teeth nipped my ear, his tongue following.

"You got so jealous ..." Chance's warm fingers sent electrifying waves through me as he moved my hair off my shoulder. "You didn't even notice *I* was fawning over *you* in that goddamn skirt."

His fingers ran up the slit of my black leather skirt.

"No number of women in this world could keep my eyes off of you, Sunny."

I shuddered a breath out and let my head fall onto his shoulder, surrendering to both myself and to him. His lips pressed into the space between my neck and collarbone.

"You're right," I breathed. "I couldn't stand it."

He groaned slightly. "I couldn't stand seeing that guy's fucking hands all over you," he growled before licking a line up the side of my neck to my jaw. "You're not his to touch."

"I'm no one's but my own." I sighed, both of his hands running up and down my sides teasingly.

"Oh, love. We both know that's not true." He chuckled darkly. "We both know this …" His right hand ran over my peaked nipple through the bralette under my mesh top. "Is for me." A breathy laugh escaped him as he gently pinched.

I let out an involuntary sigh at the sensation.

"And we know this …" He twirled his left fingers over my other peaked nipple. "Is for me."

A gave a dark, dark laugh as he spun me around, picked me up, and sat me on the bench. "And we know this …" His finger instantly pushed my black, laced thong aside and brushed my slickness. "Is for me." He pulled his fingers away and sucked them in his mouth.

"Cocky ass," I breathed, feeling my cheeks flushing.

"Oh, you wanna talk being cocky?" He grabbed my hand and guided it down his abs to the straining bulge in his jeans. "This, my darling, is for *you*."

My jaw slackened and I softly ran my palm around the strain.

"Every goddamn woman could be in front of me, begging for my cock. But no one …" He groaned as I squeezed. "*No one* but you can do this to me."

I bit back on a groan myself.

"You may not think you're mine." He grabbed my moving hand and lifted it to his lips, pressing a kiss to it. "But I'm yours."

Chance kissed my cheek, dropped my hand, and walked out.

CHAPTER 32

Chance

"For fuck's sake!" I tossed aside the third and fourth pieces of toast that popped up burnt.

"Someone's grouchy today." JJ's cheery voice had me picking up the piles of burnt toast and lobbing it at him.

He caught them expectingly.

"A little overdone," JJ said, inspecting a slice. "But solid effort."

"Ugh, I forgot you're one of those people who eats their toast burnt to a crisp," I groaned.

"I don't eat it burnt," he scoffed. "I just like it with a bit more colour."

The smell of charred toast was still pungently lingering when JJ dug into the charred slices. I put two more down in the toaster, then popped it every twenty fucking seconds to make sure it wasn't already burning.

"What burnt your toast today?" JJ asked, jumping up onto the bench next to the toaster.

"Gee, I don't know, JJ. Maybe it's this piece of shit toaster that's right in front of me." I snapped, smacking the machine in emphasis.

"Oh, I know that. Toaster has been playing up for years. Al won't let us dump it. I was meaning the other thing."

"What other thing?" I asked, popping my toast up to check.

"You know, your toast. Your fruit loops. Your parade."

"What the fuck are you on about now?"

"Did someone piss in your *fruit loops*? Rain on your *parade*? *Burn your toast*?"

"No."

"Bullshit."

"I said, 'No'."

"And I said 'bullshit'. Did something happen last night?" he asked with a mouthful of black bread.

"No, now drop it," I snapped. After hitting the eject button on the side, my toast popped up. I all but threw it onto my plate and lathered a thick layer of Vegemite over it.

Man, I really need to go and hit the bag.

My knuckles tingled at the thought of it.

"Yeah, that certainly sounds like something someone who's not sulking would say," JJ mocked.

"I am not sulking!" I dug into my brekkie. The sooner I could finish this, the sooner I could go and do bag work for an hour ... or seven. Anything to get the images of last night out of my mind. Only one thing stood front and centre of them—Mari Fucking Trevino.

Well, not just Mari. Mari Fucking Trevino in a leather miniskirt that proudly showed off those mile-long legs. Those legs that I could almost bet had been tangled in the sheets all night with that bloke she was dancing with last night. Seeing it in real time had made my blood boil to the point of combustion—it had been an active effort to not go over and rip his goddamn hands off her.

But whatever this was with Mari wasn't a game. She wasn't some plaything that I could pick up and put down whenever I wanted. I realised in the cab ride home last night that to me, she'd never been that. Everything about her was always *more*. There was a fire I felt when I was with her, a fire that burned so bright it left me feeling cold without it.

"Are you even listening to what I'm saying?"

"Not really." My brain was buzzing, curiosity and jealousy turning out to be a dangerous mix. "What do you know about a bloke named Beau Beckett?"

"BB? Haven't heard of him being around here for a few years now. He's an old friend of ours, an *old fling* of Mari's." He sent a knowing wink my way. "Nice guy, had real potential to be someone, and got the fuck outta here to go do it."

"How'd you go with Milah last night?" I asked, desperate for a change of subject that wasn't likely to spike my blood pressure.

He sighed, finishing the last bite of his toast. "About as good as you'd expect." He looked away and moved to flick the kettle on. "She refused to see me for the first couple of hours. So, I did what I had to do."

"Which was?"

"Told the staff her brother would cut my balls off if I left without seeing proof of life, that I was rather fond of my pair and was willing to camp out all night just to keep them attached." He shrugged before emptying two sugar packets into his awaiting mug and nearly half the bottle of honey. "Coffee?"

I nodded, passing over my now empty mug. "And that worked?"

"Barely. I think the staff knew I was serious and told her seeing me wasn't optional. She spent the forty minutes I did see her berating me for not respecting her choices."

"Sounds like one of her bad days," I replied. Hearing about my sister's ... ventures in rehab was never easy. Every brotherly instinct in me screamed to help her myself, to just take her home and protect her.

But I didn't have a home anymore. And her problems had gone far beyond the need for some TLC. Her brain was wired differently after five years of drug abuse, that I knew of. And I was a fighter. A good one, yes. But how could I fight something I couldn't see?

"Better than when I went to see her during withdrawals," he chuckled, gesturing to the scar on his eyebrow from the metal food tray she'd lobbed at him.

I had gone to see my sister once during her withdrawal phase. She had been in so much pain, so much agony that I refused to go back until her system had been fully flushed. So, I'd sent the only person I could trust in my place—JJ. He'd taken my request seriously, as I knew he would. Visited her every two weeks on the dot so I didn't have to. I still went to see her when I could, and now that Talia was no longer presenting an issue, I had a hell of a lot more time for it. That had been the first place I went when I left Talia. I'd told my sister everything, more than everything, more than I'd ever dared say aloud. She'd cried, we both had, and wrapped me up in the tightest hug she'd ever given me. And that moment, that time with her, had it made it all worth it. All of the hits I took, the shit I copped for paying her rehab bills—it had all been worth it.

"I guess after that every visit, seems sunshine and rainbows, huh?"

My sister wasn't a bad person by any means. She'd gotten mixed in with the wrong crowd when she lived with my mother for a few years when we were younger. Mum couldn't afford to pay the prissy private school fees that my father was dolling out for us, so she'd sent Milah to the local public school.

By the time she was seventeen, I was fully convinced she'd be dead before she hit her next birthday. But one day, when Dylan and I were sparring out in the yard, Dad's car had driven up. Milah had got out, quiet as a mouse, pale as a ghost, and that had been that. She never told us why she came back to live with us, and after how spooked—no—*petrified* she'd looked that day, Dylan and I had an unspoken agreement to never ask.

Our conversation stopped with an abrupt knock on the open kitchen door. There, in last night's clothes, stood the devil himself. Beau fucking Beckett.

"Jaxon Jones," he said in a tone that wasn't quite as comforting as a Soggla local liked to use. Though, from what JJ had just told me, I guess he wasn't a local anymore anyways.

A smile fought its way onto my lips when JJ's posture shift. He stood tall, his shoulders set back with that lack of rigidity that was required when you knew shit was about to go down.

Please, please give me a reason to hit this guy.

Images of him and Mari in that tiny fucking skirt flooded my mind on cue.

Good enough reason.

But JJ got to him before I did, wrapping him in a brotherly hug.

I scoffed at the easing of tension in the room, the welcoming and greeting of old friends that replaced it.

"BB, mate. I didn't know you were in town!" JJ beamed, gesturing for him to sit at the small dining table in the centre of the staff kitchen.

"Well, I was hoping to surprise you at the 'dig last night, but you didn't show. Figured I best come down here and make sure you were still alive and all." He smiled an easy, charming smile that I could tell had even JJ swooning.

Whatfuckingever.

I shoved the last bit of toast into my mouth, downing it with a final gulp of my coffee.

"You back at your 'rents house?"

"Nah, man. Staying with an old friend just up the road."

An old friend just up the road ... Of fucking course he is.

"BB, have you met Chance?"

"No, I haven't—"

"Seen enough of you in the last twenty-four hours, mate," I spat. After grabbing my hand wraps, I walked out.

I didn't need another spray from Mari today. Yes, that was why I was wearing hand wraps. That reason sounded better in my head than the fact that I thought I would physically combust if she got that close to me again.

"Lynnie! Look who's here!" JJ called.

I tossed the wraps at the far wall, the anticipation like an erupting cloud over my mind. My heart rate powered on, a thundering beat in my chest begging me to match it with my hands.

So I did.

I matched thunder with thunder, boom for boom. Over the laughter, the banter, and jokes happening in the other room.

You're not what she wants, mate. Get over it.

So why the fuck couldn't I?

CHAPTER 33

Mari

"He's not usually so grouchy," JJ said to Beau as we passed by the old church on the way to Rusty's. "Someone just burnt his toast this morning."

His eyes flicked over to me; I narrowed my own on his.

"What are you suggesting?"

"I did not say nor imply a thing," he stated, turning his nose up and refusing to make eye contact.

"Ignore him," I told Beau. "He has nothing going on in his life at the moment, so he feels the need to psychoanalyse others."

"Not true! I have things happening!" JJ whined, while Beau choked on his own laughter.

"Such as?"

"Lynnie and Chance slept together!" he rushed out, eager to change the subject.

"I knew it! I knew you were behind some little stunt when you dragged me onto the dance floor last night!" Beau pumped his fist in the victory of putting two and two together.

"What stunt?" JJ asked.

"Trevvy here dragged my ass onto Moonies' d-floor last night and a certain *someone* did not seem very happy about it." He smirked at me, sage green eyes alight with amusement.

I stiffened my face, hoping that I wasn't wearing the sudden panic that rushed up my spine.

Shit.

Shit. Shit. Shit.

Did he know? Did he see Chance follow me into the bathroom?

"*Did* she now?!" JJ practically launched himself onto Beau's shoulders in excitement. "No wonder he was a cranky bastard this morning."

"Oh, great. Nice going, Trevvy. Now one of the top UFL stars hates me," Beau whined.

"What?!" I gaped. "Why would he hate you? He doesn't even *know* you!"

"Doesn't matter, Mari!" he groaned, giving a 'silently cursing the world' look to the sky. "I touched what's his. I'm lucky he didn't rip my hands off this morning!"

"I am not his!!" I screeched.

"Yeah, you're lucky he just threw his little temper tantrum and went to hit the bag," JJ said at the same time.

"Yeah, I could tell," Beau replied. "That dude is seriously shitting-my-own-pants terrifying. There's something in his eyes, I'm telling you. Like ... like he looks straight through to your soul or something."

I couldn't have said it better myself. I'd drowned in those eyes numerous times already, and that was exactly what it felt like. When Chance's eyes were on me, he wasn't just looking at me. He was looking through me, straight into who I really was.

"You'll be right, mate. He's a big softie at heart. Besides, he wouldn't do *anything* to get into Lynnie's bad books."

JJ winced at the glare I shot him.

"What?" he defended. "Trust me—whether you like it or not, you mean something to him. Stop being uptight. We all know he means something to *you* too."

"I—"

"Nah-nah-nah-nah, don't even try and deny it. I've been back for less than twenty-four hours and even I can tell there's something happening there." Beau waggled his thick eyebrows at me.

"It doesn't matter how much or how little he means to me. I don't *do* fighters."

"Anymore?"

This time my glare moved to Beau. He'd been gone for so long, he didn't even flinch.

"Last I was here, Trevvy, you'd had a few fighters under your sheets."

"She's just got these metaphorical ten-foot-tall fences around her since Jayden allegedly fucked her around." JJ shrugged.

Jeez, again with the psychoanalysing?

"Allegedly?" I raised a questioning eyebrow.

"Yeah, *allegedly*. You haven't spoken a word about it since you two split. I'm literally just running on best-friend fumes here."

"Best-friend fumes?"

"Yeah. You know? She hates him, so I hate him too. No questions asked."

Shame flamed my cheeks as Beau and JJ continued walking together.

He was right—I hadn't told anyone about what had happened between Jayden and me. How could I? It was beyond embarrassing. But I watched my best friend, the one person in this world who was unconditionally on my side — the person who had seen my anger and hurt towards an ex-boyfriend and taken it upon himself to stand at my side without once even *asking*, it occurred to me—

"You never asked

"What?"

I'd lost where their conversation was up to, spinning in the past.

"You never asked me what happened with Jayden."

JJ shrugged, stopping ahead to wait for me. "I knew you would tell me when you were ready. You'd already forgiven him for being, well, him. I figured it had to be something pretty bad for you to slice it clean."

Beau gave a half nod. "It's what good friends do, Trevvy."

***

"Righto, I've gotta head off." Beau stacked his now empty plate and oversized coffee mug in a neat pile, ready for service staff to come and grab it. "Mum needs a hand on the farm today."

"Your dad still crook?"

"Eh, I think he's just leaning into it a little. It's not often Ma waits on him hand and foot." With a wink, he tucked a red twenty dollar note under JJ's heart-attack-in-a-glass drink.

"I can't believe you still drink those things," I told him, gulping down the last of my gigantic long black.

"Ugh, not you too! Rio already gave me his big diabetes speech—"

"Did he mention heart health?"

"Lynnieee!" he whined.

"Your body," I replied, holding my hands up in surrender.

We sat in silence together for a long while, taking in all of the people around us at Rusty's.

Surprisingly, I was the one to break it first. "Do you want to know about Jayden?"

His head whipped towards me so fast, I was half expecting it to tear off his head from the momentum. "Lynnie, you don't have to—"

"You're my best friend. It's not about 'having to'."

"True, but this is also *the past*. We don't need to relive it if it's not affecting the present."

I loosed a slightly shaking breath. "Jayden and I were together for a long while. Long enough that he started to ... want things from me. He started to *expect* things from me."

JJ narrowed his eyes.

"Things I wasn't ready for. He tried the nice way, with kindness and patience. But then his patience wore thin—"

"Did he try to force you to—"

"Relax, JJ. Words were exchanged. Outside of Knock's, Jayden's never put hands on me." The mention of Jayden laying a strike on me in Knock's seemed to only fuel JJ's anger, so I continued, "He tried to manipulate me, make me feel as if I was the issue in our relationship. As if not being ready to spread my legs made me frigid and soft."

An involuntary shiver ran down my bones at the word Jayden had used too often.

Soft.

"I broke up with him after all his theatrics. Dad may not have been around much after Mum passed, but I still remembered them together. He never raised a hand or voice to her, and vice versa. I knew I deserved better and that both of them would be devastated to find out I'd stayed with someone who could speak so little of me."

"They would be proud of you, Lynnie." His warm, dark hand grabbed mine and squeezed. "Leaving the comfort of reality ... it's never an easy thing to do. No matter how many lines are crossed."

I nodded, a small and appreciative smile on my lips. JJ's acceptance, his belief in me, made that silly nagging voice of Jayden's in my head die off. It was like the volume had been turned down, cut in half, well and truly on its way to muted. I could barely hear the taunts anymore, just quiet aggressive mumbling. As if that little ghost in my head was fighting to stay, fighting to sit on my shoulder some more.

There was no room on my shoulders anymore, not with JJ standing so close to my side.

This time, he was the one to break the silence.

"You know, not all fighters are like him?" he said gently, squeezing my hand again before standing and heading to the counter.

Patty, the sweet, rounded German lady, stood behind the counter. Her rosy cheeks darkened when JJ said something to make her laugh, the two wearing matching grins as they bantered.

JJ was right. Not all fighters were like Jayden. JJ was proof of that. The love, the dedication, and the loyalty my friend had for his people—I saw it. He defied the stereotype I'd created in my head every damned day. The least I could do was show him I believed *him* too.

CHAPTER 34

Chance

JJ's house was ridiculously loud whenever it rained. The wavy tin roof funnelled all the water into the gutters that lined the edging. But the sound of the rain was so rhythmic it was like a hundred kids were up there with pairs of drumsticks.

Over the noise, I barely heard the knock at the door. By the time I reached the rounded, heavy timber, I was ready to throw a fit at the noise consistency in the last thirty minutes. The knocking had become incessant as I got closer and closer, though the person on the other side either hadn't heard my, 'I'm coming' calls or just didn't care.

The door smacked straight into the wall when I flung it open.

And there she stood. On the porch, arms folded under her chest in an attempt to keep her fingers warm. Her orange Knock's shirt was soaked all the way through. Though the colour still seemed bright in comparison to all of the baby's breath that was growing in the front planter boxes.

She was drenched from head to toe. She lightly hopped from foot to foot, a soft squelching sound coming from her grassy shoes.

But those eyes. Something shone in them. Something fierce and brave and passionate.

"Hi." She smiled, one of those big, beautiful, breathtaking smiles. "Can I come in?"

"Yes!" I cleared my throat. "Uh, yeah, of course."

I moved aside, holding the heavy door open for her. She toed off what once were white sneakers but were now covered in grass.

Jesus, had she run here?

"God, Sunny. You must be freezing," I said, turning to start towards the kitchen. Her footsteps padded along behind me. "You could have called? I've got JJ's car today—I could have come to you."

"I'm fine." Her head lay back against the nearby wall she'd stopped to lean on, another one of those smiles gracing her lips. "It's nice being out in the rain sometimes. All of the grass is already looking greener."

"Coffee?" The kettle squealed gently as it began to heat up.

"If this goes well, I'm hoping I won't need it." She cleared her throat, pushing off the wall.

"Oh?" I stepped away from the kettle, leaning on the kitchen bench and folding my arms over.

"I, uh ... I was talking to JJ this morning—"

"Uh-oh. Not off to a good start."

"No, no." She laughed, the sound full of sunshine. Full of *Sunny*. "He actually had his wisdom on cap this time."

She took a step, slow and casual. Then another. Closer and closer towards me.

"And?"

She chewed on her bottom lip, the fingers on her right hand fidgeting. A habit, I'd learned, when she was nervous. Hard to pick, considering she wasn't the easiest to rattle.

"And ... I believe you."

"About what?"

"That you're not like the others." She stood in front of me, those beautiful, *beautiful* brown eyes meeting mine. "You've shown me time and time again that you're not like them—"

"Them?"

"The stupid little stereotype of people I've made up in my head to protect me from getting hurt again. You're not them. You never were." Her hands reached up to my folded forearms. She was soaking from top to bottom, dripping water all over the kitchen floor, but the warmth I felt from her skin on mine was that of the toasty morning sunshine. "I see you. I believe you. I get it now."

"Aside from telling me that I'm not the asshole you thought I was, what're you trying to say here?"

"I don't want to say no. Not to you. Not to this. Not to any of it," she replied, those honey eyes so full of clarity, of certainty.

She pulled my wrists down to my sides, pushing her fingers through mine. That warmth, that fire returned and spread up my arms.

"What do you want, Sunny?" I rasped out, shock and warmth and tenderness pumping through me in a rush.

"You, Chance. I want you."

Chapter 35

Mari

The pounding in my chest was so loud, I was sure he could hear it. Hell, I was sure anyone in a five-kilometre radius could hear it. "I just ... I need you to help me through this. Ride slow with me."

Using our intertwined hands, he tugged me closer to him. With my chest flush against his, now I knew he could hear my thundering heartbeat.

I didn't care.

I had nothing to hide anymore, not from him.

A small, disbelieving smile fell onto his lips. One that soon morphed into his signature smirk.

"Is that so, Sunny baby?" he purred, letting go of one of my hands and threading it into my wet mop of curls.

"It is," I murmured.

Heaven had found a new life form—the feeling of Chance's fingers running through my hair. A sigh escaped me.

"Well, that's great to hear," he mumbled. "Because I've been dying to do this again."

He leaned down and pressed his lips to mine, soft and warm, my soaking wet hair and clothes long forgotten. His tongue slid along my lower lip, and I instantly opened for him. The taste of him, so irrevocably *Chance*; it would always be my favourite. He let out a low moan when our tongues met, to which I mirrored with my own.

My shirt flung off and I chuckled softly, surprised he hadn't torn it straight off me again. The back clasps of my bra popped open, my breasts spilling out as the garment fell to the floor. Warmth, that *lovely* warmth, soaked into my palms as I slipped my hands under his shirt.

Off.

I need this off.

As if reading my thoughts, his shirt followed the same path mine had, minus the wet *thwack* mine made when it hit the floor.

Skin on skin, that luxurious, affectionate warmth enveloped me when he wrapped his arms around me, and I him. His mouth found mine once again, but with no ferocity. Slow, tender kisses were pressed onto my lips as he pulled me tighter. I didn't even realise I'd been shivering until I stopped.

Two requesting taps on my ass later, and my legs were wrapped around his. Our lips stayed fused together, moving in time to a dance I only seemed to know with him. Where he was carrying me to, I had no idea. But I didn't care, couldn't bring myself to when I was in his arms.

'*Finally,*' a little voice inside me whispered with a dazed sigh.

A soft landing skimmed my bare back. A bed. His bed. The one I'd snuck out of.

I snatched up the waistband of his grey sweatpants, unable to bite back the smirk when I had to manoeuvre it around his already hard length. The look on his face mirrored my own when he pulled my shorts and panties off, finding a wetness between my legs that had nothing to do with the rain outside.

Chance started to back down the bed, licking his lips as he eyed off my slick entrance. I reached for him but was only close enough to grab his hand. His blue eyes, those goddamn blue eyes, found mine. Silent question looming, he raised his brows at me.

"No foreplay," I rasped, barely audible, as I tugged him towards me. "I need to feel you."

"Condom?" He started to reach for his bedside table, so I grabbed that hand too and shook my head.

"Birth control."

A soft smile quickly morphed into a grin of feral delight as he scooted back up in-between my legs. Leaning down to meet my mouth with his own, he lined himself up at my entrance ... then left it. Slipping his tongue inside my mouth and triggering the thought of 'How the hell is this man so good at multitasking?', he ran the tip of his cock between my slick folds. Up and down, in an achingly slow pace.

"P-please," I murmured, anticipation already beginning to wind the knot inside of me.

"Mmm? You want me, Sunny baby?"

I nodded frantically.

"No, no. Tell me, darling. I need you to say the words."

"I want you," I pushed out between rigid breaths. "I want you, Chance."

With a final teasing flick over my clit, he brought the head of his cock back down to my entrance. He pushed in slightly and my body instantly rushed to grab onto him.

"Fuck," he muttered. "Fuck … baby, you're so tight. Make room for me."

I squirmed underneath him in pleasure, at the ultimate skin-on-skin.

"Mari, sweetheart. Relax for me. I need a little more … fuck. Fuck."

My walls loosened ever so slightly, and he slid slickly farther inside me. A few more thrusts later, and I could feel the end of him over that spot.

I groaned, uncaringly loud, and braced my hands on his shoulders, even though I was on my back. I latched onto him further and wrapped my legs tightly around his waist. But with the way my body was already shuddering at the pleasure, the sensation of *him* rubbing against that damn spot, frankly, this orgasm I was about to hit would be so big I'd fall off the edge of the planet if I wasn't careful.

Boy was I right.

Four more thrusts over that spot inside me that was physically reaching for him every time he pulled away, and I came undone. Loud cries tore from my throat, moans and groans weaving their way through me as I lost complete and utter control. Chance dove down and crashed his mouth on mine, his groans vibrating my throat just as much as my own were. Pleasure and pure ecstasy rolled over me, wave after wave.

But even when that was done, it wasn't over. That knot had spiralled but was already winding itself up again. Chance's eyes darkened and it was clear he'd felt it too. Shucking my legs up to his shoulders, the angle he found was divine.

He thrust home, deep and fast, the sounds of our skin meeting and our moans filling the room.

"Open your eyes, Sunny," he demanded softly. "Let me see those eyes."

His pupils were filling quickly, dilating with the rise in oxytocin. I could only imagine mine were doing the same as the knot wound tighter and tighter.

"Mine," he muttered, threading his fingers through one of my hands and pinning it above my head. His hand sent three light squeezes through mine.

"Mine," I replied.

His body went rigid beneath my legs as that knot of tension pulled every string in my body tight. When Chance climaxed, I couldn't help but follow. My eyes rolled back, though I fought like hell to keep them on the sexiest of sights in front of me. He pulsed and writhed beneath my legs, letting out matching curses to my own. My back arched as his began to, melding out bodies even closer together.

Chance's mouth, still panting heavily, moved to my neck, peppering kisses up, down, around; everywhere.

"Mine," he muttered into my collarbone.

"Mine," I whispered breathlessly in his ear.

CHAPTER 36

Mari

"You have a fantastic marketing tool right here on your team—"

I'd stopped listening to the networking team Chance's agent had sent us.

Unfortunately, sitting in the now cramped office space of my own gym whilst a bunch of guys in suits tried to sell me on a crappy marketing deal was not how I wanted to spend my morning.

Images of earlier this morning flooded my mind. Of the far, *far* preferable alternative.

"Mmmm, no," Chance grumbled in my ear, grazing his teeth up the lobe. "I've decided today is cancelled. We're staying here."

I laughed, rolling onto my other side to meet his sleepy, peaceful gaze. His arms stayed tight around my waist, refusing to lose contact. It made my stupidly-happy-and-in-love smile grow even more.

"Unfortunately—" I pressed a soft kiss to the tip of his nose. "I'm gonna have to burst your bubble there—"

"No," he said, pulling me in even closer.

"Chance—"

"No."

"We have that—"

"No." He sighed, as if he didn't have a care in the world. A soft smile tilted his mouth upwards, and he closed his eyes once again.

"Okay. You need to let me up." I tried. I really did try hard to get his grip to break, to loosen an inch so I could slip out.

But it didn't.Every grip-breaking technique I could think of, even tickling him. But of course, a man as hot as him wouldn't be ticklish.

"Stay with me, Sunny," he mumbled. That goddamn sexy morning voice. *"Just stay with me, right here."*

"Five more minutes."

"What a great idea, Channey!" Liv lay her hand on Chance's bicep, paying him a compliment for whatever idea he'd just suggested to these promotion guys that I'd already decided weren't getting hired several minutes ago.

Having the entire team in meetings like this was tradition, one my father and Al had started. A tradition I was now very much invested in breaking.

Chance's eyes found mine straight away as he shrugged off Liv's arm. To anyone else—it was a polite and gentle reminder to keep her hands to herself. But I knew that look, that tick of annoyance in his jaw. He pushed back his chair as the marketing men continued with their presentation. He picked up three bottles of water from the table behind us all before plonking down in the only other chair available, at the very end of the table. After throwing one to JJ and one to me,

Chance slid that lazy bored mask over his face again. Then, to my surprise, he pulled out his phone.

I was about to throw the water bottle back at him when my own phone buzzed.

Chance: Your green-eyed jealousy monster face is still out. Might want to tone it down a little.

I scoffed.

Me: I was not jealous.

A flicker of amusement crossed his face.

Chance: It's all good, Sunny. Your jealous face is pretty close to your 'fuck me now' face—so I'm here for it.

I rolled my eyes and shoved my phone into my pocket. I could have sworn I heard Chance chuckle from behind me.

Feeling his eyes burning into me, I caved.

Me: Stop staring. You're being obvious.

Chance: I can't help it. I can still smell you on me.

I just about dropped my phone, along with my eyeballs that had popped out from my head like a cartoon.

Oh, dear god.

I frowned as my body betrayed me, rushing heat to my cheeks.

JJ (to Chance, Me): Can you two quit it with the eye-fucking? Some of us are trying to learn.

Chance: Fuck off.

JJ: Your pheromones are stinking up the room. I've been holding back a gag for ten minutes now.

I snorted, earning the attention of Nan and Al, as well as half of the guys presenting at the front. Sighing, I tucked my phone back away.

Chapter 37

Mari

"We're doing something brave today." Chance stood about a metre away from the door, a navy blue cap on his head. Somehow those gorgeous eyes looked like they were *sparkling*.

"Good morning to you too." I ran a hand through the curly mess my hair had entangled itself in. The movement didn't go unnoticed, apparently, since those shining eyes flared.

"Go and get dressed. I'll wait." He smirked, walking inside. "Your nan around?"

I gave him a light shove into the wall, and he chuckled.

"Your relationship with my nan is beyond weird." I looked up at his face, his dimple popping on his right side.

"She's an important lady," he countered. "I'd hate to be on her bad side."

"I thought I heard you." As if on cue, Nan's head poked around the corner. "Good morning, dear. How are you going?" Nan waved a hand, gesturing for Chance to follow.

"Oh, I'm *excellent*, Marilyn. How're you doing?" He shot a cheeky smile my way before heading into the kitchen.

I rolled my eyes, failing to hold back a smile myself.

***

Twenty minutes later, my hair was pulled into a knot on the top of my head and I was in a black Knock's tank and some denim shorts, ready to brave whatever Chance had planned for the day ... and the summer heat outside.

I stood in front of the mirror and gazed over my reflection. It was impossible to stop the small smile that made its way onto my lips. It had been a long time since I'd put *effort* into my appearance for someone—or even wanted to. I smirked at the low dip of my tank top.

Oh yeah, eat your heart out, Chance Riordan.

I crept down the stairs, past all of the framed photos that lined the walls, hearing the laughter and chatter of a professional UFL fighter and my grandmother.

"Well, when my daughter and I first moved to Soggla, we certainly never expected this was the way our life would turn out." There was a faint distance in Nan's voice at the mention of my mother. She never spoke of being sad, but the devastation of losing her only daughter cut deep. I had only been young when she passed, but there had always been a hole that stayed. A hole that was mirrored by the little things my father, Al and Nan kept around.

The consistent growth of baby's breath around the house being one of them.

"We all seem to have a story like that, don't we?" Chance replied softly.

"Oh, definitely," Nan answered. "I could never complain about things that have happened in the past. I live a beautiful life with the one person on this earth who means more to me than anything ever has."

"I'm assuming she got her name from you?"

"Yes, not so subtle is it?" She laughed. "I tell you what, Chance. I never knew I could love anyone or anything as much as I love my daughter until my granddaughter was born. Labour came on too quickly to call. Leah had her in the offices at Knock's—though it went by a different name back then—at the end of an evening wrestling class. Elijah and I held her legs and Al caught Mari."

I stopped short of the kitchen, taking a wider berth from the creak in a certain floorboard.

"Knock's holds more history than what meets the eye. It feels like uncovering a tomb."

"It's more than just a gym, dear. Elijah wrote his legacy letter to ensure that for as long as Knock's was standing, it would never be 'just a gym'."

I walked around the corner. Nan's coffee cup was nearly empty, and Chance's was half full. His was black—just like I had mine. Nan's cup told me he had spent most of the time talking. Gus lay peacefully on top of Nan's red velvet slippers, getting sleepy drool all over the left one. Though he gave me sleepy side-eye.

Nan looked up from the table and smiled at me. "You look nice, bubbles."

My cheeks reddened at the nickname she *usually* only used when it was just her and I around.

Usually, my ass.

"Thanks, Nan," I mumbled, grabbing a keep cup from the cupboard and pouring the last of the coffee into it.

"Bubbles?" I could hear the fucking smirk on his face before I saw it.

"Oh, just a little nickname from when she was little," Nan replied, copying Chance's teasing smile.

"You'd think she would have deemed I'd grown out of it by now."

Nan tsked her tongue at me. "Your bubbles phase is one of the most wonderful memories I have of you as a child. You need to keep the nickname, so I never forget." She smiled over at me with a wink, the emerald green eyeshadow shimmering on her lids a mirror for her eye colour.

I huffed — she'd rigged the situation emotionally and won.

"Well, on that note, *bubbles*." Chance grinned. "We'd better hit the road."

"Have fun you two." Nan pressed a kiss to my cheek and squeezed my hand as she moved to pour the last of her coffee down the sink.

***

"So, are you going to tell me where we're going?" I asked, staring out the window. The trees alongside the long stretch of road out of Soggla were usually nice and green at this time of year, but we'd missed the big storms we usually had. Everything was so dry and arid.

"If you tell me where the nickname 'bubbles' came from?" He compromised, sending me a sly smirk.

"I guess you can just drive me unknowingly to my doom then," I replied, sighing dramatically.

"I told you. We're doing something brave," he said, one hand on the wheel, the other on the gearstick of JJ's old, beat-up ute.

From where I was sitting, the dent he'd put on the front bumper the night we stole Gus seemed deeper than I remembered. The green leather on the seats was peeling and cracked, and the once navy blue exterior was now closer to the colour of the clear sky above us.

"Brave like bungee jumping? Or brave like visiting a haunted house?"

"Brave like seeing your dad."

My heart stopped.

"My dad?" I asked with a mouth as dry as the grass outside.

"You told me you were worried one day he'd die and you'd regret all of the time you missed with him. Well, no time like the present." He shrugged and picked up speed at the 100 sign.

We stayed silent for the next few minutes, passing by all the farms and acreage properties on the outer-town line. The cows had gone to lay in the shade and horses had moved themselves under trees.

God I wish I could just lie there with them.

"And this has nothing to do with the fact that my dad is your idol?" I narrowed my eyes at him, and he laughed.

"I wish I could say it was." He was full-on grinning at this point. "But, no, Sunny. This is all about you."

The way he said *you* melted me in ways I couldn't even begin to explain.

"So what's the brave thing you're doing today then?" I asked.

He took a deep breath in through his nose and his eyes glassed over.

"The brave thing I'm doing today is in a bag in the back of the ute. I'll show you when we get back to Soggla," he said.

Though from the expression on his face and the way he was talking, I couldn't help but feel as if he was trying to promise himself more than me.

CHAPTER 38

Chance

S unny avoided the topic of her dad for the rest of the drive into Colling Creek. Though she did ramble on, rather nervously, with old stories of her and JJ when they were growing up. She bounced those glorious legs of hers up and down in anticipation of what was to come. It took every ounce of my concentration to focus on her words instead of reaching over and palming her thigh to settle her. I caved not fifteen minutes onto the highway, and my hand hadn't left her since.

"Is this it?" I asked, side-eyeing the GPS as I turned into the carpark in front of a large white wooden building with a matching picket fence. The building was exactly how Marilyn had described it, though it was still startling to see.

It was of the same concept of perhaps a storage locker—breezy and casual on the outside but contained a goddamn diamond on the inside.

"Sure is." She sighed.

I parked the car under a frangipani tree in the far corner of the lot — she would want to delay the entrance for as long as possible.

I jumped down from the car and strode over to her side, opening the door for her. She hadn't even taken off her seatbelt.

"Hey," I said softly.

Her brown eyes met mine, but she was slow and slid that mask over her face a second too late. I saw it. The fear and anxiety in those chocolate eyes.

"You don't have to come in with me," she mumbled, staring out the front windscreen. "It's not exactly a fun way to spend your day."

Taking a leap of faith, I reached over her and unbuckled her seatbelt.

"I've got you," I murmured. I picked up the hand that was closest and gave it a gentle squeeze.

Her eyes flared and met mine. The mask on her face shattered. "Y-you ... what?"

"I've got you," I repeated. "I'm with you. I'll be right next to you or out here. I'll be wherever you need me to be—just say the words, Sunny."

"H-he ..." She swallowed the stammer in her breath. "He may not be ... happy to see me."

"Why not?"

"I haven't exactly been a frequent visitor of this place." Her eyes refused to meet mine, darting around her uncomfortably.

I swallowed the burning question inside of me—*why*—and took a breath in to respond.

She beat me to it.

"Come with me."

***

The home was quite inconspicuous. It could have passed for a regular aged care home that no one would spare a second glance at, but a man who had changed the entire sport of MMA was within these walls. I picked up Mari's hand in mine before we walked through the doors and laced my fingers through hers.

"Good morning—" The short, dark-skinned receptionist beamed when she heard the bell go off that signalled our entry. "Oh! Mari! What a treat to see you!" She smiled, wide and toothy. Her curly hair, much shorter and with tighter curls than Mari's, bounced as she stood from behind the desk.

"Hi, Rhiannon," Mari said, though her fingers tensed over the back of my hand.

"It's so good to see you!" The woman's joy and brightness would have been contagious if I hadn't felt the rigidity of Mari's body all the way down to her hand. "Oh, Elijah will be so happy! He's been talking about you a lot recently."

A smile made its way across Mari's lips but never reached her eyes. They lacked that honey brown I so desperately wanted to see. The colour she wore when she was happy. "This is Chance. He's here to visit him with me today."

"It's nice to meet you, Chance! The more the merrier!" Rhiannon clapped her hands together. "Hold tight. I'll just grab your sign-in forms."

"She's ... jubilant," I mumbled.

"She was here when my dad was first admitted," Mari whispered back. "She ... helped me a lot when it all first happened."

The tightening of Mari's mouth told me not to push the subject, so I nodded as Rhiannon plonked down two clipboards in front of us.

We filled out the visitors forms and were given a pass to get us into the wing Mari's dad was in.

"It's a ... privacy feature of his package," she said quietly as we slipped through a set of double doors. "He's considered a code VIP. Same nursing staff and doctors each week—all have signed an NDA. Other than reception staff, no one else knows he's in here."

My gaze snapped to hers.

"No one else knows?"

She shook her head. "His nurses, doctors, Rhiannon, Nan, Al, Rocco, JJ ..." She counted off of her fingers. "And now you."

Sunny stopped in front of a door and took a deep breath. I took the opportunity to pick her hand up again. I gave it a gentle squeeze and she, to my surprise, returned it.

She huffed out a breath quickly and pushed the door open.

There, in the corner of the room, sitting in a black velvet armchair, was Elijah Trevino.

CHAPTER 39

Mari

D ad's mouth fell open for a few seconds. I took a breath in to speak but couldn't find the words there to use. Then, he smiled, big and wide. He pushed up off his chair and reached me in a few strides. His big, still-calloused hands were warm on my bare arms as he stood in front of me, taking me in.

"It's really you." He beamed and pulled me in for a hug.

Guess today is a good day then.

I couldn't help but hug him back, letting go of Chance's hand and wrapping my arms around his strong frame.

"Hi, Dad," I mumbled, blinking away the tears that always made an appearance in his company. Good or bad day, it had been the two of us for seventeen years now.

"I've missed you, Mari."

That did it. The tears I had been fighting off were replaced by fresh ones as my dad held me tighter in his embrace.

Suddenly I wasn't Mari, owner of Knock's. Or Mari, JJ's best friend. Or Mari, Marilyn's granddaughter and namesake.

I was Mari, a 'dad's girl'.

I was Mari, a girl whose dad loved her.

I was Mari, a girl who just needed a hug from her dad.

"I missed you too, Dad," I croaked.

To Chance's credit, he didn't back away awkwardly or make his presence known. He simply stood behind me, a small smile on his face, and waited.

"Wherever you need me to be—just say the words."

I sniffled and pulled away, turning to bring Chance forward.

"Uh, Dad. I'd like to introduce you to someone." I wiped one of my hands over my eyes, the mascara I'd stupidly put on this morning was definitely already smudged. "This is Chance. Chance Riordan."

Dad looked Chance over, up and down, left to right. Chance was about two inches taller than Dad, but somehow made sure he wasn't looking down at him. He stayed silent until Dad extended a hand, a joyful grin breaking out over his face.

"UFL 150, Darlington Harbour 2014," he said, gripping Chance's hand.

Chance, on the other side, had his jaw hanging wide open in shock and blue eyes beaming wide with surprise. "Yes, sir," Chance replied slowly.

"You were there. You came up to me after the show and asked me how the hell you could ever land in my footsteps," Dad continued, still gripping Chance's hand.

Chance nodded, lips parted. His eyebrows flicked up to encourage Dad to continue.

"Do you remember what I told you?" he asked, finally dropping the handshake.

Chance's pink, full lips tipped up at the corners in memory. "Yeah. You told me to find someone who you can well and truly fight for. Someone who completely changes the meaning of fighting," he replied. "The UFL called and offered me a spot in the prelims on a fight night the very next week."

"And did you? Find that someone?" Dad asked.

"I have now," he replied. "I used to think you meant my team, but someone has recently opened my eyes."

Dad smiled and gestured for us to follow him outside. He gently opened the delicate glass French doors, waving a hand for me to go first. There were four intricately welded, weathered green chairs on the balcony. Rectangular, long planter boxes draped over the railing, overflowing with blooming baby's breath.

"Quite the garden you have here," Chance commented, looking over the balcony and fingering one of the dainty flowers.

"Thank you." Dad smiled, picking up a metal watering can. "Baby's breath is my wife's favourite flower," he added, as if he was talking about something as simple as the weather. He pushed the thin spout of the watering can into the planter boxes one by one, pouring the same amount of water across each.

"That explains a lot, actually," Chance replied, and my heart *stuttered* when this man bent down and sniffed the flowers.

"Like?" I asked.

"Your Nan has baby's breath growing everywhere." He shrugged. "I offered to help her trim them the other day, but she was adamant about it being her 'Wednesday Job'."

"You've met Marilyn?" Dad asked, sitting down on the other side of the doors and placing the watering can beside him.

"I have—"

"They've spent quite a bit of time together," I interrupted.

Chance's face lit up with a cheeky smirk. "You do sound a bit jealous there, Sunny." He grinned. "Or should I say, *Bubbles*?"

I lifted a hand to swat his arm but stopped dead in my tracks when my dad began *cackling*.

"Oh, Mari." He snorted. "I'd forgotten all about that nickname!"

***

Somehow leaving Dad on one of his good days was harder than leaving on one of his bad.

"He always seems to remember more when you come to visit," Rhiannon had said to me.

Chance had, thankfully, grabbed me by the hand and led me out.

"Safety first." He reached over with my seatbelt in hand, buckling it over my waist. "Even with these outdated seatbelts." He shot me a sneaky smile before closing my door and heading for his side.

He jumped in and immediately launched the ute into reverse, hitting the other side of the carpark in seconds. But, instead of turning right to head back towards the highway, he turned left.

"Hey, this isn't the—"

"I know." A small smile plumped his lips out farther. "There's still daylight hours left. I wanna take you somewhere. That okay?"

I swallowed, struggling against every emotionally drained instinct to get out of the car and walk all the way back to Soggla. *Anything* to be by myself.

"You still got me?" I whispered.

His eyes found mine straight away, still that sparkly blue from this morning.

"Always."

***

"Where is it exactly that you're taking me?" I asked, rolling my window down just a touch to let some fresh air in.

"Full of questions today, are we?" He smirked, then used the one hand on the steering wheel to flick the indicator on.

"Arrenbrook Falls?" I asked again, reading the exit sign of the narrow lane he merged into.

"Not quite. We're nearly there. Relax." He moved his hand off the gearstick and onto my thigh, giving it a gentle squeeze.

His eyes widened for a heartbeat when they returned to the road before he swiftly swerved down an old dirt road.

Ahead of us, scribbling, rustling gumtrees lined either side of the dirt path. The sunlight was completely blocked out from the road by the overhanging trees, somehow with leaves greener than any of the others we'd driven past today.

Chance eased onto the brakes, taking the winding corners slow enough that the back wheels didn't catch, but quickly enough to keep us moving up the incline.

Then the trees broke, and the view was *astonishing*.

Hundreds upon hundreds of trees bunched together to coat the other side of the hill with a vibrant forest green. Some of the lighter trees, such as the taller ones with pale green eucalyptus leaves, had splashes of colour in it's branches. Rainbow lorikeets bustled about.

Birds flew over the peaceful land, some calling out to one another. Brief rustles were visible in nearby trees but faded with distance.

I used the roller handle to roll down my window and, like a child on a road trip, hung my face just outside the window. Feeling the fresh, warm, nature-filled breeze on my face, I sucked in a deep breath through my nose.

"Wow ..." I breathed.

"My thoughts exactly." He winked and offered me a sly smile.

CHAPTER 40

Mari

Chance drove us right up to what appeared to be an old look-out point. There was a picnic table under a nearby bungalow, though it didn't look like it could hold one of us without snapping in half. The bungalow looked to be in decent enough shape, but a rusty squeaking was coming from *somewhere* around us.

"I've got us covered. Don't worry." He smiled before reversing JJ's ute under a pair of trees.

"Is this the part where you kill me and throw me off the side of the cliff?" I teased.

"Yes, *Mari*. You got me. I brought you to one of my favourite places in the entire planet just to kill you and throw you off a cliff," he replied dryly, shutting off the engine and hopping out.

I went to follow, but the lever on my door refused to open. "The hell?"

I tried it repetitively until Chance reached my side. The door creaked open and a hand was waiting in offer. Hands instantly clammy from the gesture, I rested one on his and let him hop me down from the ute. Glancing at the open door, I noticed the little black lever that was normally pointing jaggedly left was twisted to the far right.

"Did you pull the child lock on my door?"

"How else am I supposed to show off all of this chivalry?"

His face was so close to mine, I could smell the mint and coffee on his breath. That teasing smirk faded, but not even his locked jaw could stop those pheromones freaking *wafting* over me.

He tucked a strand of hair behind my ear, a loose curl that had fallen. His lips tipped up in appreciation as his fingers traced my jaw.

"Come on, Sunny baby. Let me show you," he murmured.

"Show me what?"

"The view." His hands dropped to my waist. "Tuck your legs up."

He lifted me over the side of the ute tray, and I found what I had failed to notice this entire time. Blankets and a few stray pillows were scattered about, all on top of one giant flannelette picnic blanket.

"Is this Nan's picnic blanket?" I asked.

"Sure is. She loaned it to me for the day," he replied, effortlessly hopping up and over the edge.

"You two really are besties, aren't you?" I teased.

"Like I said, she's a special lady. I'd like to keep her on side."

"What do you mean 'on side'?" I asked.

"Sunny, I can't believe you've been up here for thirty whole seconds and haven't noticed what's right in front of you."

"What—"

Words could neither be lost or found for what I could see. Long, stretching vines fell alongside rich, green bushland that sprouted off the edge of the cliff face. Brown and yellow shining stones edged alongside it, a barrier for nature and its visitors, but a stage for the main attraction:

The waterfall.

The falls weren't gushing, fast and wild. They were blue, the same colour as Chance's eyes, and were smooth and swift. Seeing the source of water brought the fresh smell to my nose. Nature, sweet, sweet nature.

I looked up into those blues, the ones I could lose myself in as easily as I could lose myself in that falling water. They were gazing around us, not a cloud in sight in them. Clear and blue, the sun seemed to sparkle off them. As if those eyes, *his* eyes, were the ocean the sun longed to shine for.

They sparkled more when they met mine.

"What's on that beautiful mind of yours, Sunny baby?"

"How did you find this place?" I asked, unwilling to share just how hooked he had me with those goddamn eyes of his.

"I needed to get out of the city one night, I was ... caught up in some shit." He plonked down on one of the pillows, beckoning me to join him. "I was only new to the area and was trying to get to the highway. I was flooring it down the road when, believe it or not, there was a kangaroo — just staring at me dead in the face. I swerved just in time to miss the bastard but landed on this dirt road. Figured ... figured I had a minute or two to see where it led to."

A strong, warm arm wrapped around my shoulders, and I couldn't help but snuggle up to his warm chest. We both sighed simultaneously, looked up at each other, and laughed.

"So, are you gonna ask me?" I murmured, expertly ruining out nice moment.

"Ask you what?" He flicked a brow up in surprise.

"C'mon, Chance. I know you want to ask about my dad." A blink was all that told me he was surprised.

"Would you tell me if I asked?" he asked, lifting his eyebrows at me expectantly.

"Probably not," I replied with a half-hearted chuckle. "But I probably should."

"I won't ask unless you want to tell, Sunny. That's not how it goes with me—there's never a '*should*' or '*have to*'."

I looked up to find those goddamn blue eyes, heated and fiery, staring down at me already.

"It'll always be an '*I want*' when you're with me, love."

Blood rushed to my face, my heart rate doubling over.

Those blue eyes dropped to my mouth, and I took that as invitation to gaze at his. Full, pink lips surrounded by close-shaven, brown sugar stubble. Those lips turned upwards as he let out a breathy chuckle.

"I haven't done this for a while, Sunny."

I laughed this time. "Nice line, Riordan. Do you use it on every girl you bring up here?" I teased, moving my hip slightly so it rested on a nearby orange cushion.

"You're the only other person who knows about this place."

"You don't need to try and 'woo' me with a secret hideout, Chance. I appreciate everything you've done today just the same," I replied.

"Why is it so hard for you to believe that I'm not lying to you?"

I blanched at the question.

"C'mon, Sunny baby. Don't play dumb with me. I know how smart you are." He raised an eyebrow. "You know how bad I want you, Sunny. And believe it or not, my dear, I'm not dumb either. I'm nowhere near stupid enough to ruin whatever this is going to be over something as trivial as not telling the truth."

I gaped—stared at him like a fish out of water, my mouth opening and closing like one.

From curiosity to devilish in an instant, a smirk fell over his face like the fading sun. "Let me show you."

"W-what?" I managed to get out.

"Let me show you, my dear Sunny baby." A soft, tender kiss landed on my temple before he was moving. "Just how badly I want you."

The ute tray creaked a little as he moved, but I barely heard it. Chance crawled down to where my legs were splayed out over the blanket. In one quick motion, he scooped both of them up and positioned himself underneath. And when he dropped my legs?

My legs fell straight open.

With where he was kneeling, they couldn't not. My mouth simultaneously went dry and became full of saliva at the same time. "W-what're you doing?"

"Shhhh," he cooed, running his calloused hands all over my bare thighs. "Just *enjoy*."

With a quick flick of a couple of fingers, my shorts were undone with the zipper loose. Chance dragged them down my legs and tossed them to the back corner of the tray.

"The farther off you, the better." He grinned wickedly, shamelessly running his eyes over my exposed bright red, lace thong.

My body turned to mush, warm in anticipation of what those eyes were burning with desire for. "That apply for this too?" I mumbled, tucking my thumbs under the thin waistband of my underwear.

One feral grin later, and he'd ripped them clean off once again.

This would be the part where I made some joke about his tendency to destroy my clothes, but I was too busy basking in a flame of hunger.

He shuffled back farther until his chest was flat on the tray of the ute.

"What are you—?"

"Shhh," he hushed me again, trailing his mouth up either side of my legs in torturous, slow patterns.

"Chance—"

"Shhh, Sunny baby. I've got you." He'd made it to the top, head directly in between my legs as he continued to tease—running his tongue up and down either side and flicking across the middle every few licks.

"Mmm. You're so wet already for me, Sunny baby. Aren't you?" A slow, tasting in the centre, delicately swirling over the sensitive bud. "Such a good girl."

And with that, he dove in. A fierce combination of sucking and licking on that tender bud, kickstarting a winding, balling knot inside me.

"Fuck ... fuckfuckfuckfuck," I gasped.

A gentle vibration pulsed near my entrance as Chance groaned.

Heaven and all the angels have got nothing compared to the ecstasy I felt when Chance slipped a finger inside me.

"That's it, Sunny baby. It's just a finger, make some room for me, love."

As if he was the commander of my body, I loosened a tad, only to drip all over his hand.

"Fuck," he muttered. Curling that finger, he found that spot like he'd memorised its location. He pushed in and out of me to a rhythm his hot mouth followed. His second hand floated around to my hip, gently digging his fingers in and thrumming the tightening flexors.

I came undone with his head still between my legs, with Chance Riordan licking and sucking me all the way through my climax. Every muscle in my body spasmed in pleasure, my mouth loosing breathy moans and groans. Only when I went limp and dazed, did he sit up from where he'd lain.

He looked down at me, wiped his mouth, and grinned at me once again. "So, now that I have you on a nice post-orgasm high. Can I get you to agree to dinner with me?"

CHAPTER 41

Mari

"Woah, there! Look at you!" Mel, our front desk lady who worked the weekends, said. "Where you off to all dolled up?"

The heels of my knee-highs tapped on the concrete floor as I strolled towards the matte black desk. My navy blue dress fell just past mid-thigh, the bottom half swaying slightly as I walked. Mel's dark eyes scanned me from head to toe in knowing approval, her gigantic earrings jingling as she nodded her head. The mouse clicked loudly as she seemed to quickly close down some tabs on the reception computer. Mel did love a good Amazon find.

"Just meeting someone for dinner." I couldn't help but beam.

Chance.

Chance Riordan was taking *me* out to dinner.

Chance Riordan wanted to take *me* out.

Chance Riordan wanted *me*.

"Would this by any *Chance*—" She winked, her long purple lashes fluttering in front of a bright blue eyeshadow. "Be someone special? Maybe someone we know?"

"Hmmm ..." I teased, unable to wipe the excited smile from my face. "Perhaps!"

"We're finally going to have good use for that defib that has sat in here all these years. Because that man's heart is going to stop when he sets eyes on you, darl!"

I laughed and chatted with the woman while I waited. She told me all about her new grandkids, how they were hitting their milestones super early. Mel was an easy one to talk to, one of those people who could chat for hours about any given topic. The price of groceries? She was upset she couldn't afford her frozen apple pie for both during the week and the night when the grandkids came over. Jeans too tight? She was annoyed that she recently had to go up a size in jeans because they 'Just don't make them like they used to anymore'. The sun has been shining today? She was worried her silly cat would give itself heatstroke again from falling asleep under a sun-facing window.

My phone buzzed in the middle of one of her stories.

Chance: Be there soon. Got held up with JJ. X

My stomach was in the middle of doing flips when another message buzzed through.

JJ: If Chance tries to tell you I'm the reason he's late, he's lying.

Me: What did you do?

JJ: We're supposed to be friends—you're meant to believe ME!

"Sorry, Mel. JJ's just having trouble with something," I explained.

She began rambling on about how he was always having some sort of trouble while I typed.

Me: What did you do?

JJ: I can't believe this. 20 years of friendship for what? Nothing but mistrust.

Mari: JJ, what did you do?

JJ: Chance was the one who said you can cook chicken tenders in the microwave! He didn't tell me it was one of those things where you had to take the plastic off too!

Mari: I don't know how you haven't poisoned yourself yet.

JJ: Gut of steel. STEEL, Lynnie. Have fun on your date tonight! #teamChari

My fingers were just about to hit send on a witty reply when another pair of heels clicked in behind me.

A tall, stiletto-wearing blonde walked into the gym cautiously, cringing at the very ground she walked on, seemingly afraid the concrete flooring would damage her shiny pink shoes. Her long blonde hair was wrapped into multiple interlacing curls and slung over one shoulder. A bronze colour coated her skin, but the tiniest of orange tint told me it wasn't real. She wore an expensive-looking two-piece set that was such a bright shade of pink it was almost an eyesore. There was lipstick to match, and fake lashes so long Mel would be fangirling.

"Hi, darl," Mel greeted. "Can I help you?"

"I'm hoping so." Her plumped lips rubbed together as she clicked over to the desk. "I'm looking for someone."

"Who're you chasing?" Mel asked sweetly, though I could see her eyeing the woman's Prada purse.

"I'm looking for Chance. Chance Riordan."

"Does he know you're coming to see him?" Mel, bless her, tried to ask as respectfully as possible without sounding nosey.

"He should," she said incredulously. "I'm Talia. His wife."

CHAPTER 42

Chance

"F or fuck sake, JJ! You don't cook the packet!"

"You didn't tell me that!" he argued, joining me in waving smoke out of the kitchen windows in hopes of getting the smoke alarm to shut off.

"I didn't think I had to!" I defended.

"You said, 'Yeah, bro, just chuck the whole pack in'! No part of that sentence implies any removal of the actual packet!"

"I'm going to put you in the microwave if I'm not only late for meeting Sunny, but I *also* turn up smelling like I've just walked out of a fucking cremation," I growled.

"Don't be so dramatic. She used to smoke; she'll be fine."

"Really?" I asked. The smoke alarm finally stopped blaring, so I took the opportunity to whip JJ with the tea towel I was holding.

"Ow! The fuck, dude?!" He rubbed his ass, right where I'd snapped it.

"You owe me."

"Yeah, yeah. Add it to the list." He waved me off. "You ready?"

"I *was*. Until you sauna-ed our kitchen with burning plastic." I undid the black button-up I'd chosen and yanked it off. After tossing it into the laundry as I passed it, I pulled down a navy blue button-up from my closet in the next room.

"JJ! Where are the keys?!" I called, checking my wallet and phone in my pocket.

"Got 'em!"

I pulled out my phone and fired off a quick text to Sunny before almost sprinting down the hall. JJ tossed me the keys and a foil packet crinkled in my hand.

There, dangling off a new keychain, were three packaged condoms.

"Oh, my god. I'm gonna kill you," I grumbled.

"What?! Why?! I'm just looking out for you two!"

I picked them off one by one and tossed them at him. "C'mon, dude! I don't need Sunny seeing that shit!" I stomped off towards the door.

"It's okay, bro! There's some in my glove box if you need them too!"

***

I couldn't help the smile that came to my face on the drive to Knock's. The last twenty-four hours had been bliss—seeing Sunny drop her walls was beyond anything I could have imagined. It was like having the heat finally click over on a cool winter night—full of warmth and reassurance.

I'd called in an order to the Rustic Roo for two of Mari's favourites—courtesy of JJ's wealth of knowledge. Nancy and Patty had been more than happy to stay open a little late for us once I name dropped that the food would be for Sunny. Well, not Sunny. Mari. She was Mari to the rest of the world; she was a ray of fucking sunshine to me.

I floated down the street freely in neutral, giving JJ's ute a break from the strain of running the old motor. Not a cloud in the sky, orange and pinks painted a picturesque dusk. Even the birds seemed to be watching above from all of the nearby trees. Nothing dared interrupt the beautiful evening the sun had given us.

The gravel at the base of the driveway crunched as the ute ran over it. I didn't even bother trying to get the old girl up the driveway — we'd probably just roll straight back down. I didn't bother pulling the keys out of the ignition either. Soggla was safe; *I* felt safe.

A very angry Sunny met me halfway up the driveway. Stormed over to me would be a more accurate description, a deep frown etched onto her face, cheeks flushed a dark pink.

"Sunny what's—"

"Fuck off, Riordan."

Well, that's certainly a change in tune.

I grabbed her elbow as she went to push by me.

"Let go."

"What's wrong?" I demanded, ignoring her request. "Sunny, what's happened?"

I reached a hand up to tuck that one stubborn curl from her face but was met with angry black eyes. Not the warm honey when she was happy, or the hazel hues when she was sad—onyx black for when she was angry.

"Get your *fucking hands* off me," she growled before yanking her arm free and continuing on her path.

As soon as my foot lifted to chase after her, a voice called out to me from the peak of the driveway. "Chance, baby!"

Oh ... fuck.

Fuck. Fuck. Fuck.

Her silhouette on top of the hill stood tall. She must have been wearing those ridiculously overpriced heels that cost all of my fight winnings from the main card I'd been on over in Perth last year. Even from halfway down the driveway, I still tensed at those icy eyes on me. Not in the way Sunny made me tense, from heat and eagerness to touch her. No, this was like having a snake dance in front of you. You knew it was going to strike, but all you could do was anticipate and attempt to dodge.

I chose to dodge.

I kicked myself back into motion, moving on the path Sunny had taken. The street was empty, and JJ's ute was gone.

Fuck. Fuck. Fuck.

"Chance, love! It's so good to see you! I've missed you!" Talia screeched, weaving that faux silky voice through her tone.

It was all fake. I knew that now.

Ignoring my shitbag of an ex-wife, I took off down the street towards Sunny and Marilyn's house. The fact that she was walking down the driveway in those stupid heels would buy me a few minutes at least.

"Chance! Chance, baby! Come back!"

My stomach, along with every other organ inside of me, recoiled at that voice.

I spotted her Mercedes on the street, black and shining proudly under the orange sky that didn't feel as beautiful anymore.

No.

No, no, no, no.

Soggla was my home now.

JJ, Al, and Marilyn were part of that.

Knock's and the locals were too.

Sunny is part of that.

She couldn't be.

I didn't want her to be.

"Why are you here, Talia?" I yelled back at her.

"What do you mean, darling?"

I flinched at the name I had called Sunny — a name I'd only ever used in love.

"Don't call me that," I growled as she finally reached the bottom of the driveway.

She huffed out a breath, clearly not impressed with the conditions of the gravel she had had to navigate.

"Why on earth are you here, Talia?"

"Because I'm here to bring my husband home," she defended. "You just up and left—no note, no text, no goodbye—nothing. I thought you were dead!"

"Bullshit. I left you notes, a lot of them actually," I replied, referring to the divorce papers I'd left on the kitchen counter.

She narrowed those soul-sucking eyes on me, a move that would have had me anticipating a fist coming my way before. But she knew better than to throw down now, on *my* home turf.

"You made your point with your little tantrum. I'm willing to forgive you," she replied, lifting her chin as if *she* was the bigger person here.

"Good for you, Talia. But *I'm* not willing to forgive *you*."

"You know what this means, Chance." She pulled out her phone, a new bedazzled case covering the huge screen. "The world will have to know who you really are; how you *really* treat your wife."

"You have no proof," I gritted through my teeth.

She smirked and raised her eyebrows in challenge. "My *word* is proof enough. Why would anyone believe you—a UFL fighter—over me, your poor, innocent wife who spoke when she was told not to."

"You're disgusting." My heart thundered in my chest, echoing through the hollow cavity as it sank.

I'd been stupid—so fucking stupid—to think I could escape her so easily. To think she wouldn't retaliate.

'*If you ever leave me, I will make your life a living hell,*' she'd always said.

And here she was, here to fulfill that promise.

"Oh, boo-boo, don't be so hurtful," she cooed, one of her signature cruel smirks on her blown-up lips.

"What do you want from me?"

"I want you, baby. *All* of you." She stepped closer.

Her sweet perfume was so strong I bit down hard on my tongue to force my gag back. A manicured hand ran claws up my forearm. Her fake nails were so long they might as well have been fucking claws.

"Name your price, Talia," I ground out, stepping back. "Name your price so I can be rid of you."

"Is this all about that little skank who was here earlier?" Her face scrunched, all of the botox in her face fighting the movement.

"No, Talia," I replied, forcing exasperation into my tone in attempt to steer her away from Sunny. "This is about me being done with the beatdowns. The ... the ... the *abuse* and *shit* I've put up with for the last six years. It's about me being done with you thinking you fucking own me; my choices; my money; my life. This is about *me* being done with *you*."

My heart was thundering a million miles an hour, but it eased slightly after getting the words I'd never said out.

She rolled her eyes.

"Get in the car, Chance. We'll go back to JJ's and get your things," she said, brushing off my words as if they'd simply never been said.

"Not happening. I'd rather walk the five kilometres than get in a car with you," I replied over my shoulder and stalked off.

Her car pulled away and sped off after her third attempt at getting me to turn around. Once the black Mercedes of doom that reminded me all too much of a bond villain's car was out of sight, I swung around and ran. I ran down the street, past the old flower shop and Marilyn's beloved bookshop. I passed the towering eucalyptus tree that took up an entire empty lot of land. I passed the clock shop, where old Lucky Rollins was flipping over his 'open' sign to 'closed'. I kept running and running.

All the way to Sunny's front door.

CHAPTER 43

Mari

"**H**e's still out there. Poor thing must be freezing," Nan mumbled, staring out of the front room windows. Gus lay majestically on the window seat, fixated on where I presumed Chance was sitting. His tail would wag every now and again, presumably in anticipation whenever the man outside would move.

"Yeah, well ... he can go snuggle up in his *wife's* arms," I spat, the words twisting up my mouth and my insides. The green-eyed monster was here, well and truly hating the idea of Chance running back into that tall blonde's arms. But heartbreak was here too, and boy was she *pissed*.

"Mari, dear ..." Nan started, face filled with sympathy when she padded back over to the dining table where I was currently drinking my coffee at. Gus followed her with his big brown eyes until she sat and then turned back to his Chance watch post.

"*Don't*, Nan. You of all people should understand why I don't even want to hear him out."

She pursed her lips, telling me something I'd said had struck a nerve somewhere.

"Sure, but Gerry certainly never camped out on my front lawn for three days in protest of me giving him the silent treatment," she tried.

"He's married, Nan. *Married*. He's lucky the silent treatment is all I'm giving him," I snapped.

"If him being here really bothers you that much then I'll go outside myself and tell him to leave," she said.

"Thank you—"

"But only if you go and hear him out first," she interrupted.

I shook my head with a huff and stood. "Then I guess he'll freeze out there each morning until the sun comes up," I said, picking up my laptop and half-full coffee mug and retreating back to my room.

***

"I need to go into the gym," I told Nan as I pulled a light jacket over my shoulders. The sun was already starting to set, even though it was only four in the afternoon. Winter was well and truly on its way in.

I didn't care. I already felt cold, having that warm feeling of love traded for an icy stab to the ribs.

"I thought you'd told them you were working from home?" she questioned as a knock at the door sounded. She stared at me for a moment longer before standing from the table, another empty coffee mug in hand, and padded over to the sink.

I rolled my eyes, even though a tiny, traitorous part of my heart warmed at the fact *he* was still here—still coming to knock on my door.

"I've left some invoices in my office. Can you go and get rid of the pest on our front yard?"

"Have you heard him out?"

"N—"

"Then no." She shuffled off to go and answer the door.

I was already dialling JJ's number when the voice of the man himself trailed through from the front door. It was quickly followed by Nan gushing about him coming over to visit, how healthy he was looking, how she would have to bake for him again if he kept getting thinner. The things she always said when he knocked on our front door—which happened to be nearly every day.

"I think I'm wasting away over here, Nana Marilyn. Do you reckon' you could make some cookies for me? I think that would really help."

"Of course, dear. You go turn on the oven. I'll be back in just a moment."

The door shut and JJ happily pranced down the hallway into the kitchen.

"Gah!" he squealed when he saw me standing over the kitchen table, arms folded. "Jesus, Lynnie. Way to be creepy."

The sound of little footsteps clattered together as Gus leapt off the window seat and trotting *out* the door with Nan.

Traitors, all of them.

"Speaking of creepy—want to be a real pal and go get that lying assface off of my front lawn?" I scowled, barely able to call him an assface because even though he'd colossally fucked up, broken my trust and my heart, not even God himself could deny how gorgeous that man was.

"No can do, Lynnie. Been trying to convince him to move for three days now and come exorcise the demon out of my house," he replied, pulling countless ingredients out of the pantry that were definitely *not* used for baking biccies.

"Stop it. You're making a bloody mess," I snapped.

He held his hands up in surrender and took a seat at the table across from me, snatching up a green apple from the fruit bowl.

"How you goin', Lynnie?" he asked.

"Fine."

"You don't sound fine."

"Well, I am. The universe did me a real solid a few days ago—took out some trash for me."

Between my eyebrows ached from the permanent scowl that I'd worn for the last few days. Sleep had turned into a luxury I didn't deem necessary, since every time I closed my eyes I dreamt of the man out on my lawn. Reliving the memories of a blissful ignorance as to who he really was was a kind of torture I couldn't take. *My heart* couldn't take it.

"Lynnie." JJ reached a hand across the table and squeezed mine. "I want you to know that I'm well aware that you're lying to me right now, but I'm not going to push you. I'll be here when you're ready."

I stared at JJ for a long moment, the words creeping up my throat. But then my throat thickened, and the unworthy tears found my eyes.

I blinked and shook my head. "Then you'll be waiting a long while, J."

Chapter 44

Chance

"I thought you might need some of this." Marilyn's sweet voice startled me. Gus's front paws tackling me to the ground was a welcome surprise as he planted wet doggy kisses all over my face.

"Hey, buddy," I laughed.

He pushed off me and lay down in front of me, fixing his gaze back up to Marilyn.

She sighed before slowly taking a seat on the green grass. "Here," she said, handing me a plastic container.

I opened it wide a bowl full of pasta.

"Since you're out here every time I look out the window, figured you'd be hungry."

"Thank you." I smiled at the old woman, who returned the gesture almost immediately. "How is she?"

"She's doing what she normally does in these situations." Marilyn's face turned sympathetic. "Cutting herself off from everyone and using anger to cope. Sometimes it can be easier to wield the knife than to accept that someone else has cut you."

"I just need her to—"

She held up a hand. "I know. You just need her to hear your side, right, dear?"

My face burned with shame. I'd not only lied to Mari—I'd lied to Marilyn too. "I'm sorry, Marilyn."

"What for, dear?"

"I lied to you."

"I'm sure you had your reasons." She smiled, shifting her weight slightly to get comfortable.

Gus stood abruptly, watching her intently until she gave him a reassuring nod—some kind of non-verbal communication the two of them had.

"My granddaughter is tough. She's not an easy one to gain forgiveness from. But with every bridge that I've seen her cross, every fork in her road, she's always made the right choice. *You*, dear, count as one of those choices too."

"I don't know what to do. She won't see me; she won't answer my texts or calls; she won't *hear* me. I—"

"Sometimes actions speak louder than words ever can. Loud enough that even a deaf man could find his way." She patted me on the shoulder before clicking to Gus. He moved to her side, standing guard next to her as she rose slowly to her feet.

With a smile and a gentle squeeze of my shoulder, they walked back inside the house.

The house where my home was.

I stood, picking up my dead phone, water bottle, and Marilyn's pasta, and left.

Chapter 45

Mari

Whatever Nan said to Chance had worked, since it had been over an hour since he left our front lawn. Gus hadn't returned to his perch on the window, so I took that as a sign of him not coming back.

A small, aching piece of my heart twanged — he'd finally left. I tried and tried and tried to push relief on it, showing that broken piece how good it was that he was gone now. But it wouldn't take. Instead, it left that same hollow ache in my chest, but this time it was quiet. No thundering beat knowing he was right outside, so spike of adrenaline every time Gus moved—just *quiet*.

I grabbed Gus's lead and collar from by the doorway before strapping the red fabric around his neck. He was wary to leave Nan but was content when he realised he could walk at a faster pace and sniff to his heart's content.

I disconnected the clasp from his lead once we hit the old florist and Gus took it upon himself to pee on some of the weeds growing between the cracks. While he investigated the different smells of passers-by, I walked ahead. The sun was starting to set, and clouds were rolling in from off in the distance. Fitting, considering it felt like my life had gone from sunny and bright to an angry storm in the last three days.

"Mari!" a voice called.

Gus quickly caught up to my side. I squinted slightly at the figure standing at the base of Knock's' driveway. Her frizzy, curly orange hair swayed slightly in the wind. Paige's hair was that thick, that curly, that it was too heavy for the wind to really move.

"Hey, Paige," I said as we got closer.

She held a large brown box in her hands. Gus took an immediate liking to her bright pink pants, sitting at her glossy red-booted feet and leaning into her legs. I could practically see the black hair that would be littered on them when he moved away.

"I brought you some photos!" She beamed, her big teeth glistening under the afternoon sun as she shook her head lightly to clear hair from her face. Despite the orange hair falling all over her forehead, it was hard not to smile back at her. She was one of those special people whose happiness was contagious.

"Oh, that's really kind of you." I offered her a smile, though I could see on her face instantly that she didn't believe me. "You didn't have to come all the way down here. I would have picked them up."

"On a beautiful evening like this? No way was I passing up the opportunity for your view! The views from Knock's are the best when a storm rolls in!"

"Here, let me take that for you." I pulled the box from her arms, and she staggered forward slightly.

"Thanks! I hope you don't mind, but I had some of the nicer photos framed. I noticed a lot of Al's art and pictures were gone, so I thought some of these would make a nice replacement!" She and Gus bounced alongside me up the driveway. Paige, because she was excited about the storm rolling in. Gus, because he thought her theatrical happiness was her initiating play.

"That's really thoughtful of you, Paige. How much do we owe you?" I slid the key into the bulky padlock and pulled it open with a jimmy. Gus bolted inside, immediately zooming around the place, presumably looking for JJ.

"Not on the mats!" I called, already knowing I would have dirty paw prints to clean off.

"Oh, bless his little heart!" Paige gushed. "Photos are on the house! I owe you guys—it's the least I could do."

I forced my shoulders to relax at her timid smile. I often forgot about Paige staying with us for that six months when she first moved to town. She'd done such an incredible job with photography for Knock's that she'd had offers from a boatload of other clients. I couldn't work out why she'd chosen to stay here in Soggla and only do work trips rather than move to the big city. But Paige deemed herself a 'Soggla girl through and through' and loved this town as much as the rest of us did. Maybe even more.

I sighed and placed a hand on her purple-denim clad shoulder, giving it a gentle squeeze. "You don't owe us anything, Paige. Your debt was fulfilled a long time ago," I said, reminding her of the investment she made in Knock's when we were struggling. Of the meaning behind the tattoos she had on her hand that matched mine.

"Believe me, Mari. If you knew what I'd come from, you'd understand why I would disagree."

***

I'd ruffled and faffed around in the office for fifteen minutes before curiosity got the best of me. After stacking the pile of invoices and receipts on my desk, I grabbed my packing knife from the top drawer of my desk. Slicing through the tape, a dozen packing peanuts came tumbling out.

"No!" I told Gus, who had deemed them a worthy snack size. His ears dipped in disappointment before he turned, returning to his spot on the couch.

Sitting on folded knees, I pulled the first picture out. Like the others in the box, it was framed in a matte black frame with the slightest white edging. JJ's arm was in full extension as he rammed in his lead hand into the beat-up pad Al was holding. Wearing his signature cap, Al's mouth was open mid-sentence—most likely calling the next combo.

The next one was of some of the older guys who trained, arms linked together, teeth gritted, in the midst of a burnout round of sit-ups.

I pulled the one of Nan and Gus aside. They were walking up the Knock's driveway, the midmorning sun shining brightly over them. Nan had stopped to bend down and give Gus's head a scratch. She was smiling down at him, cooing terms of endearment at him no doubt. Gus had his ears pinned all of the way back, tongue halfway hanging out his mouth in an attempt to lick Nan's chin.

Six more photos had lain delicately in the box, each depicting another artery in the heart of Knock's. Liv mid-roll with her very first brown belt student. Ash and Hogs leaning on the edge of the MMA cage as they coached two fighters inside. Mel beaming proudly from her front desk. Beautiful images that captured the passion and tenacity of this community.

A note was taped on top of the third-to-last photo, a red velvet blanket covering the rest.

These are my favourites,

Paige x

The velvet slid off to reveal that same matte frame, but this time with the hint of gold edging the image. My breath caught in my throat at the picture, the truly candid moment in time. It was that fateful night of the party at Rock-It's. Chance and I were running down the hall and he had our favourite bottle of whiskey in his hand. His blue eyes were alight with joy, staring straight over at me. My mouth was thrown open in laughter, that open and free bliss that I'd only ever felt with him.

The next photo was of him holding pads for me. Deep concentration was etched on his face, but that signature smirk still lifted his lips.

The last photo was of us—a moment we thought we had stolen but Paige had captured on camera. We smiled at each other from across the mats. Countless pairs of people were sparring and rolling, all blurry silhouettes. But Chance and I were in colour.

Paige had nailed it, the picture showing exactly what my world with Chance Riordan in it was like. Without him, I might as well have been one of those blurry, blacked-out figures.

I sat up on my folded legs, letting out a shaky breath. I studied each photo, my heart crumbling that little bit more each time.

Each time I saw him, the man I was stupidly falling in love with.

Each time I saw her, the version of me when he was near.

Each time I saw us, the invisible thing I deemed the love of a lifetime.

"Lynnie?"

I didn't answer, just swallowed deeply. The knot in my throat refused to clear, and within seconds my eyes followed suit.

"Mari?" JJ asked, a hand on my shoulder. "Marilyn?"

The tears fell over of the edges of my eyes.

"I'm not fine, JJ," I croaked. "I'm not fine at all."

CHAPTER 46

Mari

"Y ou alright, dear?" Nan asked JJ, hushing her voice.

I kept my eyes closed, not ready to face the world just yet.

"Yeah, I'm all good. You should head off. I'll make sure she gets home," JJ replied, the hand on my shoulder giving a reassuring squeeze.

"You let me know if you need anything."

His body lightly shook from the nod I assume he gave Nan.

The door closed with a click, and he let out a sigh. I did too, cracking an eye open enough to see that the training space lights had been turned on, the office lights off.

It must be night.

I closed my eyes once again, still able to feel the puffiness of them.

When JJ had bent beside me, he'd caught me quickly in his arms when the sobbing started. The ugly, loud cries that I'd choked on.

'*Let it out, Lynnie. Your big heart needs it.*' He'd told me.

That seemed to be true, since I'd woken back to the world with that hollow, numb feeling. As if I was all out of emotions, all out of energy to even feel the hurt anymore.

"*I-I'm falling for him, J,*" I'd sobbed.

It had been a lie, a truth I had tried to twist on myself.

I was already in love with him.

"You could have tossed me on the couch," I mumbled, opening my eyes to my best friend. "There's no way that was comfortable for you."

I sat up, waiting for some kind of mocking, bantering comment to come my way. It never did. JJ eyed me, giving my face a once-over before stretching his arms out in front of him.

"You needed it," he said, shrugging.

I stayed sat on the floor when JJ jumped up and began packing my desk away, tossing certain things in my bag and certain things in my drawer. He cleared away the packing peanuts, as well as Paige's photos.

"I need to take some of that stuff home to do on the weekend," I said. I opened my phone camera and saw the puffy bags beneath my eyes had subsided, sending some of the little red veins in my eyes away. My eyes were still bloodshot, still red and puffy from the tears I'd tried so hard to swallow.

"Stop beating yourself up. I can see you're hanging shit on yourself for crying before. Stop it." He wasn't scolding me, just bringing me back to reality. "I'm covering for you this weekend."

"JJ, it's okay. I can work." I tried to reason with him, but to no end.

He ended up taking my huge pile of paperwork and my work laptop over to his bag and zipping it up.

"The passkey is—"

"120118," he interrupted. "I know." He gave me a sympathetic smile, knowing that the 12th of January 2018 was the day Chance had arrived. My cheeks burned in shame.

I'd trusted him.

And he'd lied to me.

Just like *he* had.

"He hurt me, J," I whispered, so quiet I wasn't sure he even heard it.

"Lynnie—" he started.

"I should have known better than to trust a fighter."

"What do you mean?"

"They all hurt. Every time. It's what they do," I said, numb to the very bone.

"Who?" He dropped down beside me once more, giving me his full attention.

"The fighters I love."

"Come on now, that's not true," he tried.

"Jayden, my dad, Chance—"

"Your dad?" he interrupted. "What did Eli do?"

"Of course this is when my deep-rooted daddy issues come out," I joked.

JJ, for once, didn't find it funny. "What did he do, Lynnie?" His voice dropped to a silent, serious plea.

"He lied to me," I mumbled, finding my now-fidgeting fingers very interesting.

"About?"

"He told me he wouldn't leave me," I murmured, low and quiet enough that it concealed the thickness of my voice. "When Mum died, he promised he'd never leave me."

"Oh, Lynnie—"

"It's stupid and selfish and childish—I know. But, between him and Jayden and Chance, I just ..."

"Look at me," he requested. "Chance is nothing like your dad. Eli lied to protect a little girl's heart from the inevitables of life. But Chance—"

"I don't want to hear excuses," I snapped, voice thick and hoarse. "He's married. That may not mean much to *some* people, apparently. But it does to me."

***

I was in the bathroom, splashing literal litres of cold water on my face, when I heard JJ's phone ring.

"Yeah, man, she's with me," he said with a long sigh. "Yeah, she's a fucking demon. I swear I see Nanna's old cross rattle whenever she enters the house."

I splashed another handful of cold water on my face, willing the puff-packs below my eyes to deflate already.

"I know ... I know ... I know, man. But you should have told her. I can't force her to do anything—I *won't* force her to do anything." There was an edge to JJ's voice that I had never heard before. In all of the years I'd known him, he had never taken quite that tone. "I'll call you later. I'm driving Lynnie home."

"Everything okay?" I asked, pushing the bathroom door open.

JJ smiled and gestured for me to go through the door he was holding open.

"Always, Lynnie."

CHAPTER 47

Chance

My hands shook as I opened the filing cabinet of fucking doom. That stupidly sweet smell of Talia's perfume wafted out like the smell of a rotting corpse in a coffin. The smell that was now also flooding JJ's house. I sighed, checking the time on my watch.

4.37 am.

I only had another hour or so before Talia realised I was missing—only an hour before I couldn't justify it as a 'morning run'. Her reins had tightened since I'd left Mari's place two days ago. I'd been grateful that my phone was dead when I was camping on her lawn, but that had earned me a sucker punch and a mouthful the second I'd walked through the front door back at JJ's. It had been followed by the usuals; '*Look at what you've turned me into*', '*This is your fault*', '*Why would anyone believe you when I tell them you've hit me?*'.

There had been countless nights in the house back in Darlington Harbour where I questioned my own mind—questioned why the woman I thought I loved would do this to me.

Was it really my fault?

Had I really turned her into this?

Would no one believe me when I said I never lay a hand on her?

Those questions used to haunt my thoughts over and over like some kind of fucked up merry-go-round.

But then I'd found Sunny.

Sunny, who'd shown me what it was like to live again, what it was like to grab life with two hands and say, 'It's fucking mine'. Sunny, who made the clouds part and sunshine beam through every time I looked into her big brown eyes. Sunny, who'd never tried to change me, but made *me* want to change *myself*.

I dug through the coffin of my old life until I found it. The old, beat-up, water-damaged notebook. Flicking through the crinkling pages, it was all still there. Every memory I ever got the chance to write. Every slap, punch, and kick. Every evening spent in coercive sex. Every disgusting word, every disgusting act—all in one place. A record of the nightmare that was my life.

Was.

Was. Was. Was.

I shut it, rolling it up tight and tucking it into my inner jacket pocket. I turned, slamming the filing cabinet closed and giving it a nice big 'fuck you' kick.

***

JJ: Satan is awake. She's looking for you. Did you get it?

I stared at my phone, my mind in a whirlwind of doubt and panic and fear.

Fear.

I fucking hated fear.

I learned to fight so I never had to feel fear again; so anyone I *loved* would never have to feel fear again.

My phone buzzed again.

JJ: You're doubting yourself, aren't you?

JJ: She'll make the right choice, Chance. She always does. I bet my left nut on it.

Me: Not both?

JJ: … on the off chance that I'm wrong, no.

I blew a breath out before tucking my phone into my shorts.

Just do it, mate.

What if she throws it at my head? What if she refuses to read it?

Just leave it on her doorstep.

"Bargaining with myself. Yep, definitely losing it." Sucking in and blowing out another breath, I moved.

Quietly and carefully, trying not to make a sound as Gus would alert everyone to my presence if I did, I approached her front door. I bent to put it on their doormat that had a faded 'Welcome' written across it when the front door swung open.

"Hi."

Chapter 48

Chance

"U-uh, hi," I stammered.

Because what else do you say when your childhood hero is standing right in front of you? What else do you say when your childhood hero is standing right in front of you and you've just broken his only daughter's heart?

"Fancy seeing you here." A sly smirk spread across his face.

"Here?"

"Yeah, mate. Here. On my daughter's front doorstep." A wink from those eyes that almost, but not quite, matched Sunny's. "You comin' in?"

He opened the door wider, the smell of fresh coffee hitting my senses, waving me inside.

I took a cautionary step back. "No ... uh ... not today. I just came to uh ..."

"Drop something off?" he asked, gaze flicking to the notebook in my hand.

The notebook that felt like it was blistering my skin with burns the longer I was fucking holding it.

"Yeah. Could you just ... give it to her?" I asked softly, extending the book out towards him.

"Of course, mate," he replied, skimming all the pages. "Classified?"

"Not anymore."

CHAPTER 49

Mari

"Knock, knock." My dad's gentle, familiar voice was muffled from behind the door with a soft rattle from his knuckles.

"Come in, Dad," I grumbled, my head heavy on my unwashed pillowcase. Tear and coffee stains coated it, but I found nothing in me ready to even care.

Since JJ had let me have a big sob fest on him yesterday, I hadn't recovered from that numb, empty feeling I'd woken up with. A part of my life felt dark; it felt quiet and empty. My routine was out of order; go to the gym, see Chance, do Chance's morning class, do admin work whilst Chance does solo drilling conveniently outside the office window ...

Now, I had to remove him from all of that. Which didn't leave me with much at the moment.

"Hey, sweetie." Dad poked his head in, a sad smile on his face. He pushed the door farther open before shutting it behind him. Walking softly on my carpeted floor, he sat down on the edge of my bed. He placed a book on the other side of my legs before moving in to clear the hair from my face. "How're you doin'?"

"Peachy." My voice cracked, probably from not using it in at least twelve hours.

"Nan is making dinner soon. Should be ready by the time you've had a shower and changed your clothes," he suggested.

"Dinner?"

"Yeah, sweetie. It's just after five."

Guess it has been longer than 12 hours, then.

"Oh, that's okay. I'm not really hungry."

"I know you're hurtin', darlin'. Wanna tell me what's going on?" he asked softly. "Does it have anything to do with your friend you introduced me to?"

I sighed, not having the energy to talk my way out. "He lied to me."

"We all tell lies sometimes, Mar. I told JJ he looked good with his prepubescent moustache when he was thirteen. You and I both know *that* was a lie." He chuckled.

"It wasn't just one lie, Dad."

He sighed. "Okay, darlin'. I won't push ya. But do me a favour, will you?"

I nodded, and he reached beside him for the book behind my legs.

"I was asked by *someone* to give this to you. Your grandmother seems to think it's very important you read it. I don't know about you, but I'd rather not go up against her, hey?"

In his hand was a worn and torn notebook with yellow water-stained pages. Some pages had very clearly been laid out in the sun to dry, as they made a crinkling sound when Dad placed it into my hand.

"Thanks, sweetie." He winked, pressed a kiss to my forehead, and quietly padded out.

***

It took approximately thirty minutes of constant back and forth in my head of 'Should I read it?' or 'Should I bin it?'.

Obviously, since curiosity killed the cat, the 'I should read it' won out. I sat up in bed, the night air starting to creep through the fly screen over the open window. Pulling the doona up high and turning a nearby lamp on, I squinted at the light.

And the smell of myself.

Dad really should have pushed a bit harder to get me into the shower.

The same pages crinkled when I picked the book up, a faint smell of dust and dampness coming out of them. Like a dog, sussing out a new toy, I sniffed it. The dust smell was pretty strong, but there was something else under it. Something bitter. Maybe beer? Petrol? Gasoline?

"Enough, Mari. Just open the damn thing," I muttered to myself, urging my courage forward.

Inside the front cover was fresh, messy handwriting. Not faded at all like what was on the next page.

Sunny,

I hope this book tells you about what I still can't say aloud.

I hope you'll believe me.

Chance x

Surely, surely, nothing in this book could make things any worse.

CHAPTER 50

Mari

Sometime in September 2014

I don't remember what day this happened. Frankly, I never thought I'd be sitting in my guest bathroom with the door locked to write this.

I've lost count of how many times it has happened since, but you know what they say? You never forget your first.

We were arguing on the staircase at the house as she attempted to storm upstairs and lock herself in the bedroom again. She'd snatched my phone from me when she'd seen a single message from Jane come through.

Jane: No worries. We'll up your carb load next check-in.

My dietician had messaged me, and my wife had been losing her shit.

"She's my dietician, Talia. I have to have contact with her," was the last thing I'd said before her open palm swung around and slapped me clean across the face.

"I-I'm so sorry. Chance, baby ... I'm so sorry! It was an accident!" she'd cried.

And I'd believed her.

23rd January 2017

She turned up at training today. Her phone clutched in her hand so tight I thought she'd break it. When I finished my session with Dylan, she waved him off before pulling me aside to 'talk' out in the carpark. It was so late in the day, of course there was no one else there. She showed me a screen, shoved the phone in my face, and told me to 'explain this'. I had no fucking clue what I was looking at. It was message requests on Instagram, seemingly from both men and women. I was confused, since she was the one who ran my Instagram account, and I asked her what I needed to explain. She slapped me straight across the face and started yelling at me about the fact that I had 'bitches messaging' me and I certainly did have something to explain. I reminded her that I didn't have any social media downloaded on my phone, and that she was the one who wanted to run all of those accounts for me. She started screaming, wailing about 'How I could do this to her'. I felt I deserved this, for making her feel this way. So I didn't try and duck when the next punch came through.

3rd March 2017

I met up with JJ for a fight night we both wanted to see in Darlington Stadium. My phone blew up the whole night, but I had it on silent during the fights. After the card ended, I saw I had over fifty missed calls from Talia and nearly two hundred *text messages. Ironically enough, when I called her back, she didn't answer.*

Message after message accused me of dressing up too much for 'a night out with JJ', saying the most abhorrent things about JJ (things that made me sick to my fucking stomach to read), telling me everything that's wrong with me; I'm a bad husband; I'm nothing of a man; I'm lucky she chooses to put up with me and my shit. I got home that night to find a pillow and light blanket at the foot of the front door. The deadbolt was over the door too, so my keys were virtually useless.

I managed to sneak inside through the back window and went to crash on the couch with my flimsy little blanket and pillow. Sleeping on the leather couch, cold and by myself, sounded like the warmer option.

4th March 2017

Talia wasn't happy I slept on the couch. The engagement ring I bought her cut me across the face when she closed-fist punched me.

March 19th 2017

It was raining today. She scratched long, sharp nails down my arm, drawing blood in multiple locations. Said I needed to stop sooking about something as silly as a 'slap on the wrist'.

My bad; it's my fault for making her so miserable when it rains.

1st April 2017

I accepted another fight deal from Baltis today. Our bank accounts were running nearly empty after Talia's latest shopping spree. I was on my way to training when she called me, claiming she'd forgotten her keys yet again. When I arrived back at the house, half an hour later, she was in tears, scream-

ing and sobbing about how I never want to spend time with her, I'm never home. The usuals.

I was tired, already in a steep calorie deficit; I was fucking tired.

2nd April 2017 – 12.30 am

Funny how all of those expensive, designer items hurt just as bad as their Target lookalike when they're thrown at you.

15th April 2017

She forgot her keys again tonight. But she needed the car to 'go driving'. When I reminded her I have a last minute fight I signed onto because we are financially in trouble, she told me to 'stop being so selfish'. I found two new joint credit cards I'd never signed for in the mail. When she came back two hours later, she'd already maxed one of them out with new handbags, clothes, and a gold bracelet.

17th April

I confronted her about the credit cards at dinner, how she forged my signature for them. She told me that it was my fault—I didn't make enough money to support the life she deserved. I pushed too far on this one, telling her we could live a better life if she didn't spend every cent we have on 'stuff'. She flipped out, yelled at me, and stabbed me in the arm with her fork.

The bleeding wasn't bad enough, so I bandaged it over at home.

20th April 2017

She confronted me about why we weren't having sex anymore before we went to sleep. I told her I was sorry, but I just hadn't been in the mood lately. I reminded her I was still in a steep calorie deficit and preparing for a fight in three weeks. She reminded me sex was a part of a healthy relationship, and I was the one ruining this for us. She pushed and pushed and pushed—refusing to let me sleep until she'd gotten what she wanted. So, I gave in. I didn't finish, couldn't bring myself to. She slept peacefully after we were done. I didn't sleep at all.

4th May

Mum reached out again, asking to catch up for coffee. Talia said we couldn't afford to waste money on silly things like coffee catch-ups. I told Mum I was sick.

11th May 2017

I won my fight, barely. I could feel the days, nearly weeks lacking in training with every punch and kick I threw. She congratulated me in front of everyone and made a big fuss, which felt like a really nice change. I was so proud of myself to have made her proud. But when we got in the car, she told me how disappointed she was in me for not getting the 'fight of the night' bonus. I drove us to the hospital for my routine post-fight check-up, since she refused to drive. The conversation quickly moved to the ring girls, how old I thought they were, how pretty she thought they were, how much she bet I had been itching to get near them. As per usual, I told her she was wrong, and that answer wasn't acceptable. She pulled a chunk of my hair out from the base of my skull while I drove us to the hospital.

21st May 2017

I'm tired to the bone. I've reached fight-week weight unintentionally and people are starting to ask questions. It doesn't matter. The lies feel like truth for a moment if I tell it right.

No one will ever love me or accept me if I leave. I can't afford to leave. Milah needs me to stay, she needs her bills to be paid.

1st June 2017

I met with my lawyer today and had documents changed. As of 1st June 2017, if anything were to ever happen to me, all funds and assets are to be split 50% to Milah Riordan, 25% to Dylan Riordan, and 25% to Jaxon Jones.

I felt such a relief from it, I actually slept after she forced me into sex again.

8th January 2018

She found my stash. Found this book, all of the invoices for Milah's treatment. She was furious, claiming it was money we needed, wanting to know how I could be so selfish to spend it on someone as fucked up as my sister. She doused the documents, the book and everything I own in gasoline and threw it in a fire out the back. She turned and threw a water balloon at me. Turns out that was filled with gasoline also. Luckily, the book was on top of the pile. I grabbed it and ran. She chased me for several blocks with a lighter. How she could run so fast, I have no idea. But I'm not exactly equipped with a super-stamina anymore. After three years of this shit with her, my own body is starting to give up on me. I can feel it.

When I lost her, I waited out for a long while until the early hours of the morning.

9th January 2018

It was around 1.30 am when I snuck into the house I bought with my own money, took the car keys to our brand-new BMW, and left.

I was driving down the highway with absolutely no idea of where the fuck I was going. I needed to leave; I knew that much. I didn't think I could be surprised anymore, until a kangaroo jumped out onto the middle of the road. I swerved hard and landed on a dirt path. Guessed this was the new road I was driving on.

I'm so glad I did. It was beautiful what I found at the end of it. A lookout over a cliff, bushland for miles, and a quiet, tranquil waterfall.

I sat and stared for hours and hours, wondering what it would feel like to share this place with someone. Someone good.

CHAPTER 51

Mari

"Where is he?" I asked, pushing past a half-asleep JJ who was still rubbing at his eyes. "Morning to you too, Lynnie," he replied, stretching his mouth open wide in a yawn.

"Where is he? Is he here?" I headed straight for his door, pausing when I noticed a set of folded pillows and a blanket on the couch.

JJ groggily walked over to the pile and lifted the note stacked neatly on the top. "Curse you guys and your fuckin' theatrics." Another yawn from him. "He's gone out for a while. He'll be back a little later."

"Did he say anything else?"

JJ shot me a filthy look, punishment for asking questions at six in the morning.

"Like, where he was going? When he'd be back?"

"Nope." A third yawn.

"Jesus, what are you so tired for?" I asked, following him as he skidded his slipper-clad feet over the floor as we walked to the kitchen.

"You try living with a spawn of Satan and tell me how good your sleep patterns are."

"Spawn of Satan?"

"The Queen of Crazytown has deemed this place her home until Chance decides"—*for those counting, this is the fourth yawn in less than five minutes*—"to go back home with her. Chance and I have been scheming hardcore. It's takes it out of a man."

"Would've thought you'd always be in for a bitta scheming."

"At the appropriate hours of the day," he grumbled, shooting me another pointed look. "You better head off, Lynnie. I'll bring him over to your place tonight. Trust me when I say you don't want to be here when that fucking *thing* crawls out of her coffin."

I looked towards Chance's door, with the bedroom behind it that he hadn't been sleeping in, and back to the front door. It would be so easy to go, tell JJ to let Chance know I stopped by. I could leave, right now, go home to a quiet, peaceful, safe house.

Chance didn't seem to have any of that anymore. So I pulled out one of the rickety, old yellow chairs from JJ's dining table and sat down. "I'd like to see what happens when a vampire comes out during the daylight."

***

Talia was up and out of Chance's room no later than an hour later. Face caked in makeup, hair pinned back, and those stupid fucking stilettos on that made an obnoxiously high-pitched noise when she walked.

As soon as she rounded the corner into the kitchen, I folded my arms over my chest. Yes, to look as intimidating as possible. But also, to help hide Chance's book up my shirt.

Her ice-blue eyes were piercing, but mine had to be molten lava. She'd have to try a lot harder to intimidate me than a levelling look from her behemoth ass. She was half a foot taller than me, even more so with those ridiculously impractical stilettoes that had a click to them so obnoxious I wanted to set the damn things on fire. But she could be two metres taller than me and it still wouldn't have stopped me from looking down my nose at her.

Fucking scum of the earth.

"I know exactly *who* and *what* you are, bitch," I hissed. "He's already copped enough of your Satan-in-human-form bullshit. Stay the hell away from him."

"Or what? Hm? What're you gonna do, *fighter whore*?" she spat.

It took everything inside me not to laugh and point out the creases around her lips from a life living in frown. I just *knew* it would drive her insane.

I stepped in closer, taking the space as mine. A clatter in the background sounded and JJ was at my side in an instant. Her time of control of the people around me was over. Done. Finished. I lifted my right palm, enclosed in a fist, and smiled. JJ once told me I reminded him of a lioness, and I let it show. I showed the threat, the promise of an ending on my terms. Because no one—*no one*—could hurt the ones I love and live on *their* terms.

"I'll show you what real pain looks like," I purred, grinning wickedly. "And trust me, Lucifer himself would be proud of what I would do to you."

***

"We need you here 24/7. I can't believe she just ... left!" JJ gushed, eating his nearly burnt-to-a-crisp bagel that was layered with Vegemite half an inch thick. "I mean, I know it's not permanent, but still! A temporary exorcism is better than the demon still wasting my good coffee beans!"

"It's amazing what shitty people like that do when someone will actually hit them back," I scoffed.

Fucking pathetic, she is.

"So, you read the book then?" JJ asked tentatively.

"Why else would I be here?"

"I'm assuming you being here means you made the right choice?"

"What 'choice'?" I asked, puzzled.

"The right one." He sighed, not meeting my eyes. "You believe him?"

"Why wouldn't I?" I could have sworn JJ's shoulders sagged in relief.

CHAPTER 52

Mari

Chance had taken JJ's truck with him, so I walked the six kilometres across town to the only other person who I knew could help me.

"Mari!" Al beamed when he opened his bright red front door. He made an effort to repaint it every year, keep the colour fresh and 'iconic to the house' as he said it.

He quickly stepped forward and pulled me into a hug. I could feel the sympathy in his hug and saw it in the brief glimpse of his face. It didn't surprise me though. I assumed Al would have been the one Nan turned to for a chat on the phone.

"It's good to see you, darlin'." He stepped back, checking me over before pushing the heavy strawberry-coloured door open wider. "Comin' in for a cuppa?"

"I'd love one, but I can't stay too long." I chewed nervously on my bottom lip. Aside from martial arts confusions and general problems, I'd never really turned to Al for help. I knew he was always there, of course. He reminded me of that often. But Al was always someone I wanted to please, wanted to make proud. "Hope that's okay?"

"Course. Any time spent with you, long or short, is always time well spent." He smiled at me, pulling open a chair for me at the eight-seater dining table that faced directly into his rounded, open plan kitchen.

Al's entire house interior was made up of cream walls and bench-tops, yellow lighting, and a deep brown staining on every single inch of timber. Outdated, sure. But the house always felt warm and full of life.

The old, red kettle that matched the front door began whistling quickly. Al must've already had a cuppa this morning.

"It's nice to see you, darlin'. Your grandmother has had me a little worried over here," he said, reaching into one of the many timber cabinets and pulling down two mugs.

"Nan's a bit of a worry wart when it comes to me, you know that," I replied.

"It wasn't what she was telling me that had me worried. In the decade that you've been working at Knock's, I've never seen you miss a day there." He put three heaped teaspoons of instant coffee in each mug before pulling the kettle. He poured a little milk in his before bringing them both over to the table.

"Thank you," I said, taking the pink painted mug from his hands. "And I don't think you have anything to worry about, Al. Sometimes we all just need a break."

"So, it's got nothing to do with that head coach of ours?"

I sighed.

"Even if it does, there's nothing wrong with needing a little space." The coffee was warm, but tasted of bitter, cheap instant coffee. I took long gulps, enjoying it for the caffeine hit I knew was coming, not the flavour.

"No, there isn't. But you don't take 'space' from Knock's, darlin'. Wanna tell me what's really goin' on?"

I glanced at the large clock on his wall. It was almost nine-thirty. I had to get moving.

"I would love to. Really, Al, I would. But … it's not my story to tell." I winced at his unrelenting gaze. "But … I do need to ask you a favour."

CHAPTER 53

Mari

I whipped down the highway going at least ten over the speed limit. Al's little Corolla had probably never gone this fast before.

Al had handed me the keys without further question when I'd asked. I think he'd been too shocked at me even asking to think twice.

His little Corolla smelled like his office used to—coffee and stinky cigars. A couple of butts were in one of the cup holders, along with three empty coffee cups stacked together. But other than that, there was nothing else in the car. Not a speck of dirt, a string of grass, not even one of his grey hairs.

I hit the brakes, shifting gear when I spotted the familiar dirt road. A loud clunking sound rattled the car, but the noise was lost to the sound of tyres on gravel when I hit the dirt road.

Had I thought about how a small, hardly-used Corolla would go on a rocky dirt road? Not at all.

Would I give it a red-hot go? Absolutely.

I dropped the gear to second, and at the base of the gravel hill, first. Flying down the road, I used the flat stretch to build momentum. The car screamed at me, begging me to change gears, but I held out. As soon as we blew past the ditch that signalled the start of the incline, I pumped the clutch and pulled her back down to second.

She whined and screamed the whole drive up, and for a moment I thought we wouldn't make it. Doing all of the cleaning at the gym for the rest of my life flashed before my eyes, since that was what I would have to do to pay the damn car off.

But we made it. And as we crested the top of the hill, I spotted a familiar faded blue ute. And sitting on the tray, staring out into the clearing, was Chance.

***

"I hear this is the place to be on a Friday afternoon," I said lightly as I approached.

His shoulders twitched, the only sign of surprise he gave me at my sudden presence.

"Can't work out why—it's pretty deserted," I joked.

"Hasn't anybody ever told you that the places with no people around are the best places to be?" he replied, though there was a faint trace of amusement in his voice.

That was something, at least.

"No, they haven't. Most of us don't like to be alone." I walked around JJ's ute to where his legs dangled off the end of the tray. He was leaning back on his hands, the gaps between the leaves in the tree above casting a freckling shadow over his figure. What wasn't casted in shade was glistening under golden sunlight. He looked beautiful. If it weren't for the tempestuous storm raging on in those eyes, he'd look the perfect image of contentment.

Turning my back towards the tray, I pushed up on my hands and lifted myself onto the warm metal. It creaked under my weight but held steady as it always did.

"I like to be alone," he said quietly, gazing out over the green valley of rolling hills and tall trees.

"Oh." My heart sank. *Of course* he wanted to be alone. A living tornado had ripped through his life for the last three years. "I'm sorry. I'll just—"

He stopped me with a strong, warm hand to my thigh.

"You don't count," he murmured, watching the hand on my thigh, waiting for me to move it. "You don't bring noise, you bring quiet."

I wasn't sure what to say to that, or if he even needed me to say anything at all. So, I didn't.

We sat in the quiet of the lookout for hours. Literally, hours. Neither of us spoke a word, just sat in comfortable silence.

The sun had just started to set, the sky brightening with hues of orange and pink, when he finally spoke. "I was sitting right here the day JJ called me with Al's job offer for Knock's." He was still staring so blankly, so lifelessly at the kilometres of nature that stretched out below us. "I sat right here, waiting to end it all."

Shock, pure and real, whizzed through my body. Steadying my hand, I lay it over his that was still holding onto my thigh. A surge of panic flooded my system, the panic of coming so close to losing him for good. Losing him before I'd even known him.

"That call was what stopped me from doing it. Al's offer was more than just another job offer—it was the opportunity of a lifetime. An opportunity for a new start, away from the mess that was my life. I sat up here and promised myself that I would never let it get this bad again. If she was right, and I wasn't enough of a man to have a partner, I simply wouldn't. I would rather be alone for the rest of eternity than live through the fucking nightmare that was my life again. I burned the letter I'd written to leave under one of the picnic tables, went home, packed whatever shit I could into a few meagre duffle bags, and left. I'd called my lawyer on my way back to the house of horrors. As it turns out, he'd already had divorce papers drawn up for the occasion two years ago. He's a good guy, Mitchie, so he came and met me at the house. I put the fat stack of divorce papers underneath my wedding band, top-decked the toilet, and left."

"And then what happened?" I asked softly.

"I went to see my sister." The haunted ice over his face cracked, just a little, at the mention of her. "I hadn't seen her for two years. She'd been in rehab for nearly two and a half. But the second I saw her ... it was all worth it. Every punch, every kick, hell, every *stab*, was worth it. Because she was here, and she was alive and mending her mind."

"Two years is a long time to be in rehab."

"It's one of those special facilities where they don't necessarily have a timeline program. Getting off the drugs is the easy part in comparison to staying off them. I don't know what, but something ... happened to her. When she was living with our mother, something just wasn't right," he said, a slight shake of his head as if trying to clear hazy memories.

"She never told you?"

"We never asked. Dylan and I made a pact not to. She came home with our father one day, and she lived with him and us after that. That was all that mattered. She was safe with us."

"Will she be getting out any time soon?"

He squeezed my thigh gently three times. "She will when she's ready. I was hoping to bring her to the title fight at Darlington Harbour, but I don't think she needs, or wants, to return to the place where it all fell apart." He finally looked at me. "She's gonna love you."

"Me?"

"Yeah. She always wanted a sister growing up. It was on her Santa list for a few years."

"Sounds like we'll have some fun together."

He looked down at me, a heartbreaking storm brewing in those eyes, even though it was a clear sunny day. I couldn't help but reach for him, to put a hand on his face. A subtle, small flinch ricocheted through his body. Apology written clear in his eyes, he turned and pressed his lips into the palm of my hand.

"You know, the day I first bumped into you in Lozza's …" He trailed off before shaking a thought free from his head. "Talia had been blowing up my phone. Threats, accusations, emotional manipulation; the whole lot. I was on the phone with her when I ran straight into you. She was trying to convince me to *'come home'*."

"But you didn't go?" I said softly.

"It was like … the world, the universe, fate—whoever the fuck it is that decided this was where I needed to be—threw me a bone. As soon as my phone fell into that fucking puddle of Sunkist, an unbearable weight lifted from my shoulders."

"It did?" I squeaked, fighting like hell to keep my jaw from slacking.

"It meant she couldn't contact me anymore. I knew it would make things worse in the future. I *knew* it would come back and bite me in the ass. But how could I care when that wasn't now? How could I care when this woman, this beautiful, *beautiful* woman, had brought the sunshine back into my life by drowning the fucking brick that was a communicator of my nightmare of a fucking life?"

Each word got quicker and quicker until he stopped. A stray tear dripped between my fingers from those eyes, so dark and full of hurt. My heart, already beating erratically in my chest, ached for the man in front of me.

He turned his head again, this time softly nuzzling my hand.

"You're here," he murmured, eyeing me warily. Panic flashed across his face, a sudden awareness as to where he was. His gaze flicked behind me, seeing Al's tiny Corolla that I planned to let roll back down the hill in neutral when it was time to leave.

Squeezing his face in my hand, a sad smile was all my mouth could muster.

"I'm here," I reassured him. "I'm here and I believe you."

CHAPTER 54

Mari

Chance hadn't said anything when I'd told him I believed him. He'd just stared at me. In shock? Relief? I'd had no idea what the look on his face was. So, I'd pulled up my big girl pants, reminded myself that this was serious stuff we'd been talking about, and hopped off the tray.

"Come and see me when you're ready. I'll wait for you," I'd told him. A slight nod of his head was all he'd given me before I'd deemed that answer enough and left.

And now, I sat on Nan's old cream and green couch in the living room. Watching the trashiest of reality TV shows? Yes. Paying more attention to the door and its lack of movement? Also yes.

I'd shed my tears for him on the long drive home, dropped Al's car off to him, where I'd found him and Nan sharing a dinner together, and walked the six and a half kilometres home. The sun had fully set by the time I'd gotten back to Soggla, but the sky was still as clear as it had been over the lookout. Stars, hundreds and thousands of little lights in the sky, shone brightly alongside a full moon.

The perfect night to sit in and wait.

***

The fateful knock had come at the door at 12 am. Gus's lack of panic at a visitor at such a strange hour told me all I needed to know.

He is here.

Heart on my sleeve, beating erratically in my chest and deep in my stomach, I opened the door. There he stood, tall and beautiful and loved. So very loved, I itched to say.

But neither of us said anything. Not after he brought his lips down on mine.

The kiss was soft and sensual, our lips fusing together delicately but furiously. I'd missed him.

God, I've missed him.

His scent invaded my senses, that sweet citrus cologne blended with the sweat from a warm day. This smell, it was too familiar. It was home. It was *everything*. *He* was everything.

My fingers slowly ran and tugged though his hair, and he let out a low rasp, sighing from the sensation. Fingertips tapped just below my ass cheeks, urging me to jump.

I obeyed and pushed myself up into his arms. His hands were waiting, cupping straight under my ass when his feet began moving beneath us.

I didn't care where he was taking me.

I've got you. Always. Those first gentle words came to mind, spreading a warmth through my chest.

The feel of the cool wood of the hallway cupboard gingerly graced the backs of my thighs. Chance pulled away, his lips pink and swollen. When his eyes met mine, I felt it. That pulse.

That energy turned *electric*.

I forced my fingers into motion once again as I reached for the hem of my shirt but found Chance already there. His heated fiery gaze landed on mine and he blinked, then, in a single swift movement, I melted as he *tore my shirt off*.

Holy shit.

Those sapphire blue eyes darkened to a stormy ocean blue, full of desire. I can only imagine my own were in a similar state; that raging *need* pulsed through me every second his mouth wasn't on me.

On mine.

On anywhere.

His pupils dilated as his gaze ran from my lips, down the nape of my neck, and swirled across my torso. I had never felt so unbelievably exposed, so enthralled about the *stare* of a man.

This man.

Physically unable to be out of reach from him any longer, I fisted his shirt and pulled his lips onto mine. He yanked his shirt over his head and closed the gaps between us, attacking my lips with such furious hunger. I palmed him through his shorts, and he groaned, nibbling teasingly on my bottom lip. One of his hands ran softly up the inside of my thigh, stopping inches away from the throbbing, wet ache between my legs.

Fucking tease.

As if reading my thoughts, Chance chuckled through his nose, his lips still parted as his tongue explored mine, tasting my own with gentle but intense patterns. My head was spinning; I was becoming positively high on this man.

My hands, so small next to his, scrambled hard to get those god-damn shorts *off*.

Elastic waistband. Thank you, Jesus.

One of his hands found its way around my waist, the other pinning me to the wall with a hand above my head, collapsing me into a warm cocoon of *us*.

Lightly tracing his chest, I felt his thundering heart. The fingers that were gently skimming the bare skin above my shorts pulled me tighter, as if to say, '*Only you. My heart beats like this only for you*'.

"Mmmm, I could sit here and breathe you in all day," he mumbled against my collarbone, his tongue swirling intricate lines against the sensitive spot.

"I-I've got time," I breathed.

Chance's teeth skimmed my skin as a hot, breathy chuckle followed. My inhale hitched as his low hand, now a ghost to my waist, skimmed under my breast. He traced the aching swell, circling lightly around my peaked nipple.

"I missed you," he said, so quietly our breaths almost masked it.

"I'm here."

The words from earlier must have played in his mind, causing him pause.

A small smile later, and his mouth was back on mine as he lifted me once again.

My bedroom door flung open with a *thud* on the wall and slammed shut with another. Soft blankets brushed against my bare back, but his skin on mine felt even better. Callouses brushed against my spine and my bra popped open half a second later.

Chance broke the kiss and tenderly helped me pull my bra straps down my arms. Tossing it aside, his eyes raked greedily over my exposed chest. Maybe greedily wasn't the right word. There was something more tender, softer, and warmer in his gaze.

"You're so beautiful," he said, running his fingers down my arms. A shiver ran up my spine. His fingers traced the outline of my waist, and they soon moved to my pyjama shorts. Delicately, so tenderly and lovingly, he lifted my hips and pulled my shorts off, taking my panties with them. "So fucking beautiful."

My legs dangled off the bed, and his body followed parallel to the lines of my legs. Kneeling before the bed, he began to take my socks off.

The words from our first official introduction rang through my head. *"Not the first time a woman has expected me to bow down to her"*.

And here he was. He who bowed to no one, willingly bending before me to take my damn socks off.

That warmth, the feeling of a million butterflies huddling together in my chest, exploded through my entire body at the gesture.

"Come here," I whispered, sitting up.

He dropped my socks onto the floor beneath him before standing.

Before he could go any further, my fingers dug into the waistband of his underwear and yanked his thick length free. Letting the fabric pool at his feet, I wrapped my hand around the base of his shaft. He hissed a sharp breath in.

"Sunny ..." he mumbled, and I'd never felt so relieved to hear him call me that. "You don't have to."

"I want to," I replied, looking up at him under my lashes. The head of his cock glistened with the sweet moisture from his slit. Anticipation, desire, and need—it was all on display in front of me. I ran my tongue over the droplets, replacing the moisture with that of my mouth.

"But ... *fuck*," he moaned, a twitch of pleasure skittering through his hips.

I wrapped my lips around the whole head this time and took him down as far as my throat would allow. What my mouth couldn't cover, my hand did. Sucking him deeply, pulling on every nerve ending, I looked up to find his eyes tightly closed, shoulders folded forward.

"Mmm," I moaned onto his cock, the edges of my mouth tipping up at the sides when he frantically reached a hand down to fist my hair.

A gentle, urging pressure. Both wanting and needing me to keep going. So I picked up my pace, moving quicker and drawing with more pressure to pull out every ounce of pleasure for him.

This man.

This wonderful man.

This wonderful man that I was falling in love with.

His eyes opened, looking down on me with dilated pupils filled with heat and infatuation. A gentle tug on my hair and he freed his cock from my mouth, multiple rolls of pleasure shivering through his back.

"On your back," he commanded, eyes hooded and cheeks flushed. The raspiness in his voice and the way his hands were still clenched at his sides— he had been close.

I fell back onto the bed, my eyes most likely mirroring his own. Watching and feeling him come so close boosted my libido to never-seen-before levels.

"I need to feel you," he muttered, running his hands from my toes all the way to my hips. Chance placed a light pressure on my hips, pinning them to the mattress. "I just—"

"I'm here." I reached up again and cupped his face.

His lips immediately found the palm of my hand and he released a long breath.

"I'm with you."

And then he was inside me. In one long, quick thrust, every inch of him was gripped tightly. Blinding pleasure erupted in me as I grappled for breath.

"Breathe ... Sunny," Chance rasped, also fighting for air. "I need you to breathe, baby."

Sucking in air felt as easy as breathing underwater. I drew in small gasps just trying to get any oxygen in.

"Fuck ... Fuck!" Chance began to move slowly, and I moaned, my walls refusing to move for him. All I could do was *feel*.

Feel him inside me.

Feel how tightly I was wrapped around him.

Feel how wound up he was already getting.

"Jesus, Chance," I groaned, the head of his cock brushing up against that fucking spot. Pleasure was quickly racking itself up my spine and I trembled, something I hadn't thought possible while on my back.

"Fuck ... you're always so goddamn tight," he groaned, moving slowly inside of me.

"I was made for you," I murmured. "That's why you fit so perfectly."

Long, pleasure-filled strokes of his cock inside me had me quickly ripping up that ladder of pressure. The knot winding tighter and tighter until I couldn't contain it anymore.

I came apart on his cock hard and fast, crying out his name so loudly I'm sure the neighbours would be gossiping about it in the morning. But it wasn't over, that knot wasn't undone.

"Your turn," I told him, pushing up on his shoulders as he allowed me to roll us over. His eyes glazed when he registered what I was doing, where I was.

I rocked my hips back and forth, swirling circles over his. I could barely speak, barely make a noise with how good he felt. How good *we* felt.

"Fuck, you… so good," I ground out.

He groaned a sound of agreement, digging his fingers into my hips.

His biceps flexed as he lifted me up and down on him, helping me ride. I braced my hands on his pecs, hitting the perfect angle. It was obvious he felt it too when both of us let out a string of curses at the same time.

"Yes, yes, Sunny, yes." He lifted a hand from my waist and pressed a finger to my sensitive clit, rubbing and flicking at two-speed of my riding rhythm. He wound that knot up and up and fucking up.

I was sure I would die from pleasure from what was coming.

Self-combust from orgasm seemed like a good way to go. Especially at the hands of Chance Riordan.

My Chance.

But I didn't self-combust, didn't implode into a million pieces. I dove off the edge of that building tension into pleasure, light, love, and warmth. I wasn't breathing, but who cared. Not when Chance was spamming out beneath me and had wrapped his hand in mind. That teasing finger had left, and his hand held my face. He was saying something to me, something I'm sure I would find out later. But the sings of pleasure and love were so loud in my ears, I couldn't focus enough to hear.

I fell to his chest, panting hard, as was he. He wrapped his arms around my back as I curled up over his heart.

"My, my, Sunny baby," he murmured. "You never fail to surprise me."

CHAPTER 55

Mari

The next month went both slow and fast, somehow. Chance and I spent every evening together, but every morning apart. We shared time, finding quiet spots to be alone. The parks on the opposite side of town, the old abandoned dairy farm, or the Murray Chance had had us hauling ass to all those weeks ago.

One of us always packed a blanket and after we we'd both finished and were both basking in post-orgasm glow, we'd lay under the stars. Some nights it was cloudy, so we couldn't see much. And others we came up with new, more entertaining names for some of the clusters in the sky above us.

We laughed, talked, kissed, moaned, and laughed some more. Conversation never stopped flowing. There were never enough kisses, never enough touches. There was never a 'last time'. I never tired of hearing his fighting stories, and all of the mayhem-filled memories from his earlier years. He never cut me off or grew tired of my tales, most containing the same four people: Nan, JJ, Dad, and Al.

I told him about Mum, about her accident many years ago. He told me about his parents' divorce, about his mother's second husband and his father's addiction to work.

He told me more about Milah and Dylan, and I was fully convinced they would set the town on fire the first night they were all back together again.

The nights we spent together were worth the daytime nap times and the pain of waking up early in the morning, only having gone to bed a few hours earlier.

The pretending was a fun little game for us in the gym, stealing glances and meeting eyes here and there. Though we both always lost, each as eager and aching to touch as the other. Chance taught morning classes only now that he was in fight preparation, spending hours a day with JJ, Al, and some of the bigger guys from Knock's. That was followed by sleep, sauna or more sleep. And I spent all day watching him. I was miles behind on work for the gym, but I couldn't help it.

He was *magic*.

"I can't believe I'm actually letting you do this," I laughed nervously as he pressed the buzzing needle into my forearm once again. "For all I know you could be drawing a gigantic dick on my forearm to stay for all of eternity."

"It's not a dick," he replied, though I could hear the amused smirk on his face without even looking. Nan's old radio was faintly humming in the background as we sat at the kitchen table. With the oldies out for the night, that being Nan and Al, Chance had managed to convince JJ to be on 'demon-duty'. Which, much to JJ's dismay, meant ensuring Talia didn't leave his house.

Chance had switched his phone onto silent twenty minutes ago, after the last 'You better bring a fucking priest home to exorcise this place' message.

"When can I look?"

"Not yet."

"When?"

"Not yet."

"*When*?" I sulked.

"*Not yet*," he mocked. "Relax, Sunny baby. It'll be over in a minute."

"I am relaxed."

"If you tense up any more, you're gonna snap the needle," he mused with a teasing laugh.

"I'm not tense!"

"Not anymore," he replied. "Since we're all done."

Instantly snapping my head to my forearm, my heart clenched at the new drawing on my skin. Smudged with excess ink, and with small and delicate lines, was a small *Chance* space from the game *Monopoly* just below my inner elbow.

"Chance." I beamed at the little rectangle on my skin.

"Fitting, since you're the first official tattoo I've ever given. Had to leave a calling card." He smirked, packing his little kit away into the shiny onyx zip-up bag.

"The first? Really?"

"Yup. JJ showed me how to do it. Then, of course, I spoke to someone else—someone with a lot more experience." He winked.

I couldn't make out what it meant.

"And here we are."

"Here we are?"

"Here we are, Sunny baby."

"So, do I get to give you a tattoo now?" I asked, reaching for the little black bag.

"No need." He smirked. "I've already got some new ink for today. I'd say we're even."

"How the hell does that make us even—" I couldn't finish my sentence. Couldn't breathe, couldn't speak, couldn't think when he pulled the already tight black sleeve up over his right arm.

There, filling a clearly unintentional gap in the whirlwind of art, was a small, hand-drawn sun. No bigger than a fifty-cent piece, the circle had over a dozen sun rays pointing out from it.

Sun. Sunshine. *Sunny.*

Fine lines that overlapped where he'd ...*Jesus, did he do this himself?*

"Did it all myself," he said, reading my thoughts with a proud grin warming his face. "JJ helped tidy up the lines a little for me, but I wanted to be the one to draw it."

Leave it to Chance to be instantly good at something as complex as tattooing. I reached out, running my fingers gently over the plastic that was stuck over the top of the slightly raised skin. It was beautiful.

Beautiful.

Beautiful.

Beautiful.

My heart pounded, thudded deeply in my chest like a sledgehammer against a wall. For sure, it was going to pop out of my chest and onto the floor any moment now. I couldn't stop it; I didn't want to stop it. Warmth, that familiar loving flood of warmth, rushed my system.

"What do you think?" he asked softly.

When I looked up to find those oceanic blue eyes, I found a stormy, heated, *electrified* gaze awaiting me.

"It's beautiful," I whispered, my throat welded shut with emotion.

"Yeah?"

"It's …" I ran my fingers over the delicate lines again. "It's perfect."

"I know." He grinned.

***

We'd found a new spot tonight, an old barn house at the back of an empty lot a few doors over from Al's house. His lights had long been turned off when we snuck past—every single curtain drawn closed in his house, a force of habit. Cars drew too much attention to our presence or lack-thereof, so we walked everywhere.

"Didn't we name that one after Hogs the other night?" I asked Chance, referring to the cluster of stars that looked like the gigantic, hunched-over heavyweight who trained at Knock's.

"Well, I'm renaming it to Old Man Larry." He laughed, referencing the man who came down to Knock's once a fortnight to complain about all of the cars parked along the street.

"Fair enough," I said, chuckling. "Hey, Chance?"

"Yeah, Sunny?"

"How long are we gonna do this for?" I asked.

He paused.

"What do you mean?" He sat up, leaning on an arm to stare down at me.

"This, Chance." I pushed up onto my elbows. "All of this sneaking around. When will it end?"

Silence.

His eyes left mine, disassociating into the long grass in the distance. Second by second, new nails would secure his walls back up into place. And with fight week beginning in two days, he was already in a different form of hell that I couldn't relate to. Any of the cash fights I took on were at my walkaround weight, just a cash grab.

"I only ask because I may need to pre-order six-dozen energy drinks—"

"I don't know," he interrupted. His blank, emotionless tone told me Chance had vacated the moment.

"Hey," I mumbled softly, placing a hand on his now turned shoulder. "Where'd you go? Come back to me."

"I'm here, Mari," he replied, running a hand down his face. "Just … don't push me on this. Not on something I don't have any control over."

"What do you mean you don't have control?"

"She can ruin me. With one Instagram post, she can ruin me. As soon as she tells the world that it was me who put hands on her, no one will ever believe me." He gently shrugged my hand off, before picking it up and brushing his lips over my knuckles. The muscles in his biceps were popping since he had already started to drop his calories. His big weight and water cut wouldn't start until fight week. But from my understanding, this was the point when the brain fog and depletion really kicked in.

"What if you told the world first?"

He went as still and rigid as stone.

"The fans, the world, everyone. What if you told them first?"

A second of silence, of taking a moment to think, before a sad, deflated laugh left his lips. "You think anyone will believe me? You think anyone will believe the number one heavyweight contender in the Ultimate Fighting League got beaten by his wife?" Another laugh. "You'd be insane to think that."

"Well, I believe you," I said, feeling my heart rip clean in my chest.

"You and no one else," he said bitterly, too late again. It was something I'd noticed since his weight cut had started.

"Does that not count for anything?" I asked, swallowing the shake in my voice.

"Not for my career, no."

"Right." I stood, brushing the few leaves I'd managed to lay on. "I'd better get home."

"Why?"

"I'm sorry for what happened to you, Chance."

Those blue eyes flared.

"I'm sorry that you fell in love with the wrong person, and that she used and abused you and your heart and your money. But I can't do this forever."

"Sunny—" he started.

"I deserve better than this," I said.

And when a reply failed to come, I left.

Chapter 56

Chance

What JJ had spoken about the entire drive into Darlington Harbour, I couldn't even say. I couldn't even describe the plain chicken breast I'd had for breakfast this morning, or how good the third litre of water I had in my hand felt going down.

I hadn't spoken to Sunny since that night outside the abandoned barn. I felt empty, like a piece of rubbish rolling around in the wind. And part of that had nothing to do with the scarcity of sugar and energy in my body.

I was three days out from the biggest fight of my life, and all I could think about was *her*.

Mari.

Sunny.

Her.

Instead, I was standing with Al, my best friend, and the human embodiment of evil. She always insisted on being in as much of my press as possible, feeding me lines to thank her for and everything. Right now, I couldn't even argue. I couldn't even remember the fucking things she wanted me to say. I felt so wobbly, so full of nothing. Every breath of air felt thick and heavy.

"Y'okay, buddy?" JJ asked.

"Yeah, mate," I replied, looking over my shoulder to Talia fixing her makeup with the stupidly expensive gold compact she bought from my first ever cash purse from the UFL. "Sunny here?"

"She's out with Marilyn and Paige."

"Paige?" I asked. The more I could ask to keep JJ talking, the less I had to. And—the less chance Talia would come and interrupt. She and JJ had had … confrontations before. She wouldn't dare try anything here where someone could be pointing a camera towards her.

"She does a lot of the gym's photography and videography. You'll know her when you see her."

I doubted my eyes would be searching for her in a crowd.

"Dylan?"

"One of the seccies just came and checked he was part of our party, so he'll be here soo—speak of the devil."

"How we doin', boys?" Dylan towered me by about two inches, but I was the bigger of us two.

Well, not right now. Right now, I was a plastic bag blown up with two puffs of air.

"Fucking fantastic, D-dog!" JJ cheered, launching himself at my brother. "Good to see you again!"

"JJ," he said, patting him on the back to signal him to let go.

"JJ," he said again.

"J!" I snapped, whacking him on the back. He dropped immediately.

"Ow! The fuck was that for?!" he whined, rubbing his back. "Thank god you're here, Dylan. He's been so cranky."

"Gee, I wonder why," my brother said before turning to me.

"Chance!" a feminine voice called.

A glance over my shoulder told me it was the chick from Knock's who was always running around with a big, red camera in her hands. Clutching a phone in one hand and her camera in the other, her hands had those same triangles, circles, and diamonds on them.

But that one glance couldn't tell me why my brother had gone as rigid as a rock beside me.

"Sorry to bother!" she chirped, slowing to a stop in front of me. "Mind if I get some pre-face-off photos?" She beamed a full-face smile before running an inked hand through her hair.

"Sure—"

"Paige?" My brother interrupted.

That beaming, happy, kind face of the woman in front of me morphed into a scowl. Her eyebrows pinched together, fizzing out the light that had been in her eyes just moments ago. "Prince Disgusting," she hissed. "I would ask you how you are, but we both know that I don't *fucking* care."

Hearing a girl wearing a green and white floral skirt and a bright pink vest swear at my brother might have just been the best thing I'd ever witnessed. I tucked the memory away in my mind. Later. I would enjoy this later. When I didn't feel like hot, steaming garbage.

She stormed off, and I failed to contain my laughter. Less than half a second later, JJ joined me in holding our stomachs from laughing too hard.

"Jesus, Dyl. What did you do to that poor girl?"

"I-I-I just—" he stuttered.

"I-I-I just," JJ mimicked. "Jesus, Deedee. I don't think I've ever seen someone talk to ya like that without copping a smack from ya."

"You good?" Dylan asked me, ignoring JJ's comment. I may have been depleted, may have been feeling like a steaming pile of horse shit, but even I could see the haunted look that had fallen onto my brother's face.

I flicked my head over to where Talia was standing, taking photos of all of the signage with my name on it.

Dylan groaned, muttering a not-so-quiet curse on the end of it. "Want me to take care of that?"

At my brother's words, JJ immediately squared his shoulders.

"Just leave it. I don't have the energy to deal with the fallout of that."

Understatement of the century.

***

Five and a half hours, and a fuckload of media presences later, I was standing side stage waiting for the announcer to call me up onto stage for the face-off with Randy.

My stomach was so empty, I was teetering on a fine line I could feel would turn into a cramp at any second. I had no salt, no sugar, no food on board. I was so depleted that I didn't even feel hungry anymore.

Yay. Fight week.

"And now, the number one contender, Chance Riordan," the announcer said.

My hearing muffled over as I walked out onto the stage. All of my energy poured into keeping my shoulders back, my chin up, and that fucking smirk on my face.

From the way Randy was shifting slightly from foot to foot, I could tell he was doing the same.

The referee for Saturday's fight signalled me to my mark and Randy to his. He reeked; the smell even more pungent when he stepped into my space.

"I've fuckin' got ya, Riordan," he snarled, his stupid smirk on his face.

I laughed. I laughed long and hard. So long that Randy's face morphed into a scowl as he shoved at my chest.

I'd seen it coming, knew he wanted to be first to put hands on me. So I'd planted my feet, not even staggering when he shoved at my chest. I stood tall, playing pretend like I did with Sunny.

Pretended like making weight was easy.

Pretended that I felt strong and powerful.

Pretended I was capable of fighting this cunt right here and now.

Multiple seccies and stage people separated us then, though I quickly pushed them off. Breathing felt thick and heavy, like a fucking chore. The less people taking up oxygen around me, the better.

"Would the fighters please take their seats." The interviewer stood on a podium, Randy and I on either side of him. Someone in the front row opened a muesli bar. The crinkling wrapper sound drilled straight into my ears and the smell of sugar hit me like a fucking truck.

***

Question after question we were asked.

"What are your plans for this fight?"

"How do you feel about your training?"

"How do you feel about your opponent's training?"

My head pounded, hypoglycaemia well and truly underway. I could practically feel the calories falling off me.

"Chance, a little birdie told us you have someone special to dedicate all of your hard work to?"

I hadn't seen her before. But at the question, of course I found her. She stood along the side of the crowded room. Her beautiful curls were pulled on top of her head, though the same strays fell around her face. A black T-shirt dress fell loose around her frame but was pulled around her waist by a thick black belt. Across the chest, in big orange letters, was the Knock's logo. Those mile-long legs finished with a pair of plain black heels that made her legs look even longer. She'd done her makeup for the occasion, but she clearly hadn't caked it on like Talia—

Shit.

There was something I was meant to say here.

"I wouldn't have been able to do this without the support of my wonderful, loving wife, Talia."

The crowd let out cheers of applause and appreciation. Love was something everyone could relate to.

But I didn't feel it, not when I spoke of Talia.

I felt it for the woman at the back of the room, with the face filled with devastation. Her eyes were on mine, even though she was more than fifty metres away. I could practically feel the hurt radiating off of her.

My mouth started to move when her feet headed for the door.

"Wait!" I shouted, standing to my feet.

Where did this energy come from?

She paused, glancing over her shoulder. That one stray curl I liked to brush away fell over her forehead.

"Bray," I addressed the interviewer. "I'd like to change my answer."

The man nodded me on. The crowd had gone deathly silent, and I could feel the steam coming from Talia's ears brushing up against the back of my neck.

"The only thing I have Talia to thank for, is for giving me a reason to leave her."

Gasps bounced through the crowd, followed by friends hushing them down, eager to hear more. But all I could focus on was Sunny. She'd turned back towards me, hands folded over her chest as one reached up to cover her mouth. "If she hadn't done all she'd done—if she hadn't hit me, kicked me, and tore me down—I would never have left Darlington Harbour. I would never have moved out to Soggla, where my best friend and new martial arts family were waiting for me. And I never would have met the real love of my life."

I paused, glancing around the room at the crowd hanging off my every word.

No going back now.

"My name is Chance Riordan. And I'm a victim of domestic violence."

Talia screamed.

The crowd was murmuring, yelling all kinds of things.

JJ and Dylan could have been swapped out for the clown carnival game, their mouths were open so wide.

And Al? Al gave me a single approving nod.

"No! You liar! You—"

"Enough," I growled, holding a hand up to her as she approached. She froze in her spot.

I turned to where Randy was sitting, clearly enjoying the moments he didn't have to use extra energy.

"I'll see you in the ring." I turned back towards Talia. Those piercing, ice-blue eyes had an avalanche tumbling down a hill inside of them. Collapse of the world she knew, of the control she'd thought she had. Fear and panic at the nightmares she'd built collapsing around her evident on her face.

"And you?"

She opened her mouth to speak, but I beat her to it.

"I'll see you in court."

This room was too loud, so I went where I knew it would be quiet. Straight to Sunny.

Chapter 57

Mari

All I could hear was my pounding heart, and his voice.

"My name is Chance Riordan. And I'm a victim of domestic violence."

He'd done it. He'd *actually* done it.

Pride and shock swelled through every inch of my body. That familiar fire burned brightly in my hand, the one that was safely intertwined in mine.

Al, Dylan, and JJ had quietly followed Chance off the stage after his confession. We'd all but sprinted to the underground carpark, eager to beat the rush of reporters and fans.

"Hang on, Chan," Dylan had called when Chance was holding the door of Reggie open for me. JJ slid into the back of Al's little Corolla, and I wondered how Dylan would fit in there too.

Before I could ponder it anymore, Dylan pulled me in for a bone-crushing hug.

"Thank you," he whispered in my ear.

***

The four-hour drive back from Darlington Harbour was silent, but Chance's hand stayed firmly on my thigh the entire time. His jaw was locked so tight I was surprised the bones weren't whining. I knew why, of course. His phone had also remained silent, but that silence wasn't comfortable. It was like that false sense of calm before a storm hit. Before disaster struck.

The sun was proudly shining when we passed the rusty old red and white sign that read, 'Welcome to Soggla'. There were some new fresh cracks in the paint. Chips had fallen off on the tail end of the 'a'. Soon it would read, 'Welcome to Sogglo'.

But then something strange happened. The streets, the birds, hell even nature, all seemed to pause for us. The stretches of road that usually had scattered cars parked—empty. The tiny excuse of a carpark for Rusty's was bare, not even a magpie or pigeon lingering nearby. Even the wind that usually swept through the eucalyptus and gum trees in the park halted.

Chance's grip faltered at my thigh and that stormy gaze scanned the roads, looking for that missing normalcy. Anything—a car, a butterfly, a person. Anything.

We rounded the corner, heading straight towards the gym. I lurched forward when Chance slammed on the breaks. My seatbelt dug snugly into the corner of my neck.

"What the fuck?" he muttered.

Long orange barricades had been placed over the road, fencing off any cars from driving through. On the other side, the street was crammed full of vehicles. A metallic sign glistened in the sun, rust coating the edges since it probably hadn't been dragged out for at least a few decades.

'*Event in Progress*' it read.

"Do you know anything about this?" That wary, annoyed tick in Chance's jaw was more noticeable with all the weight he'd dropped being so close to the fight.

"No idea."

People stood in large groups chatting on the road. Smiles and pleasantries seemed to be being exchanged. But the biggest crowd was standing on Knock's' gravel driveway. The sun was shining so brightly, I couldn't see the top.

My phone buzzed in my back pocket.

"It's JJ," I told Chance, feeling in awe of the gigantic crowd of people standing in my town. "Hey—"

"Lynnie! Where are you guys? You need to get to the gym now!" JJ's excitement only furthered my confusion.

I glanced around, looking for him.

"There." Chance pointed to the base of the driveway, where our best friend was standing, squirming in anticipation. His eyes widened and a grin broke out on his face when he saw us.

Chance threaded his fingers through mine and tugged me through the crowd.

Muttering soft apologies when I bumped into people, I noticed people were clearing a path for him.

"You guys have gotta see this!" He waved a hand and took off up the driveway. "Coming through! Coming through!"

Chance held tight onto my hand, squeezing it three times.

We were at the top before I could respond. Dozens, hundreds, maybe even thousands, of pieces of paper were stuck to the entire front wall of Knock's. Pink, yellow, white, blue, green. No particular pattern seemed to occur, but every piece of paper had writing on it.

Vandalism? But what were all of these people doing here for?

My eyes found Chance, as they always did. His face pale, he swallowed deeply. A sheen of mist coated his eyes, and his nose turned a faint shade of pink.

JJ reached a hand out and put it on Chance's shoulder. "Go and read them, man. They're here for you."

He pulled me by our hands over to the wall. If Chance hadn't been holding my hand, I would have fallen to my knees.

My boyfriend threw a drink in my face, a few weeks later he threw the damn glass.

My fiancée refuses to let me sleep until we've had sex.

My boyfriend's friend hit on me and groped me at a party. My boyfriend slapped me when he found out.

My wife sucker punched me for talking too long to a cashier when we were getting groceries. She told me no one would believe me, that I was a man, and I should be able to take it.

Story after story was hung up for everyone to see. Horrors at the hands of mothers, fathers, siblings, relatives, partners, and friends. These shitty, horrible, life-altering experiences were no longer a deadlocked memory in someone's mind. But *spoken*. Out in the open for the world to see.

"The Chronicles of Hidden Abuse," JJ read from the banner that lay at our feet. The crowd behind us had gone silent.

I. Love. You. I squeezed Chance's hand.

He turned his head to face me, those stormy eyes I loved so much starting to loosen raindrops. The eerie calm before the storm was no more—the rain was here.

I reached a hand up to wipe one of the stray tears away when he caught it. Brushing his lips over my knuckles, he mumbled, "It's okay."

Squared shoulders and a lifted chin turned to face those silent around us. Many of them smiled appreciatively, hope and relief filling their faces. Relief, not because they wanted anyone to experience what they had, but relief knowing someone they looked up to *had*. Relief knowing they weren't alone, and that there was at least one person out there who understood at least some small inkling of what they were going through.

Most of the people gathered around us were women, but I saw the few dozen men scattered about. Most lingered along the far fence line, but one man stood front and centre of them all. He was holding the hand of a beautiful dark-skinned woman by his side and staring at the man at mine. His eyes were glassy, and his mouth was trembling. That familiar shift in the air around me drew my eyes to Chance, who's jaw was locked down under immense tension.

He stepped forward and walked towards the man. The crowd, including myself, seemed to hold their breath. Rocks skidded under his feet as he paused, those blue eyes meeting mine. The clouds parted behind the storm, delivering a message to me on a beam of new sunshine. Ironic, since he was the one who called me 'Sunny'.

I need you with me.

I didn't hesitate—I didn't want to hesitate anymore. Not when it came to him.

"I've got you," I mumbled for only him to hear. The hand on my back pressed three short times. *I. Love. You.*

We beelined for the man whose nose was now beginning to flush red.

He stepped forward, standing about half a foot taller than me. Neither man said anything, until the former fumbled for his dark-washed jeans pocket. He stretched his arm down, digging deep into his pocket. A brief flicker of triumph on his weary face, and he pulled out a note. Folded, crumpled and lint strings attached, he handed it immediately to Chance. I didn't dare look at what was on it, not with how still the teary-eyed man had gone. That familiar wave of tension flung off Chance's already rigid stature before he neatly refolded the note and tucked it into a pocket of his own.

"I believe you," he told the man.

And that was the beginning of it all.

CHAPTER 58

Mari

Chance listened to every single person who showed up at Knock's. The words 'I believe you' were spoken too many times to count, both given and received. This time, I didn't feel that pang of jealousy when hundreds of women hugged him, cried on him, sought comfort in him and that beautiful heart he had. How could I when he introduced me to each and every one of them as 'the sunny day at the end of the dark tunnel'? Even after hearing it on repeat for hours, my heartbeat still flicked over into double time whenever he said it.

Gradually, we moved together down the driveway and out onto the road that was still closed. Some of the regulars from Rock-It's had pulled the old barbecue out and were currently getting snags and bread lined up for anyone around. Rocco and his new squeeze, who's pink hair matched the bright leather jacket she wore, laid out a few esky's filled with beer and mixed cans. Noodles, Danny, and some of the Lozza's boys had strapped some old speakers in the tray of Lozza's delivery ute. Two of the blokes had sat in the back, holding them all down. The oldies from Nan's gossip group had shown up with dozens of packets of glowsticks. The few children that were around loved it and took it upon themselves to make sure each adult had a glowstick around their wrist as the sun started to set.

I smiled as it all unfolded.

Because this is what Soggla did—they turned shitty circumstances into a party. A party filled with love, support, and peace. Fights were never started at big community events, despite having such a high-quality martial arts gym in town. New friendships were forged, memories were made, and looming shadows faded for the time being. The glowstick-clad children ran around, oblivious to the sorrowful circumstances as to which everyone had come to meet under today. The locals hugged anyone who needed it and cracked open a cold one for the others.

"How you doin', darlin'?" Al asked, bumping up beside me.

"I don't think I'm the one you should be asking that."

"Where is the big fella anyways?"

"Not sure. He went to get us something to drink about twenty minutes ago. Figured he probably just wants some time out for a minute. It's been a very big, very emotional afternoon for everyone," I replied, blowing a raspberry through my lips. "Where's Nan?"

"She's off setting up a cards tables down near Wally's house on the corner there. Some of the oldies are putting together some games. Look." He pointed over my shoulder to the faded yellow house on the corner block. "They've already got a line up waiting. They're betting with Louisa's biccies, I hear."

"Those biccies are worth more than money can buy," I replied.

"I don't want to step on your toes, darlin'. But I think after the day, week, year that he's had. I don't think he would mind a bit of familiar company."

"I better go find him." I gave Al a small smile and walked off.

***

I'd checked just about everywhere before I spotted him. Sitting halfway down the hill that Knock's was on, his hands braced behind him while he stretched his legs out in front. His black shirt blended into the night around him. The only way I'd spotted him was from the green and blue glowsticks on his wrist.

I didn't say anything when I dropped down next to him. We sat in that comfortable, peaceful silence for a few minutes, the music blaring in the background, laughter and sounds of joy off in the distance. But Chance and I? We sat in our bubble. I took his glowsticks off, as well as my own, and tucked them under a particularly long tuft of grass.

I ran a hand over his buzzed hair, now long enough that the ends didn't prickle my skin. With a gentle tug on his neck, he lay his head to rest on my lap.

"I don't want to feel like this anymore, Sunny." He sighed, and my heart cracked.

"Feel like what?"

"Wounded," he replied. "She's not worth anything more than the dirt our asses are currently on. But it's like there's a constant spotlight on this part of me she broke. No matter how much I achieve, how far I work up the ranks. No matter how far I go, no matter what I do, Sunny—it's always there."

"It's okay to feel hurt, Chance," I said softly.

"But I don't want to feel hurt for her."

"Then feel hurt for you. Not for her, or me, or anyone else. Just you. Feel hurt for the young man she sucker punched. For the man who has too kind of a heart to ever think about swinging back. Feel hurt for the man whose love of himself and his *life* was taken, Chance. It's okay to feel it but feel it for you."

And so he did. Drops of water slipped onto my thighs, one after the other. I didn't count, didn't keep track of time. I sat still, running one hand over his hair and the other one squeezing that pattern over and over.

I. Love. You.

Tears of my own fell, not for myself, but for him. For the man I'd come to know, had come to love. For the man who kept my heart in his hands every single day and climbed obstacle after obstacle without dropping it. For the man whose wife had hit him on the stairs all those years ago, who'd thought it was truly just an accident.

CHAPTER 59

Chance

I fucking hated weigh-ins.

Getting up on the scales, pretending like I didn't feel like I'd been robbed of all forms of energy, pretending like I was still me in this state.

I wasn't me. I was a fucking ghost of what I would be in twenty-four hours' time.

But she was holding my hand. She hadn't let go since she'd found me in the field behind Knock's. Had held it for the last of my water load, and for the big challenge of letting all of that water go. She'd sat in the sauna with me for every round, quietly sipping on water beside me.

She'd held my hand during the hot bath and sweat suit rounds, waiting patiently and quietly beside me. Because that was what she did, she brought the quiet.

The only time she'd let go was to check the bath temperature, or to go and eat. Which, at that stage, I had been confident in saying that I fucking really could have gone for a bit of bread.

She squeezed my hand three times, and I looked down to her with an eyebrow raised. Sunny was ready and waiting, with a soft but bright smile on her face. She looked the perfect picture of sunshine in the yellow sundress she was in today.

I'd listened to Marilyn beg her to wear it this morning, and to her softly argue about *not* wearing it. She'd taken one look at me, in what would be my third-last round in the sweatsuit, and caved.

Like I said, she brought the quiet.

She grinned up at me, and I couldn't help but plant a quick kiss to her forehead. I couldn't form words or even think of something to say to her, to tell her how grateful I was. We'd barely spoken in the last twenty-four hours, but her actions had spoken plenty.

I squeezed her hand back three times.

"Next, to the scales. One half of the main event to compete for the undisputed Light Heavyweight Championship belt of the Ultimate Fighting League. The number one contender. Chance Riordan."

"Remember to suck in your stomach for the cameras," JJ told me. I snickered.

I stepped onto the scale, standing tall with my chin up. It took everything in me not to falter, not to tremble. I was barely sure I was there—my mind felt so hazy I wouldn't have been surprised if I woke up from this.

"Chance Riordan. Weighing in at two-hundred and five pounds."

I held my arms up at my shoulders, flexing my biceps for the short, tubby man behind the camera.

"Five, four, three, two, one," he called. Then, the asshole, ate a handful of chips from a jumbo bag I could *smell* from here.

Ease up, mate. You're in no condition for what you're thinking.

The chunky prick shot me a thumbs up, signalling me off the scales.

"Next to the scales. The other half of the main event to compete to defend his current title as the undisputed Light Heavyweight Championship of the Ultimate Fighting League. The champion. Randy Rager."

Speaking of pricks…

Randy shoulder-charged me as he passed, but I caught his foot leaving him to clumsily fumble over his feet.

"Been walking long?" I sniggered.

JJ, Dylan, and Sunny all laughed behind me.

"I'm fuckin' coming for you, Riordan," he growled back.

"Keep it in your pants, will ya?" I tossed over my shoulder, sending a wink Sunny's way. Her hourglass figure looked absolutely ravishing in that goddamn sundress. And knowing she hadn't wanted to wear it? I'd happily tear it off her.

"I'll keep it in hers."

Sunny's face dropped, as did my joking demeanour.

"The fuck did you just say?" I asked in that quiet, painstakingly smooth voice.

Turning towards him, that ugly, fucked-up smile he wore. His face looked like mine—cheekbones hanging out and jawline sharper than ever. He was completely drained of water.

'*You could still take him,*' my mind whispered.

"You heard me." Another flash of that grin. "Quite a piece you got there, Riordan. Be a shame if you had to share her."

Every last ounce of energy rushed my body instantly, fuelling adrenaline as if it was a re-feed and a gallon of water. My fingers tingled in anticipation and my toes pushed me forward. I'd crossed the room quicker than I'd realised I could in this state.

The clouds over my mind cleared, narrowing in on the cunt on the scales. I briefly registered the look of surprise on his face before I dove on his hips, picking the prick up and throwing him onto a nearby table. There were vague sounds of things crashing to the ground, and I think I was yelling?

Someone caught my raised fist before I could land it square on his jaw. His face was going purple. Why was it going purple? Why was he holding his breath? Another hand tugged on my wrist, pulling it away from his throat.

Oh, that was why.

"You're dead, Riordan," Randy rasped as multiple pairs of strong arms dragged me away. I thrashed, pulling, and freeing myself gradually from their grip. But there were at least three of the fuckers, and every time I gained on one, another grabbed me twice as hard.

"I'm coming for you *and* her," was all I heard before they rounded me past a corner.

A flash of a head of blonde hair pushed past us, heading for that prick face.

Fuck, I need food.

CHAPTER 60

Chance

"Argh!!" I grunted, throwing the kick as hard as I could into the pads currently protecting Al's arms. Being the main event, Randy and I's fight was the last on the card. Pairs of fighters left and returned. Half victorious, half already being taken to the hospital. Training kits got packed away, bags and pads carted out one by one.

He sighed.

"Take five, Chance. I'm not holding for you unless you're gonna concentrate."

I kicked my water bottle over as I stalked to the bench, bursting with energy. My body had absorbed a good re-feed and some water like a sponge in a bathtub. I reached for my phone but was met with a tauntingly blank screen.

No new messages.

Fuck sake.

I huffed out a consistent stream of breaths, trying to force the frustration out of my body. I picked up the skipping rope, needing to do something about this relentless energy buzzing inside me.

Where is she?

"Relax, Rio. She'll be here."

I jumped at JJ's voice, almost stumbling out of my skin at the *content* of what he'd said.

"Dude!" I clipped him over the ear. "Keep it down, will you?!" I whisper-yelled in his face.

Dear god, this dude really needs to lay off on the onion rings.

I peered subtly over JJ's shoulder to Al chatting peacefully to Marilyn.

Thank god.

"Ah, I wouldn't worry about Al. He's totally team Chari," JJ stated, shrugging his shoulders and downing the rest of his Mountain Dew.

"Chari?"

"Yeah. Chari. As in Chance and Mari."

I stared at the person in front of me that I, myself, had labelled as my best friend. "The fact that things like that don't weird me out anymore kind of concerns me," I replied.

JJ smirked and opened his mouth to speak when I heard her.

"Let me in! I told you—I'm the owner of the goddamn gym Riordan trains at!"

I bolted to the door and swung it open, narrowly missing JJ's face from how close behind he was.

"HEY!" I bellowed.

The three hefty security guards stopped and looked to me.

If I wasn't so occupied by the fact that she was currently being restrained, I probably would have laughed at how it took three grown men to keep her still in the first place. "You heard her. She's with me."

They glanced down at her before turning back to me.

"Get your *fucking hands* off of her!" It was like the whole world around me had gone radio silent. I tunnelled in on the hands that were still wrapped around Sunny's wrists and waist. The second my foot hit the ground, they dropped her roughly onto her feet.

Pricks.

"You made it."

I heard JJ slip inside behind me.

JJ, I owe you one, mate.

"I'm sorry I got caught up after weigh-ins and then the meet and greet, and then I lost my hotel room key and then I get this call from Dad's facility saying he'd made a jailbreak trying to come and see you fight and so I had to hustle for a last-minute ticket for him and drive out to go and fucking get the trickster himself and then I get here and they said there was already a 'Marilyn' inside and I tried to reason with them but those assholes couldn't believe that two people could have the same fucking name and I—"

I cut her off and pulled her into my chest. Her gorgeous red dress was flush against me. I was probably getting sweat on it, but I didn't care.

She was here.

My home is here.

"Are you okay?" she asked.

I pulled away, the gold on her eyelids shimmering under the low light. The shiny, golden colours on her face highlighted the honey brown her eyes were today.

She is happy.

And I was beyond whipped over this girl.

"Can you do me a favour?" I asked. "Stay with Hogs and JJ tonight, okay?"

She looked at me with that fire crackle in her eyes, like she was readying to push.

"No problem," she replied.

***

"Better!" Al yelled. "Fuck yes, Chancey boy! Much better!"

I bumped the pad to signal a break.

"WOOOOOOOOO! RIO DE JANIOROOOOOOOOOO! WOOOOOOO!" JJ's loud cheers echoed through the room.

"Rio de Janioro?" Al asked.

"Yup!" JJ beamed, and I groaned at where this joke was going. "What's in Rio, Al?"

"Uh ... I dunno? The big j—"

"THE BIG JESUS!" JJ cheered, pointing down at me.

I glanced over to Mari sitting in the corner, bouncing between tapping away on her phone and scuffling through paperwork with a highlighter. Her straightened hair fell over her face, and I could tell she had been stress-sweating a little before she'd managed to heist her way in here—some of her curls were starting to come back around her face.

God, she is so fucking beautiful.

"Five minutes before you're backstage, Chance." Marilyn reappeared with a tray of coffees and a beer. To my surprise, she handed the beer to Mari with a knowing smile.

Sunny downed half of it almost instantly.

"C'mon, mate, let's get you ready." Al patted me on the shoulders as JJ shrugged a jacket up my arms.

I waited for the usual rush of adrenalin to start. I waited for the typical surge in my heart rate. I looked across the room.

At Al, who had taken on one last fighter to get me here to the big stage once again.

At Marilyn, who had taken a chance on a fighter down on spirits and pushed him to thrive as a coach.

At JJ, who had saved my ass on more than one occasion, but who would always be the one whose call saved my *life*.

And Mari, who had shown me what it was like to be loved exactly as *me*—who proved to me that love was not transactional but a consistent partner dance through every twist and turn.

I couldn't fight the smile that stretched across my face at the realisation; that survival-mode surge I'd waited for, what had used to be driven by threat and fear, was now driven by the love for the team around me. For the grit and the determination they had all taught me in their own ways.

"Well, that's my cue." Mari stood with an empty beer bottle in her hand. She passed it back to Marilyn and, to my surprise, wrapped her arms around my neck.

Her perfume, mixed with the sweet smell of *her*, flooded my senses.

"Remember to stay with Hogs and JJ," I whispered in her ear.

Gooseflesh lit up her bare back.

"You got this, Chance," she whispered in return. "You've earned this. This is yours."

"Rio." JJ gently patted my shoulder. "It's time, man."

***

"Saw your girl out there tonight, Riordan." Randy's sick, slow voice smashed through every fucking heightened sense.

My fingers began to tingle. Not in fear, but in absolute anticipation to drop the prick in front of me.

"She'll look better once she's cuffed to my headboard though."

JJ caught me just in time.

One of his cornermen had disappeared. The biggest one, who's name I couldn't remember, leaving his corner down to two.

"Fuck," I muttered. "JJ, Hogs—"

He grabbed me by the shoulders. "He's already onto her, man," JJ stated. I'd never heard him speak so calmly. "Dylan is sitting two rows behind her too."

I let out a sigh of relief. Hogs would be a pain in the ass to get through, but Hogs *and* my brother? Surely that was enough of a nightmare to steer any bastard away from her.

"This is your time, bro." JJ pulled his forehead down to mine. "Mari's safe. Make sure that *cunt* isn't."

CHAPTER 61

Mari

Sweat beaded on the backs of my legs as Randy Rager's walkout song came on and the devil himself emerged from the chute. That antagonistic, irritating smirk was planted on his mouth as his eyes scanned the crowd. They met mine as he passed by where I was sitting next to the beast that we called Hogs. I could have sworn his lips lifted farther, but I definitely didn't imagine that wicked flash that crossed over his face.

"Is this why you've been assigned guard duty over me?" I asked Hogs, plastering a bored look over my face as I held eye contact with Randy.

Fuck this guy.

"Partially." He shrugged and shoved half of his hotdog in his mouth.

I was antsy waiting for Chance to walk out. My knees were bouncing all over the place and I was trying my goddamn best not to watch Randy do his pathetic little pre-dance routine. I fought back a scowl as the crowd cheered for him.

Randy Rager—*a known monster.*

Randy Rager—*the pig who had alluded to disgusting, corrupted actions against me at the weigh-ins twenty-four hours ago.*

Randy Rager—*Chance's next victim.*

Then it came on. That strumming baseline of "Seven Nation Army" I'd familiarised myself to after Chance's little 'google it' comment from right back at the beginning. Before he was ... well, *my Chance.*

Chance waited the first ten seconds before he appeared at the start of the chute. His eyes scanned the countless people around the arena before settling on me. He smirked for a second, no more than a heartbeat, and began stalking up the walkway to the cage. His eyes were ahead, almost looking bored if I didn't know better.

One of the referees patted him down, checking his gloves, shorts, and mouthguard. Next the cut-man stepped in, smearing vaso across multiple points of his face before turning Chance back towards his corner.

His corner that was filled with people we loved; our *family.*

JJ and Nan took a moment with Chance—Nan no doubt saying the exact words she'd said to my father all of those years ago.

"You are brave. You are fierce. You are loved. *No matter today's result, that will never change. Go on, my warrior."*

Then it was Al's turn. Al, who had come out of retirement for one last fighter. Al, who had been reminded of a younger version of himself in Chance. Al, who had changed yet another life he'd touched.

Not many words were exchanged between the two, but the tight, long embrace said enough.

Chance did his quick bumps on the archway as he entered the octagon. To others it wouldn't have looked like much, but it was as close to a pre-fight routine as he got.

"If I lose a fight because I didn't kiss each step on my way up to the cage, I shouldn't have won it either." His words echoed in my head as he did a very quick, very brief lap around the ring, completely ignoring Randy's presence, before settling into his corner.

The announcer stepped into the middle of the octagon. "Ladies and gentlemen, this is—the main event of the evening!"

Screams, cheers, and whistles roared through the crowd as he introduced the judges for the evening.

"And now! For those in attendance and UFL fans watching all over the world! This is the moment you've all been waiting for! Live! From the sold-out Lockdown Arena in Darlington Harbour, Australia!"

"It's time!! Five rounds, for the undisputed UFL Light Heavyweight Championship of the world!"

"Introducing first, fighting! Out of the blue corner, a mixed martial artist, holding a professional record, twelve wins, one loss. He stands at six-feet-two-inches tall, weighing in at two hundred and five pounds, fighting! Out of Colltown, Australia, presenting, the current UFL light heavyweight champion of the world! Randy Rager!"

I watched Chance, pacing coolly in his corner. The red shorts he wore, shaping his muscled legs and ass perfectly, matched the red at the base of his gloves. I glanced down at my own attire.

Had a little surprise up your sleeve, did you, Chance?

"And now! Introducing, fighting, out of the red corner, a mixed martial artist, holding a professional record of ten wins, no losses. Standing six-feet-three-inches tall, weighing in at two hundred and five pounds, fighting! Out of Soggla, Australia. Presenting! The number-one contender for the UFL Light Heavyweight Championship! The challenger! Chance 'Rio' Riordan!"

***

Chance was losing.

It made my body physically ache watching every hit he took. The cut on his left eyebrow was deeply split now, blood pouring down his face. He wouldn't be able to take many more hits before they stopped the fight because of it. Chance knew it too. He'd switched back to predominantly using a southpaw stance, leaving the right side of his face further exposed.

His cheek was busted as well as his lower lip. Bruised marks were already beginning to form on his high cheekbones, and I dreaded what his beautiful face would look like tomorrow morning.

The bell signalled the end of the fourth round, the referee pulling Chance and Randy apart.

Time is running out.

"Where do you think you're going?" Hogs asked, his huge arm pinning my body back into my seat.

"Hogs, you gotta let me get in there, man," I begged. "He needs my help!"

"You can help him by keeping your little ass in this seat until the end of this fight," he replied, sipping on his coke whilst he single-handedly held me down.

"Hogs."

He sat quietly.

"Hogs."

Silence.

"HOGS!"

More. Fucking. Silence.

"I'll give you a free gym membership for a year," I bargained.

"Not worth losing my dick when Chance cuts it off for letting you go."

"ARGH!" I huffed in raging frustration. "I'll give you unlimited Knock's gear."

"My dick is worth more."

LIGHTBULB MOMENT HERE, MARI.

"I'll get you a date with JJ." I smirked. His thinking music was all I needed to jump out of my seat and onto the floor. I ducked and weaved security guards like a woman on a mission before heading straight to the open cage door. I was on the first step when one of them caught me.

"NO!" I screamed. "Chance! Al!"

A wave of relief went through Chance's eyes but was quickly replaced with concern. The cut on his eyebrow was brutal, but he waved off JJ holding a cotton tip to it and started to stand. Though he wasn't the first to speak.

"Put her down!" Al bellowed, and I swear the whole stadium went quiet. The two hands that were holding me off the ground quickly left my sides, and I dropped to the floor.

I scrambled to my feet, ignoring the pain shooting up my ribs. I'd lost my heels by the time I hit the top step. "Chance!"

He scrambled past the small crowd of people and came to me, checking me over quickly and frantically. "What are you doing up here? I told you to stay with Hogs—"

"I love you."

He was speechless as he stared at me with wide open eyes. I'd loaded up on words, ready to snap him out of his daze, when the most beautiful, breathtaking grin broke out over his face and he slammed his lips on mine.

The crowd went silent, though I knew they were cheering.

The bell went for the round to start, though I couldn't hear it. All I could hear was my thumping heartbeat as he kissed me.

"Time's up, Riordan," Randy said with a faux yawn.

Al ushered me out of the ring, pushing me to one of the security guards who was more than happy to carry me back over to my seat. A very angry Hogs stood waiting for me, but all I did was flash him a bright smile and a double thumbs up.

As soon as my ass hit the seat, I saw it.

The change.

The shift.

Chance was standing up taller. His back muscles rippled as he rolled his shoulders and swung his neck. Any tension he'd carried in his juicy, *juicy* lats had vanished as he stalked Randy on the edge of the cage.

Surely I am dripping through my dress with how turned on I am.

Randy came forward to bump gloves, but Chance declined, shaking his head and circling him like a predator stalking his prey. Randy hit him with a lighter one-two, but Chance circled out and dropped his bomb of a right hook.

Randy, the prick, fell to the ground cold.

Chance didn't even chase him down for follow-up punches; he knew his job was done.

Chance—my person, my love, my *home*—was the new Light Heavyweight Champion of the world.

I was up and out of my seat once again before Hogs or Dylan (who was beside my father bellowing for his brother two rows behind us) could stop me. My heels were long gone as I sprinted along the side of the cage. Most likely knowing I would try to get through again, they had stationed more security guards around the ring so I had no chance of sneaking in. I screamed at him.

My Chance.

My champion.

My *love*.

The referee had called Chance and Randy into the centre of the ring when he saw me. Before anyone knew what was happening, Chance ran, jumped, and climbed the cage. He leapt off the side, landing in front of me and taking me in his arms. Blood was still streaming from a cut on his eyebrow, with more blood spattered across his tired body.

He smiled at me, neither of us having the words to speak right now. Chance took my hands in his and pulled me up into the cage. Finally, the referee took his wrist.

I screamed with nothing but pure joy when the referee raised his hand.

I screamed with nothing but pure joy when they wrapped the belt around his waist.

I screamed with nothing but pure joy when he jumped up the side of the cage once again, but this time in celebration.

I screamed with nothing but pure joy when he pointed down at me then to his left pec—right where his heart was.

***

Once Chance was done basking in the love from his fans and spectators all over the world, the interviewer quickly pulled him in for a chat as Randy made his way out of the cage. I flipped him a hard bird when he met my eyes. His lip curled back in a snarl as he passed by.

"Oh ... man ... it's incredible, really." Chance puffed into the microphone. "It's not so much of a secret, but I've recently changed gyms. Absolutely no bad blood to all those guys I was with before, but it's very public knowledge why I moved. It truly takes a team to get us fighters up here, and I feel so goddamn lucky to have had the opportunity to work with, train with, and to love such wonderful people. JJ, Al, Marilyn, all of my guys at Knock's—I owe you more than I could ever repay. More than this belt around my waist." Chance turned back to face us. His lips curved upwards as he met my gaze, JJ's arm lazily draped around my shoulders. Poor JJ, the softie was crying.

"Those first few rounds were tough for you, Chance, but after the break in the fourth round, it was like you'd flipped upside down," the interviewer started. "Is there a special someone here today that we have to thank for that?"

Just when I didn't think he could smile any bigger.

"Yeah, yeah definitely. That incredible woman who broke through your security line has a very special place in my heart. For those of you who don't know ..." His eyes found mine, sparkling and shining my favourite shade of sky blue—the one that gleamed with happiness. "Mari is the most fierce, compassionate, *badass* woman I've ever had the pleasure of meeting, let alone loving. I've loved you for longer than you know, darling. This fight, this belt, this *life* ... it all means nothing without you."

My heart pounded against my ribs, filling my entire body with love and air and light.

Chance grabbed the microphone out of the interviewer's hands and walked closer to where we were all standing.

"Sunny baby ..." he said gently. "Everything I am is yours. Everything I will ever be is yours. Life is only beautiful when I share it with you. I will *never* finish falling in love with you."

JJ's hand came up behind me and pushed me straight into him. I staggered forward but, as per usual, a pair of strong arms caught me. I could not get enough of this man, couldn't get close enough when I pressed my lips to his. His tongue gently probed my bottom lip, and I welcomed it instantly. Despite having just fought a grown-ass man, he still tasted like *him*—somehow still minty and sweet.

I was utterly *lost* in him, and I didn't ever want to be found.

CHAPTER 62

Chance

"WOOO!" JJ hollered for the fifth time in less than five minutes. "Fuck yes, Chancey boy! WOOO!!"

"JJ, I appreciate your hype, man," Dylan started. "But in case you didn't notice, we're currently inside a moving vehicle."

"WHO CARES, DEE-DEE! MY BEST FRIEND IS A WORLD CHAMP! WOOHOO!"

"I promise we'll leave you a nice tip," I told the driver. He laughed, muttering something about young-ins.

"Oh my god, do you know how much clout I'm gonna get being friends with *the* Chance Riordan, Light Heavyweight Champion of the world? I can practically see the girls falling at my feet!" JJ sighed dreamily, resting his head on a fisted hand.

"Proud of you, mate," Dylan said, turning from his seat up front with the driver to face me. "You deserve this more than anyone."

My brother stared at me. Eyes a shade darker than mine, he studied me. We still hadn't talked about what I'd said at the press conference, but that conversation was coming. He clearly did too, since he ended the conversation with a slight dip of his chin.

"I'm proud too! I feel like a proud mother hen over here. You've just won your title. Lynnie's finally found herself someone she fancies. And I got one of the ring girl's numbers. It's been a successful night for all." JJ wiped a faux tear of pride from his eye, clutching his hands to his chest in theatrical awe.

"What about me?" my brother asked.

"You managed to get through the entire night without starting a fight of your own," JJ retorted.

Dylan and I snickered— that really was an achievement for him. My brother had been kicked out of a few of my early-day fights for ... disagreements.

"Where's Mari?" he asked me.

"She was heading back here to get changed to head out with us. I told her not to hang around for the post-fight interviews, so she took Al, Elijah and Marilyn too. Apparently, it's tradition for the oldies to go out for dinner together after a big win."

The driver pulled in front of our hotel, a tall skyscraper with over twenty floors. I handed him a fifty-dollar bill out of my wallet and apologised for my best friend's craziness. "I gave Sunny the key to our room, so she's gonna meet us in there."

We all piled out of the car and into the large, warm, golden foyer. The seccies stood tall at the door, warding off the press that suddenly had the knowledge we were staying here. Guests and people bustled around the lobby, but I stood out like a sore thumb with a couple of cuts and shiners on my face.

"So, where are we thinking for celebrating?" Dylan asked when we got into the elevator.

"I was thinking either Vikki's or The Reef." JJ was bouncing with excitement.

"Dude, no. That's where all of the midlife-crisis women go," my brother groaned.

"So?" JJ asked.

"You wanna hang around women where a common topic could be what colour their kid's shit was that day?"

"Who said we'd be talking?" JJ waggled his eyebrows, causing both of us to swat him in the arm.

"Awe, man. I thought at least one of you would team up with me on the other. Not with each other *against* me!"

The elevator finally dinged on the nineteenth floor. Our footsteps were muffled by the carpet as we walked down the long hallway, JJ and Dylan bickering like an old couple.

I was four doors away from ours, room 1507, when I tripped on something. Catching my fall with my front foot, I inspected the culprit. A gold stiletto heel.

I recognised this shoe.

There was another about two or three metres away.

No, no. Something wasn't right.

"Whatcha got there, Chan... Are those—"

"Sunny's shoes," I interjected.

My heart sank, and I had no idea why. Something about this—the quiet, the shoes, the lack of people around—something was wrong. Within a few paces, I was at the door that read 1507. To make matters worse, it was slightly ajar. It was being held open with what looked to be some kind of baking dish.

My heart sunk even farther.

"Shit," I mumbled before pushing the door open wide and letting myself in. "Sunny?" I called, racing through the spacious, luxurious apartment. "Sunny!" I called again.

And again.

And again.

I stopped when JJ and Dylan found me, telling me of all the areas they had checked. Turned out to be everywhere.

Sunny wasn't here, so where the hell was she?

CHAPTER 63

Mari

A sharp pain twanged from one side of my head to the other as I opened my eyes. Stifling a groan, I groggily took in my surroundings. I shifted to lift a hand to my head, finding them bound behind the chair I was currently sitting on.

I shoved at the hazy blanket that had fallen over my mind, trying to force myself into gear. I needed to get out of here, wherever the hell *here* was. I was just so fucking tired, and my head felt so, *so* heavy.

A clatter sounded nearby. My internals flinched at the noise and my heart jumped at the sudden sound, but all I could manage to do was reopen my eyes again. My red dress had a few tears across the skirt and a gaping hole across my left ribs. I scoffed. The lack of blood meant someone had torn up my dress *for fun*. A white powder was littered across the delicate fabric, some in what looked like fingerprint patterns.

No wonder I feel like I've downed half a bottle of tequila.

"She'll be up soon," a sickeningly sweet voice said. "And then we wait."

"What if he doesn't come?" a man's voice said. Was that …?

"Trust me. He'll be here. Then the real fun will begin."

I forced my head upright, urging my body to cooperate with me and not whatever drug they'd shoved into my system. Those lifeless, icy eyes were already on me, so focussed my loose, aching jaw trembled. I swear she could see right through the mask I'd strained desperately to put into place.

"Well, if it isn't the life of the party."

Even in the dark, her tall frame was beautiful. But when I looked into those piercing eyes of hers, I could still see it. The *rot* inside of her.

"That's a bit generous, don't you think?" I clenched my jaw painfully to keep it from dropping as the man from before stepped out of the shadows. Randy wrapped an arm around Talia's shoulders, a wicked gleaming grin on his face.

I focussed on the blue and purple bruises on his face and bit down on a smile, remembering just where they had come from. *Who* they had come from.

I focussed on the pain in my jaw, the haze that was slowly easing from my mind.

I focussed on keeping that blank mask across my face, the one I'd seen Chance use when he was around *her*. I pinned every ounce of my concentration into that image while I scanned them from head to toe. They would have to have something, a weapon of some kind, surely.

"Always know what you're up against before the fight begins. At a minimum, they'll have two arms and two legs. Worst-case scenario,

they'll have something more sinister." Dad's words rattled through my mind.

Randy's disgusting laugh filled my ears, followed by a mocking remark I didn't deem worthy of hearing.

There.

Tucked into the waistband of his jean shorts, a sparkle of light flickered off the blade. Even with such little light in the room, the knife shone like a fucking beacon.

Well, that was going to present an issue for my escape. So was the gun Talia held in her slim, acrylic-tipped fingers. A thick black tube was wrapped around the end of it.

A silencer? I'd only ever seen those in the action movies JJ chose when it was his pick for movie night. Guns, being as illegal in Australia as actually shooting someone, were not seen very often around Soggla. Maybe a shotgun here and there for some of the local farmers. But hers? Talia's gun wasn't like the locals'. It was shiny—too clean from what I could draw from the little amount of knowledge I had surrounding firearms. The gun had a wispy darkness oozing from it, the kind that drew a certain persona in. The kind that promised a life of wickedness and corruption to follow.

A life that someone from little old Soggla wouldn't know.

Behind her slender figure was a pile of rope that explained the burning sensations in my wrists and ankles. The rope was chucked lazily onto the dingy red rug that was half faded, half stained—

The rug.

That rug.

With a wince and an internal scream from every single one of my neck and shoulder muscles, I looked to my left. There it was, highlighted by the moonlight shining through the skylight above us. The gigantic stain halfway down the left side of the rug from where

I'd violently thrown up on it the night I turned eighteen. Like some drunken, disgusting shining star to help me escape.

I am in JJ's fucking house.

It was genius, really. Who would ever think to look here first when they realised I was missing? What kind of kidnapper brings their hostage back to their hometown, let alone their fucking house?

Well, former house … sort of, but close enough.

They continued talking, not giving a single shit that I could have picked up on all of their evil plans … if only the buzzing in my head would stop.

"He won't be able to resist coming here himself. There's no way he'd leave it to the cops," I managed to catch.

"Trust me, baby, I've laid it out for him and only him. He's the only one who can solve the great puzzle of 'where we are'." She waved her hands in a rainbow, like she was announcing her name in lights.

Chance.

They were baiting him. They wanted him to come here and … now would be a really nice time for my fucking head to stop pounding.

I had to get out of here. I had to escape before Chance found us and somehow got in contact with them before—

I caught myself falling into a spiral loop of anxiety and dread.

Priority one—get the fuck outta here. They may have been smart bringing me back to JJ's, where cops wouldn't think to look for me. But they forgot about one thing—I knew this house like the back of my own hand.

"You're making quite the death wish here," I said, clenching my jaw to force the wobble out of my voice. I looked to Randy. "I think you're forgetting who knocked you out less than twenty-four hours ago."

I had a grin on my face when Randy slammed his fist into my temple.

***

Randy's fist drove across my left cheekbone, splitting skin and smashing through what felt like straight bone. How Chance's cuts hadn't been worse from his fight with him, I have no idea. Randy's knuckles arched high across his hand, each and every one forming a pointed peak. I concentrated on the gashes Chance had left on *his* face when he backhanded me. I smirked at the fact that he couldn't draw as much power from his left side, from the switch kick Chance had delivered. That costed me a heavy boot to the gut.

"You should really learn to submit, slut," his voice whispered in my ear, and I could feel the darkness on the edge of my mind, threatening to take me again. "I wouldn't have to get my hands dirty *all over you* if you did."

I held my breath to stop the gag reflex that followed. He smelled of booze, cigarettes, and blood. His? Mine? Chance's? I pushed my teeth into my lip as he grabbed my bound hands and put a foot on my lower back through the gap in the chair. He snickered, the most disgusting sound I've ever heard, and began to pull.

I will not scream.

I will not cry.

I will not please him.

The ligaments in my shoulders began to stretch, begging me to stop and firing off panic signals to my brain. I bit down harder onto my lower lip, using it as if it were a strap of leather, and pushed away the pain of driving my teeth into the split in it. I imagined that pain and locked it into a box, deep in the archives of my mind. A metallic taste filtered into my mouth. My teeth were sticking to my lip as I withdrew them.

Talia sat in the large, green armchair across from me looking as if she was enduring nothing but a regular, boring day. The armchair I'd cuddled in with Chance less than a week ago. I scowled at her—her disgusting, abusive, evil ass was tainting that goddamn chair.

A fire lit in my gut—that familiar searing hatred. I fuelled it, using it as a shield to block out the reality I was present in. I remembered the words he'd said, the memories he'd shared with me during our secret nights.

"I made weight for my fight eight weeks out because I couldn't fucking eat ..."

"I got home from my contender 'bout and she sucker punched me when I walked through the door. Apparently, a ring girl got too close up on me that night ..."

"The first full night's sleep I'd had in two years was the first night I had you in my bed ..."

"You'll suffer for what you did to him," I snarled at her, blood coating my lips and drenching my tongue.

Randy paused, and I could have gasped in relief at the halting of pressure in my shoulders.

She sighed, as if it was an inconvenience to bother with a response. "Oh, babe. You really don't know me well enough to say things like that."

A knock at the door sounded and I let out the hot, fury-filled air that had been burning in my lungs in a weird combination of a sneer, cough, choke, and growl.

Randy, to my surprise, let go of me and headed into the dining room nearby where the pentagon open windows were. He squinted for a moment, studying whoever was at the door before stalking back over. He nodded at Talia, then stood in front of me, landing a blow that busted my lip farther open.

"Does she hit you too?" It was intended as a growl, one strong and powerful like Chance's, but it came out a raspy and broken whisper.

Randy stood, studying me with a heat in his eyes I couldn't read. I didn't know what to make of the fact that he didn't punch me again but instead walked out of the room.

"Finally." She tsked in dismay. Another pound on the door sounded. "I'm coming!"

"Open up!"

My heart sank. My head throbbed and my shoulders were screaming, but I would know that voice anywhere.

Chance.

He'd fallen for the trap.

"Oh, Chance! What a surprise!" She opened the door wide, beckoning him in. "How nice of you to finally join us."

A hand pushed on her chest, those two golden rings glimmering like North Stars bringing me home.

Talia stumbled back into the wall. "Watch it," she growled.

I bit down into my bloody throbbing lip when Chance's beautiful face came into view. Still wearing the damage Randy had given him, his expression was wild with panic and thunderous wrath. The circles ran deep under his eyes, as if he himself had been up all night.

"Took you long enough to get here," Talia purred, pressing the barrel of her gun between his shoulders.

Tension radiated off Chance's entire frame. He wriggled out his fingers, as if straining not to close a fist and swing. "You didn't exactly leave a trail," he gritted out. His eyes found mine and I could *feel* it down to my bones what he was trying to tell me—*there was a trail, but I needed time.*

I may not have escaped as planned, but that was another thing these two idiots were too stupid to take into consideration—the bond Chance and I shared.

"My bad, I guess, for expecting better of you."

My blood boiled at the insult.

She sighed and used a hand to brush loose, purposeful stray hairs out of her face.

"What do you want, Talia?" Chance growled. His jaw was locked, and the sound barely made it past his teeth. Every single muscle in his body was locked and steeled under his control. The tension emanating off him, the strain to spring into action—it was *him*, fighting every instinct of his roaring to life inside of him. He gripped them like a vice, had to in order to be smarter than these two assholes. Better than them.

A fighter.

My fighter.

"You know what I want, baby." Gun now pressing against Chance's abdomen, she trailed her long nails up his torso.

Those beautiful, *beautiful* blue eyes never left mine.

Talia sighed theatrically. "But I guess that's now out of the question."

Chance all but growled when he turned to face her. "I'm here. We had a deal—I'm here, so let her go." He slowly took steps around her, moving in a way that made Talia think it was her own motions. They turned a full 90 degrees before Chance met my eyes again. He stared at me—if I'd blinked, I would have missed it.

His eyes, they quickly flicked to my left.

"Baby, you know I can't do that," Talia purred, now trailing her fingertips up and down Chance's forearms. "And if *I* can't have you ... no one can."

A subtle flaying of a hand to my left, just past the grandfather clock that JJ and I had accidentally broken when we were fifteen, grabbed my attention.

JJ's eyes flared when I met his gaze, and he pressed a finger to his lips. A steel baseball bat was in his other hand. He twirled his finger, telling me to turn back around.

I nodded and my legs began to shake in anticipation to run.

A knife and at *least* one gun against a baseball bat.

Running was the best option.

"Of course you can have me," Chance's voice softened, his heated gaze falling onto Talia's face.

I knew that heat, not the wild, flowing, carefree flames he had when he was with me. No, this was straight from the pit of a bushfire—the part that burned the most.

"Come on. This will draw way too much attention for us to get out of here together."

Talia's free hand was now grazing Chance's face.

I swallowed the fury that built up inside me at the sight, even when the lines of tension formed at the corners of his mouth.

He leaned into the touch, moving her head off centre as JJ crept close and closer. His bottom lip was no longer swollen. The cut that graced it was closed but still present.

"Trust me, baby. I won't get caught." The she-devil let out a revoltingly sweet laugh.

JJ's footsteps were quiet, barely audible, but getting closer as he moved along the open hallway and into the room we were all currently in. But he knew this house better than anyone—knew where every creak in the floor was. Hell, he was the expert sneaker-outerer when we'd both hit our 'rebellious teenager' phase.

I couldn't help but internally laugh at what our younger selves would think of this situation we were in—we thought we'd been through tough shit then. This? This was real stuff. Big, scary, evil, real-world shit.

Chance stared Talia down, and he swallowed the grimaces fighting to surface.

She was mid-sentence when a creak sounded, right under JJ's boot-covered foot.

"I hate things on my feet. I'll only wear my Doc Martens when I know shit is gonna go sideways. Like if I know Jayden's very punchable face is going to be anywhere near me."

I opened my mouth to speak, to try and cover for the noise when she whirled, firing blindly but missing JJ's thankfully moving target. She fired again. Adrenalin rushed so quickly to my skin it prickled.

Fantastic. Gunfire was going off around me, and I was tied to a fucking chair.

Chance grabbed Talia's arm, forcing her into a severely uncomfortable shoulder lock.

Oh, Chance.

A gun didn't require two hands.

Another shot went off and a scream ripped through me as Chance, the love of my life, dropped a hand to his abdomen. Dark, wine-red blood was already pouring past his fingertips.

"Not very nice of you, *sweetheart*," Talia hissed, rolling out her shoulder. "Now, where is that friend of yours?"

***

My head screamed, every single neuron inside buzzing in panic. My heart pounded.

Chance.

Chance.

Chance.

Each beat could do nothing but repeat his name. Over and over again in soothing yet frantic calls for him.

He was on his knees in front of me. So close, and yet so far away.

If my fucking legs weren't tied to the chair, I'd be able to reach him with my toes.

His hand, the one with the rings, was covered in blood now, along with the side of his shirt. He hung his head low, letting out slow but even breaths.

A *thud* sounded from the back of the house, near mine and Chance's room. Talia's heels clicked like a horse running as she sprinted across the tiles. When I looked back, Chance was on his feet, eyes blazing as he staggered towards me.

"Chance!" I choked. "Stop! You're bleeding!"

"Well ..." He grunted as he bent down in front of me and began to fiddle with the ropes. "... aware, Trevino."

"Chancey-boy," JJ called, sliding a pocketknife across the wooden floorboards before turning and running back the way Talia had gone.

It hit Chance's booted foot within a second. His shoes were bigger, clunkier than JJ's.

"You came," I whispered, smiling at the bleeding man in front of me as he sawed through the ropes around my ankles.

"Whatever it needs to be, darling," he said, looking up at me under heavy, pain-stricken lids.

"Even if it means you playing superhero?" I stretched out my legs, rolling my ankles to wake them up so we could get the fuck out of here and I could get Chance to the nearest hospital.

"Especially then." He pressed a soft, tender hiss to the back of my neck as he cut through, layer by layer, of the rope that bound my hands. "I've got you, darling."

A muffled voice came from nearby as a light flashed. A phone screen lit up with an active call. Chance shoved it into my hands when he'd finally freed them. Three white zeros stood boldly on the screen. Hope bloomed in my chest. I opened my mouth to start shouting instructions down the line, starting with JJ's address and finishing with, 'Get the fuck here now!'.

"Hang up the phone." That cold, cunning, malicious voice.

I'd been cut off. Painfully, piss-poor-timingly cut off.

Chance's face hardened to stone, and I knew Randy had the gun held to my head.

CHAPTER 64

Chance

I wasn't even touching the gun and I could feel how fucking cold it was. Despite the warm blood trickling against my hand, ice-cold rage poured itself through my veins.

I'd fucked up, been careless and gotten so lost in Mari that I'd forgotten about the *mysterious man* witnesses had seen Talia lurking around with. Now Randy fucking Rager held a gun to Mari's head.

My woman's head.

Not happening.

I'd cut his hands off before he could even think of pulling the trigger.

That icy swell pumped its way through my body, igniting the fight response that was so conditioned in my brain. I clenched my hands, digging my blunt nails into my palms, forcing my brain to slow down and think.

Fucking think, man.

I pulled the phone from Mari's hand, letting my probing fingers skim her cheek. Being careful not to press the hang-up button, I tossed it to the ground then slowly kicked it away, attempting to buy us as much time as possible.

"Get your hands up." He wrapped an arm around Mari's chest, holding her back to him, the gun still pointed at her temple.

My legs traitorously wobbled, my abdomen burning at the movement. The world turned fuzzy and hazy, but I urged the adrenalin to hit my system.

C'mon, body. Level me up.

JJ, who had at some point found his way next to me, stepped slightly behind me. To others, Randy included, it would have looked like JJ was hiding behind me. But it was his knee wedged behind mine to stop my legs from buckling that told me my best mate was okay. He was here. He was ready.

"The only way my hands are coming up is to fucking flog you," I growled, the words burning through my throat as I fought like hell to remain in control. "Let go of her, before I have to."

He laughed. The sound was putrid, and I promised myself to never remember it.

"You're not as scary as you think, Riordan." He threw a sharp, wicked smile my way. "I was so close to finishing you off. Somehow, this little whore—"

"Watch it," I snarled, my back teeth beginning to ache from biting down, a lock on my jaw.

"She comes in and kisses you. Kisses you! And somehow you win twelve seconds after the round starts." He ran the barrel of the gun up and down the side of Mari's beautiful face. It caught on her cheekbones, but she didn't flinch. She kept her eyes on me, and I gave her a subtle nod.

I know what you're doing, keep doing it. I've got you.

"Was there a point to your little tale? Aside from pointing out the obvious," JJ chided.

Slowly, slightly, I inched forward. I was all too aware of JJ's handy little pocketknife in my back pocket. It was rusty from years of sitting in the crowded glove box of his ute, but it would be our saving grace now. Not yet ... just a little longer.

"That belt is mine, Riordan. I'll make it mine again."

The hand that gripped Mari's shoulder moved to cup her neck. "Hmm, I'm curious just how good this pussy must be to have you so wound up over it." He leaned his nose in and scented her like a *fucking dog*.

No.

No.

No.

All thoughts flew, lost to the fire, as every ounce of control burst into flames inside of me. After ripping the flimsy little blade from my back pocket, I drove it—short, sharp, and fast—into the forearm holding the gun to Mari's head. It struck true in one of his outer forearm muscles, forcing his grip release on the gun.

Randy roared in pain and threw Mari into the wall, leaving a dent behind and crumpling my beautiful woman to the floor. He chuckled at seeing her in pain, seeing what it did to me.

But that was where he went wrong.

Loving Mari didn't make me weak.

It made me *unstoppable*.

He pulled the knife from his forearm and flung it at me.

Already moving, I easily evaded the blade flying through the air. The clatter of it falling sounded behind me, but I'd already struck. I jammed my fist hard and deep into the sealed-over cut on his eyebrow that I'd caused less than twenty-four hours ago. Using the sharp point of my knuckle, I dragged it, enough to split the cut into double the length. Blood immediately spurted down his face, but I was already on his other side, completely out of range when he swung in retaliation. My adrenalin took a toll and I stumbled into the wall, but then JJ was there.

There weren't two professional fighters here.

There was *three*.

JJ's attacks lured him away from the wall, away from Sunny and me. I groaned or roared—I couldn't tell—as I kicked my body back into motion. Somehow, JJ had landed himself a split lip, filtering his front teeth crimson red. Randy rolled out of a left hand JJ had thrown but didn't miss the body shot he followed through with. His brow was bursting with blood, and he let out a guttural groan at the blow to his liver. Randy hunched momentarily. Thinking he'd landed a hard enough blow, JJ stepped in to throw a knee to his asshole face. But JJ was wrong, so fucking wrong.

Randy snapped up tall as JJ closed in, a large, long blade now in his hand. He sliced a deep, ruthless slash across JJ's chest. JJ's teeth gritted in agony, but all I could hear was roaring in my ears when my eyes landed on Sunny, still crumpled on the floor.

Unconscious.

Battered.

Bleeding.

Bruised.

Randy grinned and turned to face me once again. The sick fuck was enjoying this, hurting the people I loved.

Never again.

Stepping through on my left foot, I used the momentum to double pump my calf. Leaping into the air, I launched a vicious superman's punch. Glorious, wonderous pain sang out across my hand when I struck true on the very end of his chin. The landing of the blow sent his head swinging, knocked out cold by the time he hit the floor. I let out a raspy breath and stared at Randy for a moment, half-expecting him to jump up and go for another round. He didn't. His body was as still as Sunny's.

I snatched up the gun on the floor, removed the clip, and tucked it into the waistband of my jeans before shoving the clip deep into my front pocket. Police, Ambos, Firies—whoever came here could take it off me. I'd be gone by the time they found us.

I dropped to my knees, then to my side next to Sunny. The adrenalin was fading and the searing, blazing pain from the bullet wound in my abdomen felt like my insides were being personally shredded by Lucifer himself. Fitting, considering the deep orange sunrays that were filtering through the windows. The sun was rising.

I looked over to the woman laying next to me. Her eyes were lightly shut, as if she was simply sleeping. Ignoring the bile that rose from the sight of her split lip, cheekbone, and bruised jaw, I smiled. I smiled at the love of my life beside me—the other half of me; my soul; my world. We'd found each other, after all of the pain and suffering and loss. It'd all been a long, winding road that led to her, the most extraordinary destination of all. Stifling a groan, I picked up her warm hand and pushed my big fingers through her small ones. After releasing the precious metal down onto her fingers, I squeezed her hand three times.

I. Love. You.

My insides felt like they were being tasered, but I just kept looking at her. Her curls were frizzy and messy, but I still itched to run my hands through them, to tug them the way she liked. Her chest moved up and down rhythmically, in a sequence of steady breaths.

"Come on, Sunny baby," I gently urged. "Let me see those eyes."

I ran my spare hand over the band of freckles that striped across her nose and up her cheekbones, unintentionally smearing blood across her face. I never knew I could be laying here, a bullet inside me that was squirting blood fucking everywhere, and still feel *lucky*.

I was so lucky.

I was so lucky to love this woman.

I was so lucky to die next to this woman.

I was so lucky to die for this woman.

"Let me fall in love all over again, Sunny. Open your eyes."

The floorboards thudded beneath me, and I groaned. JJ was beside me yelling into my retrieved phone. From the corner of my eye, he ripped his shirt off and shoved it into my leaking gut.

"You know," He sniffled lightly, "If you wanted to play the whole damsel in distress, we could have gone to the beach instead. I could have dragged your heavy ass out of the water instead of shoving my shirt into your insides."

"I know you're a sucker for a damsel in distress," I rasped.

Sunny took a slow, deep breath but still didn't open her eyes.

I held her hand tightly, still warm, and squeezed it three times again. *I. Love. You.* "I love you, mate." I wrapped my spare hand around one of his wrists that was coated in my blood. JJ sobbed and growled simultaneously.

The faint sound of sirens tickled my ears.

"Thank fuck," he muttered under his breath, loosing a shuddering breath. His hands were shaking, or maybe that was me. I was so cold. "Stay the fuck awake, Chance. I mean it."

"Get Milah out. You have to help her, J. She's a tough nut, but she'll listen to you."

His face softened as I broached the subject that would catch his attention from anything.

I squeezed Mari's hand three times. *I. Love. You.*

"Your sister will cut off my balls if I show up to get her without you. Open your eyes," he demanded.

"They ..." I rasped. "They weren't that big anyways."

"No way are your last words to me going to be you telling me I have small balls. Open your eyes, Chance." His voice cracked, and I groaned when he put more pressure down on the burning fucking hole in my stomach.

"'Til forever falls apart, brother," I whispered the vow we'd kept for all of those years.

"Put the pieces back together mate," he replied. "'Cause you're not dying today."

I squeezed Mari's hand, soothing and warm, three times. *I. Love. You.*

I was so cold and so tired. I dragged my eyelids open, desperate to watch the woman sleeping beside me. *Sleeping*—I told myself—because I couldn't die knowing she was in pain. Her face wasn't scrunched up like it usually was just before she woke up to her morning alarm. The crease between her eyebrows was absent, smooth skin in its wake. Her face was relaxed, despite the chaos and gloom and hell that surrounded us. I swallowed the boiling anger that rose knowing how they had tainted JJ's house for her, how they had punished her for mistakes that weren't even close to being hers—

No.

I refuse.

I dragged my eyes to that silly little 'chance' space she had tattooed on her inner arm. An eternal reminder of our love, of our time sharing this planet together. I'd find her—I always could. She was the sunshine in the word of unending darkness—a beacon whose call home I would always answer.

My eyes failed me, drooping and dragging. Mustering any form of consciousness I could, I snapped my gaze up to her face. Even bloody, bruised, and cut up, there was no better sight to behold.

When the cool shadow finally came, it erupted over my mind and body. But there, in darkest of corners, I found that quiet peace amongst the abyss. The place where my Sunny baby's light would shine brightest. I squeezed her hand one last time.

I. Love. You.

I. Love. You. She squeezed back.

Chapter 65

Mari

"She's not fucking conscious, that's why," a voice growled beside me.

I knew that voice.

"I think it'd be best if you blokes came back another time," a second voice said with a tone that didn't leave much room for disagreement.

Other voices, maybe two or three, were mumbling low enough that I couldn't hear.

The door slammed, the sound echoing in my throbbing head.

"Fucking inconsiderate pricks." That was JJ's voice.

The storm clouds in my head cleared ever so slightly and I opened my eyes. It felt like dragging sandpaper over my eyeballs, but I was awake.

I was here.

I was alive.

"Hey, darlin'," the other voice said to me, leaning over the bed to look down at me.

Al.

"Lynnie!" JJ squealed before throwing himself on top of me.

I sputtered a cough as I tried and failed to force air into my lungs with a gigantic man on top of me.

"Jesus, JJ, get off her. Poor thing already has a concussion—she doesn't need to have her lungs collapse on her too," Al said, grabbing onto the back of JJ's shirt.

"Where's Chance?" I rasped. Al handed me a plastic cup of water.

"I'm fine, thanks for asking. Only gave me forty-two stitches and a giant-ass lecture when I discharged against medical advice to come up to your sleeping ass." JJ's voice dripped with sarcasm, but he didn't meet my eyes.

"Where is he?" I asked again, taking another sip of water. The cold liquid was so soothing on my dry, aching throat that it tasted like God himself had poured it straight from his sacred fountain.

"He's still in surgery," Al said softly, brushing the stray curls off my face. He smiled sympathetically at me, sadness swirling in his hazel eyes.

"Wh-Wh ..." I sputtered.

JJ sighed and looked up at the ceiling. I would have thought he was putting on the theatrics, if I hadn't seen the single tear that slid down his far cheek.

He sat on the bed, lifting my clean hands into his. There was a cannula on my right hand, and two heavy gold rings on my left.

One was a sleek gold band, with patterns on it that were giving me a deja vu. The other, I'd recognise anywhere. The band thickened at the peak of my finger then dropped slightly for the engraving of letters.

DCM

M

An extra 'M' had been tagged beneath the initials of Chance's family. My heart swelled and my throat closed up. I looked to find JJ staring down at the rings, his jaw locked tight, lips tucked to the side.

"He took a pretty brutal shot to the gut," JJ mumbled, clearing his throat. "Docs said they would do everything they could, but that there were no guarantees."

"That was three hours ago," Al chimed in gently.

I slipped my hands from JJ's and pushed myself up. My ribs ached and my shoulders throbbed, but I needed to go. I needed to get to him.

"What're you doing?" JJ asked.

My head felt as if someone had blown up a too-big balloon inside my skull.

"Take me to him." I lifted a leg to slide off the side of the bed, gritting my teeth at the agony it delivered into my ribs.

"Lynnie, he's in surgery. I *can't*." His voice broke.

"Then I can't sit here and wait. Take me as far as you can," I demanded. A groan slipped past my lips, but I was sitting up.

"Mari." Al placed a firm hand on my shoulder and gently tugged. "You won't be any good to him if you don't get yourself sorted."

"But—"

"No 'buts," he stated. "I told the same thing to your dad. Many times."

That hit me in the gut as hard as Randy's boot. I sighed and nodded to JJ, who scooped an arm under my knee and lifted my legs back onto the bed for me.

"Where's Nan?" I asked.

"Right here." Her sing-song voice floated in like a ray of sunshine as her head popped around the door. Her face filled with relief, though I could see the mascara smudges behind her glasses. Her long hair was out, tucked behind her ears that were, for once, earring-less. Wearing a pair of navy blue three-quarter length sweatpants and a loose grey T-shirt, I don't think I'd ever seen my grandmother look so casual.

Tears stung my eyes at the sight of her, and she let out a choked laugh as she pushed the door open. My father trailed in behind her. His big smile was nearly as lively as Nan's, until he cast a glance over my tenderly sore face. No matter how unwell he was, he was still *Elijah Trevino—one of the scariest fighters to ever walk the octagon*. His eyes darkened to that murderous black I knew as well as looking in a mirror.

"Hi, Dad," I whispered.

***

"Lynnie. Lynnie, psst, wake up." A frantic shaking of my non-injured shoulder had me startling awake.

"Shit, JJ." I rubbed at my eyes, urging my heart to slow the fuck down.

I'm okay.

I'm still okay.

It was just JJ.

"Sorry, Lynnie. But we're sneaking outta here," JJ whispered, looking over his shoulder to the sleeping crew at my bedside. "Now be quiet before you get us caught again."

He scooped a hand under my legs and pulled them upwards before slipping a hand around my shoulders. In a slow, quiet movement, he sat me up.

"It was not my fault we got caught last time. You were the one who let the wind catch the door," I whisper-argued.

The dark blue woolly socks maintained warmth in my feet when JJ helped me onto the floor, both of us glancing left at the oldies still snoring away on the other side of the bed. Nan's head was resting on Al's shoulder, while Dad's head had fallen back over the chair he was in. His mouth was wide open, little snores escaping every few breaths.

"You were the one who thought hiding behind the TV was a bright idea," he replied with a swift shake of his head.

"You hid under the stairs! That's even more obvious!" I hissed.

Feeling like I'd done five hundred rapid kicks, my legs dragged and protested at every painfully slow movement. Not to mention the headache that had now returned with a bang. With the painkillers worn off, a rave of post-concussion aches bounced around inside my skull. JJ's arm was around my back, holding me as steady as possible and trying to take some of my weight. My jaw creaked when I gritted my teeth and continued to move forward. But I didn't stop, wouldn't stop.

"Did you have to park the wheelchair half a kilometre away?"

"Beggars don't get to be choosers," JJ reminded me. "Besides, I know your stubborn ass would rather crawl to that wheelchair than let me carry you to it."

I gritted my teeth, knowing he was right. My refusal to accept help had come back to bite me in the ass again.

"Thank you for helping me," I said quietly. Just a few more steps. I could make a few more measly steps on flat ground, *right*?

"Of course, Lynnie." JJ, surprised already by my acceptance of his help—let alone my gratitude, softly smiled down at me. My heart ached at that. He'd risked his life to come and save me, and he was surprised I'd recognise him helping me from my bed into a wheelchair?

"Not just for helping me out of the bed," I continued.

"Well, I went and heisted a wheelchair too."

"You know what I mean, J. Thank you for coming to save me."

"Don't sweat it." He shrugged. "I just wanted those fuckers out of my house."

Catching onto the humour he was using to put a wall up around himself, I didn't push it any further. There would come a time when we would talk about what had happened, all of us, but that day wasn't today.

I plonked down in the fabric seat and swallowed the breath of relief that filled my throat. JJ quietly opened the creaky door, using my meal tray to prop it open while he pushed me through.

I shaded my eyes with my hand immediately, the dimmed white lights around me burning my eyes and every inch of my skull. It was an effort not to bend at the waist and hide in the folds of my hospital gown.

"Sorry, Lynnie," JJ mumbled, picking up his pace.

"It's ... it's okay. These lights make me feel like someone's shot me in both eyes." The joke fell flat as a high-pitched *ding* sounded and JJ pushed me into an elevator.

Silence filled our ride before another *ding* and JJ was pushing me out again. There were less lights on this floor, but more beeping and scuffling of people. With more space between the doors on this level, there didn't seem to be any visitors floating around.

JJ pushed me alongside the nurses' desk where an older lady with smooth brown skin and short ringlets of jet-black hair gave him a bright smile.

"He's just gone back to sleep." She swung around the side of the desk, passing by us. "He was asking for you, sweetness," she cooed down at me.

Chance, my Chance, was *alive*. My throat welled with a spaghetti ball, millions of emotions tangling and knotting together. The relief, god the relief. A shimmer of light zinged through my chest, a broken part of my soul kneading itself back together. After all, if my Chance was alive, there was no need for it to be broken.

"He's okay?"

The pretty nurse opened her mouth to speak when JJ interrupted.

"He's alive. That's what matters," he finished quickly.

She read whatever look JJ was giving her before smiling. A smile full of pity and sympathy that I'm sure she'd mastered from years of using it. "Absolutely. He's been asking for you, Ms Trevino."

"Mari is fine," I said softly, channelling every ounce of energy into urging someone to take me to him.

Him.

My heart thrashed inside my chest, pumping over double time in anticipation, angst, and overwhelming relief.

"Where is he?" I croaked.

The nurse, who's name badge read 'Effie', waved a hand for us to follow.

The rubber wheels of my chair grumbled and squealed a little on the shiny floors. We passed door after door after door. Two cops rounded a corner and gave us a nod in passing.

"Here we are!" Effie beamed, pushing the door open to poke her head in before allowing us to enter. "She's here for you, honey."

And then he was in front of my eyes. Pale, bruised, and hooked up to more lines and wires than I could identify. But here, he was right here.

I dug my fingernails into my palm—urging my subconscious to wake me right here and now if this was some cruel joke it was playing on me. Pain flashed, here in the flesh, and I grinned.

JJ pushed me up next to the bed before taking a seat on the other side. Chance's hand, the one that was closest to mine, had an IV line running fluids into it. I brushed a finger over the purple bruises on his knuckles, the rest of his hand starkly pale in contrast.

"Hi, darling," I whispered, a soft request for him to open his eyes.

The ocean in his eyes was cloudy and hazy. Slightly puffed circles ringed just below his lashes. Little red veins rushed to support that warm lagoon I'd grown to love more than the sea itself. Those little creases below his eyes appeared and I glanced down to his mouth, where a drug-hazed smile tugged his lips up.

"I found you," he rasped, clearing his throat. His fingers, despite being pale and bruised, were warm. They pushed through mine and tender comfort wrapped my chest in a warm embrace.

Home. We're home.

"I think I'm the one who had to find you." I smiled back, unable and unwilling to fight it off. Moisture burned my eyes and my smile wobbled.

"No ... no ..." he started before looking over to JJ. He smiled brighter. "JJ, I found her, man. I told you, she's my sunshine. I'll always find her."

"Think I found her for you this time, man," JJ replied, patting Chance's forearm.

"No, no. I found you." That dopey, drug-induced grin focussed its grip on me and violently ripped down my wall. "I found you. My sunshine. My beacon home."

I lifted our linked hands to my face. When his scent hit my nostrils, my eyes couldn't hold more water if they tried. When the familiar smell of mint and home found me, tears fell freely down my face. It wrapped me, every part of me, in an embrace so tight and warm. A cocoon of love and light and liberation; my heart no longer hurt. It had no reason to, not when the other half of it was right here before me.

"Sunny baby, why are you crying? I found you. Aren't you happy I found you?"

I was caught between an ugly, sobbing cry that was sure to make Chance reconsider his decision to wake up, and a laugh.

I, apparently, opted for both. "O-of course I am. You found me," I repeated, smiling down at his high-as-a-kite worried face.

"I told you I would. No one believed me." He pouted.

"I believed you. I'll always believe you," I defended.

He paused, as if one of the clouds had cleared and he remembered. *I believe you. I'll always believe you.*

"Yeah, you do, don't you?" The look he gave me was coming straight from his heart, a look so full of love and adoration, it pushed more tears from my eyes.

"Can I get in on this?" a misty-eyed JJ joked, though I noticed he had Chance's other hand in his.

"Thank you for what you did." His smile was still happy, dopey, and pain-free, but a heavy weight dropped in the room at his words. *What he did.*

I was confused and felt like I was still missing half of what happened that night. I looked to JJ for an explanation, figuring I was unlikely to get a straight answer with the state my Chance was in right now.

His face paled and his eyes darted away from both of us. Despite the obvious discomfort, his grip stayed firm on Chance's arm. "No need, mate. But just so you know, I'll be telling everyone back home it was me who got shot," he replied, cool and crisp.

Anyone else would have seen JJ just being JJ; funny, straight to the punchline, *always* good for a laugh. But a darkness hung heavy in the room. The ghost of the last three days stood tall in the doorway. It sat casually in the chair next to JJ's, sucking what little life we'd managed to regain. It loomed over Chance's bed, a reminder that things had come so close to being incoherently, painfully different.

But while the reaper draped a black void around us, we weren't alone in the abyss—we had each other. Always and forever, we'd have each other.

So, we sat quietly together. We all pretended not to notice the ghosts swarming the room, or the darkness-incarnate who clung tightly to the hopeful and relieved emotions buzzing around us. It plucked those strings of emotion like a tightly wound guitar, playing a symphony of grief, fear, anxiety, and anger for the three of us.

CHAPTER 66

Mari

Ten days with nothing else to do but lay with Chance was a new form of paradise. Over the last fortnight, he'd gone from sleeping as much as a house cat to staying awake with me during the day.

Due to JJ's name dropping of who exactly was staying in their hospital, the nurses had set up my recovery and observation bed right here in Chance's room. With all of the machines and wires, we couldn't lay completely side by side, but Chance still held my hand.

We played TV trivia, guessing all of the answers to the gameshow questions. Turns out, we probably wouldn't last very long on one of those shows. We ate ice cream and shitty hospital food, but stuffed ourselves stupid when Al or Nan brought goodies with them. Usually going on to fall into carb-comas and take long and uninterrupted rests.

JJ had been coming to visit too, just not as much. All of us had co-hosts standing behind us now, demons sitting on our shoulders. We needed a bit of time to learn those demons, to work with them instead of against them.

I wasn't sure about Chance and JJ, but I remembered that night as if it was a bad dream I woke up to every morning. To be fair, it was. Randy had been found, arrested, and charged just hours after the ambulances arrived to take all of us to Brown's Hospital in the next town over. But Talia? She was missing. Cops hadn't found her yet, so she showed up in my nightmares every night.

But that didn't matter right now.

Because after two weeks in hospital, we were finally going home.

Al had picked Chance and I up in his little Corolla. Since, if we put the seat back all of the way, he could stretch his legs and stomach out when he needed to.

Chance began softly snoring five minutes in. But Al waited forty, when Chance's soft snores had turned into a nice, steady sleeping rhythm.

"I'm really proud of you, Mari," Al said suddenly.

"What do you mean?" I replied with a yawn.

"Mari, look at all you've done," he said softly. "You always say that it's me and your father who made Knock's what it is and built its legacy. But it's not. It's you, darlin'. It's been you all along."

"I—"

"And what you've done for this young man here. Well ... that's something beyond special," he went on.

"It's always special when two people fall in love," I countered.

"You didn't just make him fall in love. You gave a man his worth back. A man who, for the last three years, had been told he had none. That's not something to take lightly."

"I didn't give him anything, Al," I said softly, looking over at the man still peacefully sleeping against the window. "I showed him."

***

I must have fallen asleep during the drive back to Soggla, since it was Chance's kisses and soft murmurs that woke me up.

"Hey, Sunny." Those blue eyes greeted me with open arms, gleaming from the outside sunlight when he smiled down at me. "Wakey, wakey."

"I fell asleep?"

"I can't believe you didn't wake yourself up with all of the snoring you were doing," he teased with a wink. Leaning over my legs, he clicked the button to free my seatbelt.

His hands gently found mine and helped me out of the car. Chance was the one who had been shot and knocked up on death's door, and yet here he was, helping me out of the car.

As I stretched my legs and raised my arms over my head, Chance's eyes raked down my extended body. When his gaze finally found mine again, he wasn't even subtle with giving me the eyes.

"Come on, lovebirds." Al waved us on, up the driveway to Knock's.

Chance and I took the walk nice and slow, neither of us in a hurry to get anywhere. His hand was in mine, and mine in his. There would never be a rush when we were together.

The sun shone down on us from directly above in the middle of a clear day. The perfect 'welcome home' for us in the place we both could call home—Knock's.

Chance squeezed my hand three times, to which I eagerly returned the action.

Those three little squeezes had meant much more than touch all along. I'd figured it out during Chance's weight cut. Those three squeezes had said what words couldn't. And in those long twenty-four hours before weigh-ins, actions were how we'd communicated.

A slim figure crested the hill along with a large furry figure beside her. Gus came running down towards us, skidding on the gravel, and landing belly-up in front of us. A groaning laughter came from him when we scratched his belly. Then he was up and bounding off for Nan, looking back every few seconds as if to say, "Come on, guys! Hurry up!".

"Welcome home!" The entire town of Soggla was standing before us, bringing us home. Gym-goers were standing inside, mostly warding people from standing on the mats with shoes on. Patty, Nancy, and all of the Rustic Roo oldies. The ladies from Nan's gossip group, and the four ladies who worked between the bookshop and the florist. Paige stood next to Dylan, laughing at something he'd said before quickly snapping a picture of a nearby kid whooping and cheering for us. Kids—there were so many young ones here too. Children who might have a poster of Chance on their wall, who could look up to him and say, 'When I grow up, I want to be just like him'.

And there, front and centre, stood Al, Nan, JJ, and Dylan.

"The king returns!" Wazza hollered from over the mats.

Chance grinned before bowing down to me, lifting my fingers to his lips.

"And so does his queen," he replied, holding my hand in his, high for everyone to see.

CHAPTER 67

Chance

Two years later ...

"That's it, Lenny! Bridge and roll ... Excellent!" My wife stood circling two six-year-olds, who were rolling. Her new BJJ Gi fit perfectly around the growing bump of her stomach, but we would have to switch to no-Gi classes soon.

"Great job boys!" she cheered for them as the timer beeped loudly. "Change partners!"

She wandered between different pairings, switching from instructing to cheering within the span of half a second. Sunny really was an incredible coach, and all of the kids in the class responded well to her methods of teaching.

She'd taken over kids' classes permanently after my last championship title defence three months ago. When we'd come away with the win, a submission in the second round, she was bouncing off the walls, excited about my grappling execution. For the eight-hour flight and the four-hour drive home from the airport, it had been all she could talk about.

Seeing her participate every day in the two things she was truly passionate about—BJJ and shaping young minds—was fucking incredible. She was glowing, and not just from our baby boy who would continue growing inside her for the next four months. She was happy. Finally, beautifully happy and at peace.

Those brown eyes met mine, and I did the same thing I always did when our gazes met—I fell in love all over again. Those warm, honey brown eyes sparkled when her lips tipped up in that fucking breathtaking smile she had.

"Hi, darling," she said, skipping over to me.

"Hey, Sunny baby," I replied, dropping a kiss to her lips. "How're you going?"

"Can't complain." She beamed, subconsciously rubbing a hand over her swollen stomach.

JJ, Sunny, and I had all attended therapy for what happened that night after I won my first championship. We had done some sessions together, some apart, but we weren't haunted anymore. We spoke about what happened freely and openly, and we stood by each other on both the good and bad days.

There had been a lot of both.

But these moments, these special memories of the last two years made everything worth it. Seeing Milah come home. Seeing JJ make it into the pros as a heavyweight fighter. Hearing Sunny say the words 'yes' and 'I do' had been particularly special times. Hanging up the pads Al had held for me the night I first won the belt in his house for him. Sitting with Marilyn while she got her first tattoo and comforting her to have faith in JJ to know what he was doing. Seeing the two lines pop up on Sunny's pregnancy test.

All of these moments in time were priceless, and if the life I'd lived before was the price I had to pay—I would pay it ten times over if it meant I ended here. Because sometimes you've gotta bear with the storm to see the sunshine. And boy was that warm, quiet sunshine worth the rain.

ACKNOWLEDGEMENTS

Thank you to my partner, Jonno, for being the best creative muse. All of the best characters have a piece of you in them. Thank you for holding my hand and saying you believe in me, and that I should run with any and every opportunity to take a chance on myself. Thank you to my wonderful parents, who always encouraged me to dream big— I can safely say, this has been my biggest one yet. Thank you to my amazing editor, Anna Bishop, for all she did for this book— you're the real MVP! Thank you to my brilliant cover artist, Kari March, who made me the perfect cover first go. Thank you to Shae for helping me market my book and for being a fantastic listener, hype girl, and best-advice-giver— Facebook ads still confuse me but that only serves to make me even more grateful for all that you've done! Thank you to Max Leali, Ryan Doyle, and John Fraser for answering all of my questions about being a fighter— no matter how repetitive. Thank you to Lucy Score and Chloe Walsh, without the *Knockemout* and *Boys of Tommen* Series this book would cease to exist. Thank you to every person who's ever made me feel safe training in a gym. Martial arts holds such a special place in my heart and that's only made possible from having good, genuine people in the sport. And finally, thank you again to Jonno. The best stories I have start and end with you.

Keep an eye out for
'Under Wraps' - JJ
and Milah's story!

www.ingramcontent.com/pod-product-compliance
Lightning Source LLC
Chambersburg PA
CBHW030508120726
47904CB00005B/1388